A BATTLE OF SOULS

A SHADE OF VAMPIRE 59

BELLA FORREST

NEW GENERATION LIST

- **Avril (vampire):** adopted daughter of Lucas and biological daughter of Marion.
- **Blaze (fire dragon):** son of fire dragons Heath and Athena.
- **Caia (part fae/human):** daughter of Grace and Lawrence.
- **Fiona (vampire):** daughter of Benedict (son of Rose and Caleb) and Yelena.
- **Harper (sentry/vampire):** daughter of Hazel and Tejus.
- **Scarlett (vampire):** daughter of Jeramiah (son of Lucas Novak) and Pippa (daughter of Cameron Hendry).

FAMILY TREE

If you'd like to check out the Novaks' family tree, visit:
www.forrestbooks.com/tree

1

HARPER

I t would've been redundant and annoyingly repetitive to say that I was in trouble. I was, but it was deliberate and of my own making. I'd gotten myself captured on purpose, just so I could get inside the Palisade compound, closer to the swamp witch.

When we'd planned for this mission, we'd known that we had to stay one step ahead of the Exiled Maras. We had to think outside the box and take unprecedented risks in order to succeed. Most importantly, we knew that Lumi would be warded and guarded up to her neck by both Maras and daemons, as she was a shared asset of inestimable value to this nefarious alliance.

My heart hurt whenever I remembered the look on Caspian's face—specifically when the glass sheets came out of the walls and isolated me from the rest of the group. We'd known I'd be the one to take the fall, but we hadn't been sure how that would come to pass. Recalling the pain in Caspian's eyes made me feel uneasy.

He was terrified, and I couldn't blame him. He loved me, and I loved him. But the mission came first. There would never be a "we" if we didn't bring the shield down. After we'd stumbled upon

Vincent's magical contraption, used to hijack the Telluris spell, we understood how they'd been keeping GASP and Eritopia at bay. Until that moment, we'd assumed our people had probably been trying to get in but couldn't, because of the shield. Now that the hijacking spell was done for, GASP was bound to come looking for us, since they could no longer reach us—not even the fake "us."

This, in itself, was simply one more reason to get Lumi out of there.

My team was already preparing for stage two of our master plan. There was going to be a siege against Azure Heights, with the help of our newfound allies. The seed of discord had been planted among the Mara Lords, as well. Their alliance with Shaytan was already hanging by a thread—a fact evidenced by his refusal to let Darius return to Azure Heights after the jig was up with us. The Maras needed that extra push to take action against the daemons, and Nevis had been kind and devious enough to provide it. He'd also served Caia and Blaze up on a platter, but they had their contact lenses on, rendering them immune to mind-bending.

All I had to do was brace myself for the return of my team, since I was shackled to a wall with charmed cuffs. Perhaps the greatest surprise was that I'd been put in the same room as Lumi. Knowing the Mara Lords, there was some psycho logic behind this. My immediate guess was that they wanted to torment me by keeping me so close to her, yet unable to set her free. I'd learned enough about them to not be surprised by this reaction. The Exiled Maras took pleasure in hurting others, not just physically, but also psychologically.

The room was dark, but I could still see. The walls were covered in swamp witch symbols and were reinforced with meranium, making it impossible for me to see what was going on outside. But my olfactory sense had already picked up the traces of four guards. I was even able to distinguish the difference between two Correction Officers and two daemons, posted just beyond the door.

No magic could be performed inside the room, but they couldn't stop my sentry nature from manifesting itself, as much as it could, given the circumstances.

Hours had passed already. Morning had yet to come, but I figured the Maras had their hands full with the trail of bodies we'd left behind. Vincent and Amalia were dead—that alone was enough for the Lords to pay me a visit, soon.

Lumi sat in her chair, bound and gagged, unable to speak. Despite her Azure Heights garb and up-do, it was easy to tell that she didn't belong here. I had a hard time looking away, her bright orange hair and strange, white eyes with a pale blue border keeping me in a permanent state of fascination. Her tattoos were traditional swamp witch markings, with each swirl and pattern representing a level of witchcraft mastery she'd attained prior to crash-landing on Neraka. They reminded me of the Oracles' tattoos, only they weren't runes and didn't cover her entire body.

She was calm but in a lot of pain, both physical and emotional. Her red aura burned bright, with occasional wisps of black. Those made me feel uneasy, because they echoed hopelessness. She was close to caving in, after thousands of years tied up in this place.

"Lumi, my people are getting ready to lay siege upon the city," I said to her, keeping my voice low. My arms were partially numb from being chained in an upright position against the wall. The cuffs were tight, further impeding blood flow. I was anything but comfortable, but it was nothing compared to what she'd been enduring for close to ten millennia.

Lumi scoffed, then shook her head slowly.

"I'm serious," I muttered. "Me being here was part of the plan. We've got warriors coming from my world and yours."

I'd spent the last couple of hours bringing her up to speed with what had been going on in Eritopia, with a heavy emphasis on Azazel's reign of terror and the alliance that followed. There was peace now, and GASP was working closely with Draven and the

Daughters to rebuild the entire galaxy, one day at a time. There was hope—and Lumi needed plenty of that.

"As soon as my friends get back in here, we'll set you free. I promise," I added. "It's why we've aligned ourselves with the Dhaxanians, the Adlets, the Manticores, and the rogue Imen. We lack strength in numbers, but it doesn't matter at this point. We just need a distraction so I can get you out of here. We've thought this through. The Exiled Maras didn't expect us to bring a dragon. They didn't even know we had them. Their whole plan went up in flames when they sent *us* over here."

Footsteps echoed outside. I had a pretty good idea as to who was coming to visit.

I braced myself for the worst.

The door opened with a clang. Chills ran down my spine. Rowan and Emilian walked into the room. They were both fuming, their eyes puffy and red. The corner of my mouth twitched, but they didn't notice. They were both too busy projecting all their rage and hate onto me. I couldn't read their emotions, but their expressions told me everything I needed to know.

"I take it you found the presents we left you?" I asked, keeping a straight face.

Rowan was the first to respond, rushing across the room and backhanding me so hard, it threw my head to the side. My jaw burned from the strike. I licked my lips and found blood at the corner. Despite her ladylike appearance, Rowan was impressively strong, with the added grief of a mother on top.

"I don't get why you're so mad, Rowan. We did you a favor," I said. "Sienna's the only one of your offspring who's actually worth something."

She hit me again, this time even harder. It took me a couple of seconds to see clearly again.

"You killed my son! Emilian's daughter!" Rowan hissed. "You'll pay for what you've done!"

"They both took pleasure in tormenting and killing innocent creatures," I shot back. "You're all next, by the way."

"You don't get to waltz in here and tell us how to treat our food!" Rowan barked, unable to contain her fury. Her fists balled at her sides, her whole body shaking.

I gave her a brief scowl. "Kind reminder here that you're the ones who brought us here in the first place! Just because you can't admit that what you people are doing is wrong doesn't mean we can't call you out on it. It's wrong! It's horrible! It's unacceptable!"

Emilian stepped forward, a muscle in his jaw ticking.

"My daughter didn't deserve to die like that, you monster!" he spat.

"Oh, really? She loved feeding off and killing Imen children. Children!" I replied. "You people think you can just slaughter Imen left and right like there are no repercussions whatsoever. Well, I have news for you! You're all going down for this one."

Emilian raised his arm to hit me but stopped himself and took several steps back. After a couple of deep breaths, he narrowed his eyes at me.

"It doesn't matter what you think about our feeding practices. Only the fittest survive, and we are living proof of that," he said. "You will spend some time down here, within reach of your ultimate goal, getting comfortable with the idea that you will never touch her. You will never get her out of here. You will rot in a cage, your soul chewed on, bit by bit, for thousands of years, until you beg for death, Miss Hellswan."

I scoffed. "You think a pair of charmed cuffs will keep me down? You've got another thing coming, buddy. I killed Shaytan's first son! By comparison, you guys are target practice!"

Emilian put on a confident sneer. "Who did it, huh? Who killed Amalia? Vincent?"

"I did," I replied, looking to test Emilian and Rowan's limits. Had they not needed me alive, they would've killed me by now. I needed them so enraged and on edge that they would, eventually, slip up with something. One mistake on their part, and the tables could be turned even harder against them. The one thing I'd learned from Bijarki during training sessions on Mount Zur was that an emotionally fragile enemy was easier to bring down.

Chip away at their psyches, he'd said. *Make them angry enough to no longer think with their heads. A rattled enemy is yours for the taking. Emotions can topple a kingdom if they're manipulated correctly.*

They were both boiling at this point. It took titanic amounts of self-control for Emilian not to come at me. Rowan, on the other hand, was weaker. She pushed him aside, then started punching me, over and over.

"You bitch!" she screamed. "You heartless, devious bitch!"

My face hurt. Sharp knives cut through my muscles and scraped at my bones—that was the precise sensation of each of Rowan's hits. I saw white, and my ears started ringing. Soon enough, I became numb. Being repeatedly punched did that to a person.

"Hey, stop that!" The voice of one of the daemon guards boomed through the room. "She's not yours to kill!"

Emilian grunted, then pulled Rowan away from me. She flailed and screamed, desperate to hurt me some more. I couldn't help but breathe a sigh of relief, as burning pain settled in every molecule of my body. The Mara Lady had a killer right hook; I had to give credit where it was due.

I coughed, then spat blood, licking my lower lip to get rid of the warm liquid trickling out of my mouth. She'd broken some teeth, and it would take me some minutes to heal on my own. I looked up and saw Emilian gripping Rowan's arms. They both glowered at me.

"Shaytan wants you alive for his own delight," Emilian muttered. "He'll feed on you, slowly. I'll make sure I get access to flay you, once a week or so, just to blow off steam."

"You take Fridays; I'll take Sundays." Rowan snickered, baring her fangs at me. "She'll need a day to recover before I start over."

I chuckled briefly, finally able to focus my vision again. "You two won't make it past tomorrow," I said, "but I do look forward to watching you try."

Rowan tried to attack me again, but Emilian held her back. The door was open, and I caught a glimpse of an invisible daemon's red eyes as he moved closer, ready to intervene if either of the Mara Lords tried something. It was then that I had a full confirmation of what I'd been assuming. Shaytan's ego was badly bruised. Killing me or anyone else on my team would be too easy and too unsatisfactory for someone like him. He needed me alive and whole, so he could torture me himself—and considering what we'd done to Infernis, Draconis, and his troops at Ragnar Peak, I was in for quite the horror show.

"I promise you, Miss Hellswan, that no matter where you end up, you'll be in a world of pain," Rowan snarled.

"The same goes for Caspian, too," Emilian added. He noticed the subtle change in my expression as soon as he uttered his name, and smirked. "I knew it was only a matter of time before he caved and betrayed us. I saw the way he looked at you. Tell you what, Miss Hellswan. I'll make sure to take my time killing him, and I'll make you watch."

That set me off, but not in the way they'd expected. I didn't get emotional or wrestle against my restraints. That would've given them satisfaction, and I wasn't going to oblige. Instead, I felt my lips achingly stretch into a cold grin.

"You lay a single finger on him, and I promise you'll suffer the same fate as your children, only much... much slower," I replied dryly.

Emilian took a few seconds to react, as if wondering about the odds of me getting out of here and fulfilling such a gruesome promise. He smirked, crossing his arms.

"You're done for, Miss Hellswan. You're all doomed. We have captured your dragon and your fire fae. Your so-called allies betrayed you," he said. "You will all die."

I stilled, doing my best to feign shock. It wasn't that hard, with several facial muscles still numb from the pain. It was enough to make Emilian think I didn't know they'd caught Caia and Blaze.

He put an arm around Rowan's shoulders and escorted her out of the room.

As soon as the door was closed and locked after them, I exhaled sharply. It felt as though I'd been holding on to that breath since they'd first walked in.

"Don't worry, Lumi," I murmured. "I'm definitely getting you out of here."

She didn't scoff this time. Instead, she gave me a sympathetic look and a soft moan, as if telling me that she could almost feel my pain. I was willing to bet my aura was nowhere near her shade of burning crimson, though. My bruises would heal within the hour.

Her suffering required a much longer time to overcome.

I moved my head around to release some of the pressure gathered in the back of my neck, then relaxed against the cold wall and told Lumi all about our Nerakian experience, from day one. I figured she'd been deprived of all forms of socializing for thousands of years—the least I could do during my stay here was give her some kind of comfort.

On top of everything, she needed hope, desperately.

And everything we'd been through, all the challenges we'd overcome on Neraka—if those didn't give her hope, nothing else could.

2

AVRIL

We got back to Meredrin after our first incursion into Azure Heights. I felt horrible for leaving Caia and Blaze behind, and I partially resented Hansa, Jax, Harper, and Nevis for not telling us about their plan to serve them up to the Mara Lords. On the other hand, I understood why they'd gone about things this way. It didn't feel right, but I got it.

I barely slept that night, despite being wrapped up in Heron's arms and huddled beneath soft layers of bedcovers and furs. He was the only creature who kept me somewhat calm, adequately settled somewhere between angry and determined, with the right amount of each to focus on stage two of the mission.

I worried about Velnias, too. Sure, the guy was a huge daemon with plenty of warfare experience and the purveyor of many a nightmare in Draconis prisons, but I still spared him some thought, hoping he was okay and either on his way back to Meredrin or waiting for us back in Azure Heights. Him staying behind had not been part of the plan—we'd simply been over-whelmed by the number of Correction Officers ready to intervene.

We'd thought the Maras weren't expecting us to go back into the city, but they had sure gone to the trouble of being extra vigilant in case we did.

In the morning, we all met downstairs in the dining room to recap the mission so far and prepare for the next steps. This was a team effort. We all had our parts to play, and each was important and downright crucial to our overall success. If we wanted to deal a substantial blow to Azure Heights and recover Lumi, each of us had to pitch in. Fortunately, none of us had a problem with that.

Judging by the looks on everyone's faces, they'd all slept as little as Heron and I had. Technically speaking, we really only needed to rest every twelve hours or so. However, given the intensity of our tasks and the constant stress of watching our backs to avoid capture, none of us could be blamed for wanting that extra hour of sleep.

To my surprise, Dion had brought Alles downstairs. The young Iman looked a lot better than he had the day before. He seemed alert and fully conscious of his surroundings, a clear sign that the Maras' activated mind-bending had finally worn off. He'd been normal until he was awakened and set to turn on us, much like a sleeper cell. Now, however, he was quiet and ashamed as he sat in a corner, mostly out of sight, almost hiding behind Dion as the rest of us gathered around the table. I felt bad for him.

Scarlett and Patrik stayed closer to the door, while Hundurr and Rover sat outside, listening in. The pit wolves were too large to fit through the actual doorframe. Hansa and Jax stretched several maps out on the table, while Nevis, Neha, and Colton analyzed them. Pheng-Pheng and Arrah stayed close, somewhat bonded after their experience in the Palisade. The rest of the Druid delegation, along with Vesta, Peyton, and Wyrran, stood facing the door, on the other side of the rectangular dinner table.

"So far, so good," Hansa said, pulling her rich, curly black hair into a loose bun. "We've got Harper in the city, though we don't yet know where she's kept, exactly. My immediate guess is the

Palisade. Based on what intel you've gathered, that basement was designed for high-value prisoners, warded all over."

Fiona nodded slowly. Zane was standing right behind her, unable to take his eyes off her. The daemon prince was head over heels, and, based on Fiona's permanent blush, she was totally on board with that. Given our circumstances, I wasn't exactly surprised. We'd all bonded and gotten closer to one another—not just romantically, but also as friends. For example, after everything that Zane had abandoned to help us, I was more than ready to burn this entire planet down, if that's what it took to keep him safe.

"The walls are reinforced with meranium," Fiona replied. "There are swamp witch charms and hidden traps everywhere. I doubt they'd bother to get her out of there."

"Which kind of works for us," Jax muttered, crossing his arms as he looked at the city map. "We know Lumi is in the Palisade, too. I'm not sure they've got a safer place in which to keep her. I don't think they'll move her from there, even though they know, by now, that we're aware of her location. After all, from your group, only Harper got captured."

"They'll probably strengthen security in and around the building, at most," Peyton said, then briefly glanced at Caspian, who was dark and gloomy in the opposite corner. "Lord Kifo would tell you more about the Palisade himself, but his blood oath won't permit it. The basement holds approximately fifty rooms, sprawling on two underground levels, deeper into the mountain. Chances are there will be more prisoners in the other rooms, though I'm not sure who they are or what the Lords' plans for them are. It's independent from the prison, so I've never really understood its purpose."

"Either way, the situation as it stands is working to our advantage. We've got Harper close to Lumi. We've got charms and explosive charges planted all over the city, thanks to Patrik's team," Hansa replied, then gave Patrik, Scarlett, Heron, and me an appreciative nod. "And we've got Caia and Blaze with the Mara Lords, listening and gathering intel, while keeping them busy until we implement stage two."

"In short, for the time being, we hold the advantage," Nevis interjected. "Our soldiers are positioned all over the gorge, hidden and ready to strike," he added. "All we need is a signal."

"We agreed on an Adlet flare for every squadron to leave the Valley of Screams and converge on the mountain," Hansa said, and Colton nodded in agreement. "We still have two of those."

"True, but we shouldn't strike before Shaytan gets there," Neha replied. "We did our job of nurturing discord between the Lords and the king of daemons. We need them in the same place if we're to deliver an effective blow."

Jax scratched the back of his head, frowning as he stared at a map of Azure Heights. "We'll need eyes on the city, then. It may not happen today, though. I don't know how long it'll take for the Lords to get Shaytan into Azure Heights. They may need a day or two to prepare for his arrival. You know, laying traps and everything. I doubt they'd meet him without some kind of contingency in place."

"Wait, you're saying Harper, Caia, and Blaze will be stuck in Azure Heights until Shaytan gets his huge ass into the city?" I snapped, still irritated from yesterday.

Hansa sighed. "We may not have any other choice. We can't squander the few resources we have on just half of our problem. Shaytan and the Lords need to be there when we strike. Otherwise we risk the daemon king coming up from behind, and, trust me, the last thing you want is a horde of daemons up your ass."

It was my turn to sigh. She had a point. We had a better chance of crippling the enemy if all the leaders were in the same place.

"Obviously, Shaytan will have armed guards with him, as well as invisible backup," Jax added. "But it's better if they're caught unprepared, while quarreling among themselves. Our allies will provide the brute force, while we infiltrate and attack from the inside. We've got Caia and Blaze as elements of surprise, already.

And we'll have a separate team to handle Lumi and Harper's extraction."

Caspian stepped forward, his gaze fixed on the map. "I'll lead that team," he said, then looked at Fiona, Zane, Heron, and me. "But I'll need backup, and I trust you four will be able to provide it. That is, of course, if Hansa and Jax approve it."

"We do. It seems reasonable," Hansa replied. "But you'll need to find out where they're keeping Harper in the Palisade. You may have to split into two subgroups to cover ground effectively."

Just then, Hundurr and Rover growled. Scarlett rushed out of the room to see what they were agitated about. We heard her shush them. She came back, joined by an Exiled Mara we didn't recognize. She'd already drawn her sword, keeping it close to his throat as they stopped in the doorway.

"That may not be necessary," the newcomer said.

He wasn't armed, but he wore a Correction Officer patch on his arm. My first instinct was to draw my weapon, worried we were going to be ambushed.

Peyton rushed to the door and positioned himself in front of the Exiled Mara, his arms out in a defensive gesture. Upon a brief examination of the room, I noticed everyone's instincts had led to the same reaction, as they were all gripping their sword handles, ready to take them out and cut down the enemy.

"Don't hurt him, please!" Peyton said. "I know him. He's a friend."

"What is he doing here?" Hansa replied, her brow furrowed.

The Mara offered a confident smirk in return. "I'm Aymon," he said, "and I'm here to help you."

"Help us how?" I asked, my shoulders relaxing.

"Aymon is a spy," Peyton replied. "He works with us. He's on the Palisade detail."

In light of that new development, I couldn't help but smile. Maybe Jax was right. Maybe this was definitely our chance to bring the alliance of Exiled Maras and daemons to an end, once and for all.

With one of their own on our side, victory felt closer than ever before. Hope was a fickle and treacherous thing, but I had to give it a try. We'd been through enough already.

Maybe Aymon was the final nudge we needed to tip the scales in our favor. Permanently.

3

SCARLETT

This was an interesting new twist. However, we welcomed this one.

"You didn't mention you had a Correction Officer in there," Jax said to Peyton, who smiled.

"I said I still had spies in Azure Heights. I just didn't mention their positions," he replied.

A couple of seconds passed as Jax accepted the argument and cast away the last shred of doubt he had left. "Okay. What do you have for us, Aymon? And how are you able to move around with so much ease, given the circumstances?"

Only then did we put our weapons away. Aymon looked young, in his early twenties, at most. He wore his pale blond hair short, in a crew cut, while his blue eyes pierced everyone with chilling intensity. I figured he was part of the younger, more rebellious generation. According to Sienna and Peyton, the newer generations had been more likely to rebel over the past century, proving that the Maras' nature didn't have to be the horror currently manifesting in Azure Heights. Just like the White City Maras had been reformed, so could the likes of Sienna, Peyton and anyone else from their species who opposed the Lords.

"I'm a Correction Officer," Aymon replied nonchalantly. "I go wherever I want, especially if I suspect I might return with rebel Maras. They pay heavy bonuses to those of us who bring back the runaways."

"And do you do that?" Hansa asked, raising an eyebrow.

Aymon sighed, appearing somewhat saddened by the choices he had to make. "I have to. Otherwise they'll sense I'm working against them. But my numbers are lower than the others'," he said. "If I get caught, the resistance will be in trouble."

"There's an Exiled Mara resistance?" I replied.

"No. It's mixed and scattered all over," he said. "Maras, Imen, even daemon pacifists. You know some of them. I'm involved, and I put my life at risk to do it, in case you're doubting my allegiance."

"It's okay, Aymon," Peyton replied, resting a hand on his shoulder. "They don't doubt you. They've just been betrayed one too many times already. They have to be diligent. Now, tell us what news you bring."

"Ah, yes," Aymon said, lighting up with a smile. "I walked in and heard you talking about splitting up to scour the Palisade to look for the swamp witch and your friend. Like I said, there's no need. They have her in the same room with Lumi."

"No freakin' way!" Heron gasped, his eyes wide and a grin slitting his face from ear to ear. My heart skipped a beat. Was fate finally playing in our favor?

Aymon chuckled softly, then leaned against the doorframe, hands resting in his pant pockets in a most casual pose. "I said the same thing, believe me. Thing is, it's meant to be psychological torture for Harper. Keeping her there, inches away from Lumi but unable to touch her or get her out—or that's what the Lords are thinking, anyway."

"If she'd been taken for real, I would curse at how devious the Lords are," Hansa muttered, slightly amused. "But given the circumstances of her capture... Well, I have to admit, this is a little hilarious."

"It just proves that Rowan and Emilian's emotions got the better of them," Jax replied.

Aymon nodded his agreement. "They're both stricken with grief and seething at the same time," he said. "It's nearly impossible to get them into such a state of mind. Of course, losing a child will make you flip out. But yes, they're definitely emotional and prone to making mistakes."

"What about Caia and Blaze?" I asked. "What do you know about them?"

"The dragon and the fae, you mean? They're cuffed and held in Lord Obara's mansion," he said. "They're safe, for now. Shaytan will come for them, though."

"What about Velnias? Do you know anything about a daemon pacifist who fought COs in the prison yesterday?" Avril asked.

Aymon frowned, then shook his head. "No one was captured down there. But they've reinforced security now. It'll be harder to go in, next time."

"What makes you think we'll want to go down there again?" I replied, raising an eyebrow.

"It's one of the first things I would do, if I were you, to wreak havoc in the city and distract them from Lumi's extraction. The prison is filled with Exiled Maras and other creatures they've captured over the years. It isn't just the daemons collecting 'soul food' in cages. You know that," Aymon said.

We looked at one another for a few moments, before Caspian asked his most burning question.

"Did you see Harper in the Palisade?"

"I did," Aymon replied. "She's okay, for now. I was on the midnight detail outside her and Lumi's door. I heard the conversation between her, Lord Obara, and Lady Roho. Those two were fuming. Lady Roho got a little physical with her, but one of the daemon guards reminded her that she's soul-chow for Shaytan."

Caspian nodded slowly, darkness settling in his jade eyes. It kind of terrified me to see him like this, deprived of Harper, knowing she was in danger. It did a nasty number on him. I didn't want to be in his way of getting her back. To some extent, I even pitied the daemons and COs he was going to encounter in the process.

"She's chained to a wall with charmed cuffs," Aymon added. "One of you will have to take them off. There's no magic in that room, though. It's warded up like crazy."

"What about weak spots, access and observation points?" Jax asked. "We'll need good angles of attack all over the city. Before we launch our signal for the allies to lay siege on Azure Heights, we'll need good locations to stay in, undetected and ready to strike."

Aymon stepped closer to the table, then picked up a piece of writing coal from a small brass plate and marked ten points across multiple levels of the city. "These will give you good vantage points. Kind of a bird's eye view of each level. COs rarely venture to these parts."

"Thank you," Hansa replied.

"It's my pleasure, believe me," he said. "I have COs willing to rebel with me. They're ready to help you. They're not liking this situation either."

Hansa and Jax looked at each other. Jax offered a faint nod, and Hansa shifted her focus back to Aymon. "Can they be trusted, though?"

"Absolutely. Once the siege begins, they will take up arms against the Lords with the rest of you," he replied. "They've had enough. Believe it or not, many of us do have a conscience. Some fall in line to avoid punishment. There are plenty who eat souls and drink the Imen's blood dry just for kicks. But there are dozens of us who would certainly choose another path if given the option.

If you get the witch out and she brings the shield down, I assume your forces will storm the planet." He exhaled sharply. "Then all my COs and I will require is amnesty. Whatever you do to the Lords and their acolytes, don't do to us. I assume it's a simple, manageable demand?"

"We have no quarrel with those of you who wish to bring this nightmare to an end," Hansa said. "The Exiled Maras who receive pardons or amnesty after all judgments are made, however, will not be allowed to stay on Neraka."

"We'll bring you all back to Calliope and resettle you in White City," Jax continued. "We cannot allow the Maras to settle in this world again. We've thrown it out of balance already. We need to remove the toxic element from these lands."

"I agree," Aymon replied with a brief nod. "I would do the same, if I were you. Besides, to be honest, this never really felt like home to me." He straightened his back. "That being said, there is something more you should know. First of all, the Lords are watching the stars through their special lenses. They confirmed foreign elements trying to come through several days ago."

"Wait, what? Foreign elements?" I breathed, my temperature suddenly spiking.

"A capsule in an interplanetary spell," he said. "They tried to get in, but couldn't, and eventually settled on one of the moons. They've been there for days."

"Whoa. If they used an interplanetary spell with Neraka as the destination, how come they didn't get blown up like I did?" Avril muttered.

"And, follow-up question, how were they able to steer and change its course to land on the moon?" Ryker added, visibly confused.

"Ah, I think the Daughters might've had something to do with it," Patrik replied. "Viola has become pretty adept at complex swamp witch magic. Given her natural powers, I wouldn't be surprised if she figured out a way to adapt the spell to work in her favor."

"Plus, she's probably got Corrine, Ibrahim, and the other witches from The Shade on board," I said, then gave Hansa and Jax a hopeful smile. "This is it, guys! Our troops are out there, ready to come in!"

We needed a minute to let that sink in, to relish the temporary relief and flicker of joy that followed, before Aymon brought us back to the obvious and unpleasant repercussions.

"The Lords are planning an attack on your friends," he said, crinkling his nose. "They've got enough swamp witch spells and knowledge between them to disable the capsule without leaving Neraka. They've got incendiary projectiles that can explode upon impact and cause catastrophic damage to large areas. The capsule itself would be obliterated."

The good mood suddenly evaporated, as the state of emergency set in. My stomach churned at the thought of our people out there, sitting ducks for the Exiled Maras. I was willing to bet that our families were in that capsule—our parents, specifically.

"Jax, we have to do something," I said, struggling to keep myself calm, despite the growing restlessness that made my heart pump faster.

"When do they plan on attacking them?" Hansa asked.

"I'm not sure," Aymon replied with a shrug, "but it will be soon. It takes a few days to prepare the spell itself, but I don't have any precise information on the matter. However, you won't have to wait another day for Shaytan to come to Azure Heights," he added. "There's a funeral service for Amalia and Vincent today. They've invited Shaytan, and he's accepted. Chances are he'll bring Darius with him, too. The Lords have specified that they wish to meet with the daemon king after the funeral."

"Consider that our silver lining, then!" Hansa quipped. "We'll have to get ready and deploy as soon as possible."

"The ceremony takes place at three. It starts at the Lords'

mansions, and then it goes down to the cemetery at the base of the mountain," Aymon explained. "They've already mobilized the COs for war, just so you know. A battle for supremacy is about to ensue, and I doubt Shaytan will come unprepared. They'll get into a fight, and you'll need to step in and cripple them in that precise moment, with your allies. Catch them unprepared. They won't see you coming. They're too concerned with stabbing Shaytan in the back."

Fiona cleared her throat, looking at Avril and me. "I think it's safe to assume that Corrine and Ibrahim will be in the capsule, too," she said. "Which means they'll keep some protective measures around it. I'm guessing there's low gravity and no atmosphere on the moons, so they'll have a living system in place to allow them to stay there for days on end. And if they've been in the area since before we destroyed that Telluris hijacker, it means they've already caught on to what's happening here. I'm willing to bet they're prepared for whatever gets hurled at them."

I nodded. "Fiona's right. GASP is always prepared for the worst," I replied. "We need to focus on this second stage of the mission, then, and allocate resources to finding out where the Maras plan to launch their attack from. We could stop them, while everybody else goes ahead with the original plan," I added, then looked at Aymon. "Are you able to find out where they'd launch the spell from?"

"I think so, yes," he replied. "I'd be more than happy to assist with the disabling part, too. Your people will need someone to guide them and cover their backs. I volunteer. Now is the perfect time to strike, with the Maras and daemons quarreling. The bigger and more confusing the distraction, the higher the odds that you'll get Lumi out of there."

"I agree. Good. Thank you, Aymon," Hansa said. "Now, every-body, get ready. We have a funeral to attend."

We had our work cut out for us. It wasn't the first time we'd had to move and act fast to prevent a catastrophe, nor would it be the last. We'd succeeded before. And damned if I was going to let the Exiled Maras and the daemons ruin it for us.

We were so close to victory, I could almost feel freedom itself fluttering like a butterfly, just inches away from my face. *One more push, and we're out of here.*

4

FIONA

One hour later, we were all geared up once more and ready to return to Azure Heights for the second stage of our plan to cripple Neraka's leading coalition. Had it not been for the secret tunnels and the swamp witches' invisibility paste, we would've lost this fight days ago. I had to take a moment to thank the universe for throwing these artifices into our paths.

The sun was out and bright as ever, prompting the vampires and Maras in our group to cover our heads and faces as usual. Zane stood next to me, his towering presence casting a shadow in which I took comfort. Just having him close to me was enough to pull me through whatever lay ahead of us. The looks he gave me helped, too. We'd slept in the same bed, his arms wrapped around me. He'd held me close, dropping kisses on my temple as I slipped into my dreams. The memory of waking up in his embrace continuously filled me with the kind of energy and strength that could make me move mountains.

"Okay, now that we're all here, time to split into teams, like we discussed," Hansa said, standing next to Peyton, Jax, and Alara,

Meredrin's Iman leader. She first nodded at our allies. "Colton, Nevis, and Neha will lead their forces from the Valley of Screams in the siege against Azure Heights. They'll wait for my Adlet flare to go off before they charge. All squadrons will come out and converge on the city at once."

Nevis clicked his teeth, then gave Neha and Colton a playful smirk. "Ready to slaughter some Exiled Maras, then?"

"I thought this day would never come," Neha replied, feigning excess emotion. "I might just tear up."

"Good grief, we're about to kill creatures. Maybe dial the enthusiasm down a notch." Colton scoffed, crossing his arms.

"Oh, please. At least our people got killed by these monsters. Yours got turned *into* monsters," Nevis shot back, then stilled when both Hundurr and Rover growled, uncomfortably close to where he stood. "Hey, just being honest here," he said to the pit wolves.

Colton grumbled, but gave Hundurr and Rover a playful wink. "That's true," he replied. "But now we get to fight our way to freedom, no matter what it takes."

"Okay, you take the high road," Neha said, smiling as she put an arm around Pheng-Pheng's shoulders. "I'm perfectly happy to enjoy this moment on behalf of all the Manticores that have bled for the daemons and the Maras."

In any other circumstances, I probably would've been creeped out, if only partially, by Neha's morbid enthusiasm. But after everything I'd witnessed in this world, I had to admit, at least to myself, that I completely understood where she was coming from. Most of the Exiled Maras thrived on making other creatures suffer, and so did the daemons. I wasn't one to pass judgment, in general, but these bastards had it coming tenfold.

"Fiona, Zane, Caspian, Avril, and Heron will handle Harper and Lumi's extraction," Jax continued. "You've made your ingress plans, I presume. Aymon here was kind enough to provide additional intel on the Palisade's underground structure, so as to avoid their alarms and traps in the process."

Caspian nodded, patting his chest. Beneath his dark blue coat, tucked in an inside pocket, was a hand-drawn blueprint of the Palisade, with key traps and triggers marked to help us avoid them. "Yes, we're good to go," he said.

I could almost feel his drive, though I didn't have Harper's or, as of recently, *his* sentry abilities. But his expression was like an open book: Caspian was determined and would stop at nothing to get Harper back.

"Patrik, Scarlett, Cadmus, Pheng-Pheng, Tobiah, and Sienna, you guys find out where they're planning to launch the attack on our moon-based people, disable that endeavor, then handle the prison. Aymon will join you for support. Sabotage the living daylights out of it all, until the Correction Officers lose control over that part of the city," Hansa said, smiling at them. "Let all the prisoners out. Those who can stay and fight are welcome to help us wreak havoc through the city once the signal is launched. The others can be escorted out of the city via our tunnel."

Sienna gave Cadmus a gentle nudge and a knowing smile. "Cadmus will handle their extraction."

"Don't you think that will make them reluctant to follow me back to the sixth level tunnel entrance?" Cadmus replied with a frown. "They've known me as a House Kifo lieutenant for a long time. There's no trust between us."

"Do you think they'd be more willing to follow a daemon out of the city?" Sienna retorted with a raised eyebrow.

She made a good point, though. At least Cadmus was a familiar figure. I wouldn't have followed a daemon out of prison. After everything those captives had been through already, I had trouble seeing them following a potentially soul-eating daemon.

"Fair point," Cadmus replied with a sigh.

"Besides, we've got your back down there, if you need any help convincing them to follow you out," Scarlett added.

Ryker came over and showed them a duffel bag filled with small jars, all topped with shimmering paste—a large supply of invisibility spells, ready for consumption. "I'm not sure how many prisoners they've got in there, but this reserve should cover at least half," he said. "They'll need to keep a low profile on their way out of town, especially if they're weakened or wounded."

"Thank you, Druid," Cadmus said, taking hold of the duffel bag. "I'll pass the contents along as needed."

Alles stayed close to Dion, listening to the conversation with sad eyes. He still felt horrible for what had happened, even though it wasn't his fault. Scarlett, Avril, and I had already spoken to him, reminding him that he'd been mind-bent without his knowledge. No one could have predicted he'd been tainted—especially him. He was no longer under the Maras' influence, and that was what mattered the most.

"Dion, Alles, Arrah, Idris, Rayna, and Ryker," Jax said, "you will all assume your assigned positions on the sixth and seventh levels of the city. You'll stand by and be ready to intervene as soon as the Adlet flare is launched. Given where Hansa and I will be located, we will most likely need your support up there, more than anything. At the same time, some of you will need to keep an eye on the Palisade. Once the swamp witch is out, the Maras will stop at nothing to get her back."

"Duly noted," Arrah replied with a nod. "We're stocked up on invisibility paste and red garnet lenses, too. I'll have a good bird's eye view from my position, thanks to Aymon. I'll be able to spot any inconsistencies and foreign... horned elements," she added, giving Zane a brief glance.

He scoffed in response, feigning offense. She chuckled.

"Sorry, Your Grace, but we both know Shaytan won't come alone," she added. "I'm willing to bet he'll have at least one of his other sons with him."

"I'll raise you all five, actually," Zane replied. "Father is no idiot. The younglings and a handful of generals can watch over Infernis, easily. He'll want his strongest and most able with him to provide cover. Expect five princes, plus armed guards. Keep your red lenses on at all times."

The group nodded in agreement, and Hansa and Jax stepped forward.

"Hansa and I will tail the Lords and Shaytan, from the beginning of the procession down to the cemetery, and back to whatever meeting place they've set up to discuss their fracturing alliance," Jax said, then reached out to gently pat Hundurr on the top of his ginormous head. "Hundurr and Rover will stay close, in case anything unexpected happens. They've caught the scent of everyone in this place now, so they'll find you if we need you. And by 'you,' I mean any of you or all of you. Hopefully, however, that won't be necessary. I'm more comfortable knowing we've got pit wolves watching our backs in there."

"Yeah, I don't blame you. Emilian alone gives me the heebie-jeebies," I replied dryly. "Not to mention Rewa, the giggling psychopath."

"Don't worry, Rowan and Farrah are just as bad, if not worse." Arrah scoffed, her lips twisted with disgust. "My personal issues with House Roho aside, believe me when I say that you don't want to see Rowan's bad side."

"Oh, what we've seen so far wasn't her bad side?" I replied, chuckling softly.

"Not even close," Zane muttered. "She can be exceptionally cruel. Personally, I'm not comfortable with Harper, Caia, or Blaze being in there right now. We killed her son. She'll want retribution, and I'm pretty sure Harper, for example, doesn't need all her limbs for my father to feed on her soul."

We all gasped and looked at Caspian, whose expression darkened instantly.

"Maybe you should've kept that little nugget to yourself," I murmured.

Zane shrugged. "Sorry, but it's the truth, and Caspian knows it better than anyone. He just can't tell you anything about it because of the blood oath."

"As for Farrah, she is an evil opportunist," Arrah continued, dragging the conversation away from Harper's potentially unfortunate predicament. "She will tank her own people for her survival and profit. You'll have to be extra careful with her, Hansa," she added, frowning.

Hansa gave her a confident smile in return. "Worry not, Arrah. I've seen enough of these people to know what to expect from them," she said, then shifted the focus to another group. "Moving on now. Laughlan, Vesta, Rush, and Amina, you guys will take your position in the fields between the mountain and the gorges. You'll be the welcoming committee for our people once the shield comes down. They'll need someone to stop them from going into Azure Heights blind. Chances are there will be dragons on board, so we want to make sure they don't go in blazing. There are hundreds of innocent Imen still living in the city."

"They'll most likely be aware that there's something weird going on here," Jax added. "Once the shield comes down, we'll be able to resume Telluris communications with Draven, too, but we might be too busy fighting for our lives at that point to effectively convey what's really going on here. So we'll need you to bring them up to speed before they swoop in and finish the daemons and Exiled Maras off."

Laughlan nodded, scratching the back of his head. "It also stands to reason that we can assume that they've made modifications to the interplanetary travel spell, if they were able to settle on one of the moons, despite the original destination. If they could do that, then surely they'll be able to divert their course by a measly mile upon landing on Neraka."

"I'll use my aerial skills to intercept them as best as I can," Vesta offered. "Our position gives us a good view of the entire section between Azure Heights and the Valley of Screams. We'll be able to spot them early and determine their trajectory before we step in, anyway."

"And I'll help you however I can," Laughlan replied.

"Good," Hansa interjected, then shifted her focus to Peyton. "You and Wyrran will bring your rebels into position as well. I would advise sticking to the upper levels of the city. Once the allies lay siege on the base, the COs will have to retreat upward. You should be there to... welcome them," she added, smirking.

Peyton and Wyrran exchanged brief glances, then nodded.

"There are many innocent creatures in Azure Heights," Jax said, looking at each of us. "The Maras will use them as shields. Please, be advised that some of the innocents will include Exiled Maras, as well, so you'll have to be careful in your assessments before going for the kill. Some will even pretend to be rebels like Peyton and his people, just to get close enough to hurt you, or to run away. Neither can be allowed."

A minute went by as it all sank in. Jax then cleared his throat, demanding our attention once more.

"There's something else we need to be aware of," he added. "We're not sure of all the factors pertaining to this meeting between Shaytan and the Lords, but, like Zane said, assume that Shaytan has come prepared for an attack. So, to those of you who will be in the city with us, remember to watch your six and keep your lenses on at all times. No exception. Laughlan and his group will have a good position in the field to warn us if they spot any suspicious activity headed toward Azure Heights."

Laughlan exhaled. "I'll have blue fire signals ready to go if I see anything that doesn't belong in those fields. You know, like an army of daemons, for example," he said, the corner of his mouth twitching with dry amusement.

"We must also be ready to consider the possibility that my father may try to take Lumi away, for himself," Zane replied. "At this point in time, given how high tensions are running between him and his bloodsucking allies, I can definitely see him trying to pull an extraction stunt," he added, then looked at Caspian. "We'll have to be extra vigilant in and around the Palisade."

He made a fair point, and that sent shivers down my spine. No one wanted to compete with the king of daemons in stealing back a swamp witch. Shaytan was cruel, devious, and ruthless. The last thing we wanted was to bump into him or any of Zane's brothers in the Palisade corridors. This was the one part of Nerakian warfare that we didn't want to compete in.

If the Maras were ready to cut off ties with Shaytan, it also made sense that they would reinforce protections around Lumi. Surely, we weren't the only ones thinking the daemon king might want to snatch Lumi for himself. We certainly had our work cut out for us in there.

5

HANSA

With all our supplies checked and blades sharpened, we split into our predetermined groups and prepared to leave Meredrin behind. Alara came forward and motioned for a group of twenty armed Imen to join us.

"Please, Hansa, let my Imen help you on your mission," she said, as her Imen settled into formation with Wyrran and Peyton's troops. I could see the fear in their eyes, but it was weak compared to their determination and desire for freedom. "These are all the fighters I can spare for you. I will take the others, along with the elders and younglings, and leave Meredrin for the time being. Nevis was kind enough to grant us protection on Athelathan. We'll go there until your fight is over."

I had to admit, she was a wise leader. "I assume you're taking your people away just in case we fail."

She offered me a weak smile. "I have to take that possibility into consideration. If any of my Imen are captured, they could be mind-bent into revealing our location. I know the Druids didn't have enough resources to provide everyone with protective lenses.

While you and your team members may be immune now, our Imen are still vulnerable."

"No, I completely understand," I replied. "Thank you for lending us your strength, nonetheless. I'm sure they'll provide crucial support."

She squeezed my shoulder gently, then stepped back, watching us as we all headed toward the shore. I took one last glance over my shoulder, so that the image of Meredrin would stay with me for a little while longer as an example of peaceful coexistence between Maras and Imen. Proof that it was possible.

"We're not expecting anyone," Peyton muttered, frowning as he pointed at something ahead.

We all stilled at the sight of a small boat that quietly cut across the lake waters and headed toward us. My instincts were quick to kick in, but the fae in our group were even quicker to react. They dashed over to the water's edge and used their elemental abilities to coax the waters into bringing the boat closer to the shore, while Ryker and Laughlan stood by their side, ready to intervene.

"Wait!" I croaked, recognizing one of the two occupants of the boat. "That's Davo!"

Davo, our first guide through Draconis, was hilariously huge compared to the size of the boat, as was his companion, another daemon whom I'd never seen before. They both put their hands up in a defensive gesture as the fae brought the boat to the shore.

They both got out and bowed before us.

"We weren't sure you'd still be here," Davo said. "We're here at Zane's request. The pacifists are eager to help. This is Beryn, by the way."

"Mose's brother!" Fiona gasped.

Caspian smiled as he stepped forward and shook both their hands. Beryn pulled him into a tight bear hug, then chuckled as he measured him from head to toe.

"Good grief, you've grown!" Beryn exclaimed. "You've had a growth spurt since the last time I saw you!"

"I take it you know each other?" I asked, offering a polite smile.

Beryn mirrored my expression, nodding. "I've known Lord Kifo since he was a little Mara, always voicing his displeasure with the treatment of his Imen friends. He got himself in so much trouble on a daily basis," he said, then narrowed his eyes as he noticed Caspian's blood oath symbol behind his ear. "It was only a matter of time before they branded him."

We introduced ourselves, one by one, before Davo and Beryn brought us up to speed.

"Wait, you said Zane called you here," Fiona muttered, then looked at Zane. "Why didn't you tell us anything?"

Zane smirked. "I figured you could all use a good surprise," he replied. "Besides, I wasn't too sure they'd be able to make it in time."

"Your Grace, we've gone to great lengths to get here," Davo said. "But we just couldn't let you down. It is an honor to know you've sided with us in this fight."

"Not like I had much of a choice," Zane replied with a shrug. "Out of the few options available, anyway. This way, I get to be with the little vampire," he added, giving Fiona a playful sideways glance that made her blush like a primrose. "Anyway, tell us, what's new on your end?"

Davo and Beryn looked at each other for a second.

"Milord, there's a pacifist riot about to unfold in Infernis," Beryn said. "As soon as the king leaves for Azure Heights, our people will storm the palace. We've freed about a hundred pit wolves for this. In return for their support, we'll help them return to their packs in the west."

"That's amazing!" Scarlett replied.

"What about the pacifists we released from Draconis?" Fiona asked.

"Three dozen survived the collapse," Davo said. "They're on their way to Azure Heights as we speak. They'll be close by. Once your allied forces storm the city, they'll join in and assist however they can."

I couldn't help but smile. We were on edge already, limited in numbers but driven to succeed. The difference that three dozen pacifist daemons alone could make in our mission was significant, to say the least. Having that many daemons on our side was sure to turn the tables further in our favor once we infiltrated and attacked the city.

With Infernis coming down as well, we had an even better chance at inflicting irreparable damage to Shaytan's kingdom. By the time GASP came over after the shield's collapse, they were bound to find a nefarious alliance in complete disarray, utterly crippled and prone to fatal mistakes. Whatever tools and weapons we had at our disposal, we were ready to use them in order to restore Neraka's freedom.

Nevis snapped his fingers, drawing our attention as he moved to the edge of the lake. "It's time to go," he said, as his Dhaxanian frost stretched out from beneath his bare feet.

Within seconds, a thick layer of ice created a path for us across the lakes, all the way to the northwestern side. From there, only two miles lay between us and the abandoned red garnet mine, where the secret tunnel to Azure Heights awaited.

We made our way across the water, invigorated as we short-ened the distance between us and what I hoped would be our victory. Fate had not been kind to us, but it had rewarded us for our perseverance with incredible new allies and the knowledge that our people were out there, waiting to get in.

6

CAIA

They kept us chained to a wall in Emilian's mansion overnight, with no apparent intention to move us elsewhere. The upside to our predicament was that all the Exiled Maras we'd come in contact with thought we were mind-bent and submissive. They left us alone in the room on the first floor, which gave Blaze and me some time to discuss the possible outcomes. Nevis still had a punch coming his way from each of us, though we'd understood and accepted his reasoning—albeit begrudgingly.

We had it relatively easy, because we were nowhere near Vincent and Amalia when they got their heads cut off. I was worried about Harper, as I knew both Emilian and Rowan were aching for revenge. Word traveled fast, even in the Obara mansion, and the Correction Officers who came to check on us talked about what had happened, thinking we were too dazed to understand what they were saying.

All Blaze and I had to do was pretend. But Harper wasn't that lucky.

My stomach churned at the thought of her caged somewhere

in the city. Were they keeping her in the Palisade, or had they moved her to the prison? I had no way of knowing—not yet, anyway. The only thing I was certain of was the fact that our group was coming to get us. Sooner or later, we'd hear the invasion alarms blaring all over Azure Heights. Our allies were patiently waiting in the Valley of Screams, hidden from daemon hunters and hostile Maras passing by, and ready to lay siege on the city.

We just needed to hold on and gather as much intel as we could from our position, and, when the time came, unleash a little bit of that fire and fury that both the Exiled Maras and the daemons feared the most. We had the element of surprise and a lot of determination to get ourselves out of here. All they had was mindless greed and a grudge. *Manageable.*

"I'm still annoyed, you know," Blaze muttered, sitting next to me, his charmed cuffs keeping him against the wall. The morning sun burst through the windows, casting its amber light all over the period furniture and floral wallpaper prints. "They could've given us a heads-up about this."

"They most likely just wanted our shock to be genuine," I replied.

"Why? We're both capable of faking something like this!"

I couldn't help but chuckle. "Blaze, let's be honest. It worked. Whether we liked it or not, it worked. That's all that matters. We've got the lenses on, anyway. It's not like we were at risk of getting mind-bent. And frankly, I think it was better this way. I mean, the looks on our faces when we were made... That must've been quite the sight for the Lords."

He sighed in return. "I'm still going to punch Nevis's lights out when I see him," he grumbled.

"Just hold on," I replied, stifling another bout of laughter. Humor was our only company in this place, and I was determined to make liberal use of it. "There's a plan here, for sure. We certainly provided the authenticity, and now we just need to keep our heads down, our eyes and ears open."

"What do you think will happen next?" Blaze asked.

I shrugged. "You heard the COs last night. They're getting ready for Shaytan's arrival. There are only two ways in which that meeting could go. One, they'll shake hands and get Darius back, or two, they'll try to kill Shaytan and claim supremacy over Neraka."

"Whatever they choose, they'd better do it fast. I cannot take another session of Rewa shoving her tongue down my throat. I'll need to wash my mouth out with a gallon of soap after this."

The thought of her coming back to taunt us again reminded me why Nevis hadn't told us about this change of plans. It took every ounce of strength I had not to kick her face in whenever she stopped by to sneer at me and slobber on Blaze. Rewa was out of her mind and the poster child for serial killers at the same time—delusional and murderous.

"It's cool. As long as we play along, we'll be okay. Besides, I doubt she'll be able to keep you, like she said. We both know Shaytan 'really wants the dragon,'" I said, rolling my eyes as I remembered our last encounter with the daemon king.

Just then, a tiny flash of light caught my eye. One of the windows was open, the morning breeze flowing in. A tiny snowflake slipped in, its bluish surface twinkling gently. My heart skipped a beat as I watched it fly around the room before it reached us.

"Blaze, look," I murmured, unable to take my eyes off it.

"Is that..."

His voice trailed off as he watched the little snowflake settle on my left ear. It felt cold, but that wasn't the weird part. Within seconds, I heard whispers. It took me a while to figure out what they were saying, but once I understood, I started beaming at Blaze.

"What is it?" he asked, and I shushed him.

"A message. Hold on," I muttered, then listened carefully.

I'd yet to wrap my head around how Nevis's Dhaxanian frost worked, but there was definitely some element of foreign magic to it. It had nothing to do with witches like Corrine or Lumi. It was something entirely different.

The little snowflake didn't melt as it rested on my skin. It acted as a recorder of sorts, playing back a whispered message on a continuous loop. I heard Nevis somewhere in the back of my head.

Sorry for this, Caia. I could've told you about the sudden change of plans, but Hansa and Jax approved it like this. So, if there's anyone you would want to punch, I'd recommend looking at those two. I like my face the way it is, and I don't heal as fast as the Mara.

Now, moving on. I assume you're chained to a wall in one of Emilian's rooms. Stay there and keep playing your parts. No matter what happens, do not let them know you can't be mind-bent. We're on our way now. The Lords will most likely use you and Blaze as leverage against Shaytan.

Your people from back home tried to get into Neraka but couldn't penetrate the shield. They're currently stationed on one of the moons, and the Maras are keen to launch a swamp witch magic attack on them. We've got a team going in to stop them. The rest of us are converging on the mountain. As soon as Hansa launches the Adlet flare, we'll bring our troops in and attack the city. You and Blaze will be crucial to this development, as the Lords think they have you under their control. I need you to make sure they think that until you're given the signal to engage. Chances are you'll be in the same room with Hansa and Jax when that happens.

Harper is being held in the Palisade, in the same room as the swamp witch. What the Lords thought of as psychological torture, keeping her so close to her objective yet unable to get her, is, in fact, a great advantage to us. We've got that side covered, as well. They're going to bury Vincent and Amalia today. Shaytan will attend, most likely with one or more of his sons, after which they'll probably meet in the Obara mansion to address the terms of their alliance. Hang in there, little fae. If the fates align, this will all be over soon. Whether we all survive or not, well, that I cannot promise. But I'm sure we'll go down swinging.

I gasped, then looked at Blaze, as the snowflake finally melted, having relayed its message.

"So. Got some news for you," I said slowly.

I brought Blaze up to speed with everything that Nevis had told me. Out of everything I said, he got himself hung up on Nevis's suggestion to redirect our anger toward Jax and Hansa.

"I'm still punching him," he muttered, his brow furrowed.

For a brief moment, I stared into his midnight-blue eyes, mentally preparing for what would come next. There was going to be a fight, and we needed to find a way to rid ourselves of the cuffs. His gaze lit up.

"Hey, remember when we were in the meranium box, in Shaytan's palace?" he asked, and I nodded in response. That was impossible to forget. "Well, they charmed that thing like crazy to stop us from using our natural fire abilities, but I could still blow fire."

I thought about it for a second and realized he was right. There were slim chances that the daemons would have communicated with the Maras over this, since they'd held on to Darius and further fueled the tension between their camps.

Blaze blew out a wisp of fire, making me gasp.

"Hah... So, you can still use your natural fire, even with the cuffs on," I concluded. "Finally, something that works in our favor."

"We have to get rid of these cuffs," he added, as if reading my mind. "That way, we'll be ready when the cat gets out of the bag with Jax and the others."

"We're presumably mind-bent. I'm sure we can find a way to—"

I froze as the door to our right opened. Rewa came in, careful not to step into the sunlight. She slapped a button on the wall behind her, and all the shutters came down with a thud, sinking the room into darkness. I needed a couple of seconds to adjust my eyesight to the sudden change.

"How are my favorite chew toys doing?" Rewa asked, her voice sweet like honey but reeking of poison. We were in for another taunting session from Little Miss Psycho.

I cleared my throat, prompting Blaze to follow my gaze. He noticed the gold keys hanging from Rewa's belt, then quickly switched to his mind-bent stare as she approached us. The only influence she'd exerted on me had been to make me stay quiet. She needed me conscious and aware of what was happening, so I could watch her making out with my dragon.

She slithered across the room and leaned in to Blaze, cupping his face and pressing her lips against his. I almost retched when she flicked her tongue over his lower lip, then bit it, a little harder than usual. She enjoyed inflicting pain even on her "favorite chew toy." I was seething, and I didn't hide it, either, giving her the kind of death stare that could've made her heart stop forever, if I had such an ability.

What a shame that I don't.

"I slept like a baby last night," Rewa cooed, keeping her cheek close to Blaze's, her eyes half-closed as she enjoyed the physical contact. "Thinking about all the ways in which we'll have fun together. I'll have to work hard to convince Shaytan to let me keep Blaze, but you?" She sneered at me. "You, I look forward to handing over. But there's something missing from this whole arrangement. You're getting off easy after how much of a nuisance you've been."

She took a couple of steps back, picking some lint from her black velvet dress before she gave me one of her insufferable smirks.

"I don't think the idea of me making love to your dragon will be enough to torment you for all eternity," she muttered, putting on a pensive expression. "I wonder what else we could do to make sure you never forget the price you pay for crossing me..."

In that instant, she lit up like the night sky on the Fourth of July.

"I know!" she exclaimed, giggling like an ecstatic little girl.

"Blaze, darling, I need you to burn Caia. Just on the face, though. We don't want her dead. We don't want to waste any of the soul food she's got for the daemon king. But it doesn't say anywhere that she needs to be in perfect working order for Shaytan's consumption habits. Burn her face. I want her ugly and disfigured, so whenever she catches a glimpse of herself in a mirror, she remembers that I, Rewa of House Xunn, defeated her."

That entire statement sent chills down my spine, but the look on Blaze's face—which she'd yet to notice, since she was busy grinning at me—told me what we had to do next. First off, it was time to drop the act for a minute.

I couldn't help but smirk. "You know what, Blaze? I've had enough of this bitch. Burn her ass to a crisp," I said flatly.

Rewa froze, realizing that her mind-bending wasn't working. I was supposed to be mute and helpless. Watching that grin get wiped off her face was, perhaps, one of the most satisfying moments in my entire life.

"Wait. How—" She stopped herself from talking when logic finally caught up with her. If it didn't work on me, it didn't work on Blaze either. She stared at him for a second, finally seeing the grim look on his face. "Wait. You... How did you—"

Blaze blew out a thick column of fire. The flames were so powerful and so intense, they instantly killed her. Within two seconds, Rewa was a blackened husk with a humanoid shape, the golden key hanging by a burnt thread. It would take just one gust of wind to completely disintegrate her. Blaze had put enough fury into those flames to perfectly replicate death by standing right at the back of a rocket. The charmed cuffs didn't do anything against a dragon's natural ability to breathe fire, after all...

Rewa was dead, and I could breathe again.

"Wait, wait, wait," I murmured, then managed to slip one boot off. I put my foot out to catch the keys with my toes as they fell off her. I dragged them back, then clutched them with my toes and brought them up in a yoga-like stretch. It took some grunting and panting to lift my leg to a height where I could reach the keys, since my hands were still cuffed against the wall, but I did it. "There we go."

Blaze stared at me, evidently impressed. A smile tugged at the corner of his mouth.

"I didn't know you could stretch like that," he breathed.

"Oh, there's a lot you don't know about me yet," I replied with a playful grin, then nodded at Rewa's carbonized corpse, still standing and sending chills down my spine. "Now, let's clean *that* mess up before others come in."

Nowhere did Nevis's instructions say we couldn't get rid of Rewa. Besides, she was despicable and annoying as hell. It didn't feel good to take a life, but the world was definitely a better place without her in it.

7

BLAZE

I watched in amazement as Caia twisted her hand around, key firmly between her fingers, until she found the keyhole and we heard that first, liberating click. With one hand free, the other cuff didn't stand a chance.

Two seconds later, we were both free, standing in front of Rewa's charred remains and completely weirded out by the fact that she'd yet to fall apart. Caia narrowed her eyes at what had once been Rewa's face, pursing her lips.

"You brought this on yourself," she muttered, then exhaled.

That brief blow of air was enough to finally do the deed, and Rewa disintegrated into a pile of charcoal on the floor, prompting Caia to yelp and take a couple of steps back. We instinctively froze, listening to what was going on outside. We breathed a sigh of relief when nothing concerning came through. The chances of someone walking in at this point were slim.

"We need to move fast," Caia muttered, frowning as she looked around. "Gah, where's a broom and a dust pan when you need one?"

I stifled a smirk, then went over to one of the wooden cabinets on the other side of the room. A brief search through the cupboards and drawers answered our prayers—sort of. Armed with a handful of cloths and a porcelain bowl, we proceeded to transfer Rewa's ashes into the china container.

It took us about two minutes to get most of them. I stashed it into the cupboard, while Caia blew over the floor, scattering the rest away. It was literally the best we could do with what we had.

"Now what?" I asked, resting my hands on my hips.

She sighed, then pointed at the cuffs. "We'll have to go back there and pretend nothing happened," she said.

I rolled my eyes, then walked over and wrapped my arms around her, pulling her into a deep and feverish kiss. There was something about Caia that constantly kept me on my toes, equally nervous and exhilarated. Being around her made my heart beat faster, even when we were chained to the wall. She'd been so resilient, so patient and self-contained, until we got rid of Rewa. I was genuinely in awe of her.

She moaned gently against my lips, then put her arms around my neck and held me tight. The move set my soul on fire, and, for a split second, I completely forgot where we were.

It took all the energy I could muster to pull my head back and give her a weak smile.

"Sorry, I just had to," I whispered.

"No, no, it's okay. You kind of read my mind," she replied, giggling.

We went back to the wall and loosened the chains on our cuffs, enough for us to reach our hands and each other if needed, then locked ourselves back under the swamp witch charms. Caia held on to the key, slipping it into one of the back pockets on her leather combat suit.

"Okay, so, what if they come looking for Rewa?" I asked.

Caia shrugged. "We pretend we're two mumbling, drooling messes. We don't know where she went after she came by just now.

She just taunted us and left. They have no reason to distrust us. After all, we're mind-bent," she replied, her lips stretching into a smirk.

I wanted to kiss her again, but, at the same time, the weight of what I'd just done finally kicked in, the adrenaline wearing off.

"I don't like what I just did," I muttered.

"I know. Me neither. But, Blaze, she would've tortured and killed as many innocent creatures as she could get her claws on," she replied softly. In my heart, I knew she was right.

"Yeah. The weird thing is I feel bad, but I also feel... relieved."

"Because you did the right thing, even though it was, in a word, awful. It just proves you have a conscience, and it's one of the things I love most about you," Caia said, giving me a warm smile.

A minute passed as we gazed at each other. I wondered what I had done to deserve such a wonderful creature's undivided attention. Caia was like the sun, and I was desperate to get closer to her, even if I got myself burned. It was a price I was willing to pay.

She made me feel something so ardent, so intense that it made it difficult for me to breathe if she wasn't around. The world was a better place with her in it. My world, in particular, was infinitely better since she'd stumbled into it. No matter what came next, I was determined to make sure we both walked out of it alive. I had plans for this fae, and they involved breaking that celibacy oath over and over again.

"Would you mind taking my cuffs off for a second?" I asked.

She frowned, somewhat confused. "Why?"

"Because I *really* need to hold you and kiss you until I run out of air."

Caia burst into laughter, then quickly silenced herself, pressing her lips into a thin line. She didn't want anyone hearing us, and for good reason. We were still neck-deep in enemy territory, after all.

"It's best not to risk it, even though every fiber in my body is screaming, 'Yes!'," she replied.

I let out a heavy sigh, resting my head against the wall. "Have you ever been to New Zealand?" She shook her head, prompting me to smile. I instantly made plans in my head. "Once we get out of here, I'll take you there. There's a volcanic lake area called Rotorua. It's absolutely stunning," I said. "You'll love it."

"First date?" she replied, smiling.

"I was thinking more like first elopement," I muttered.

"That sounds… appealing," she said. "I'll hold you to it."

I chuckled. "Already looking forward to it."

There wasn't much else we could do, given our position. We were in for the long run, playing the waiting game as we mentally prepared for the final gag. Having something enticing to come back to was just extra motivation, an additional incitement to make sure we won this fight.

I knew one bungalow in Rotorua that offered a superb couples' suite, with floor-to-ceiling windows and a plethora of flowers framing the terrace, which provided direct access to a thermal spring. I could already see myself and Caia there, with no clothes present between us and nothing but love for each other. I could already feel her heartbeat echoing in my ribcage as she opened her eyes in the morning. I could already see the look of pure happiness on her face as I showed her the lake in its multitude of colors.

That alone made me want to fight harder than ever. The chance of living a life with Caia was something worth burning a thousand Rewas over. I didn't voice that thought. I kept it to myself because my conscience made sure to send a dagger through my stomach just for thinking it. But I secretly accepted the concept as a part of who I was becoming—a dragon willing to endure and do anything to defend freedom and peace.

After all, circumstances didn't always allow one to spare one's enemy. Sometimes, death was the only option.

8

HANSA

Fate worked in our favor. The mansion behind which our secret tunnel ended was inhabited by more than just the Mara we'd killed the day before, when we first came out. Yet no one had come around searching for him. It was close to noon when we got there, but the back garden was empty.

We could hear pots clanging in the downstairs kitchen, along with various doors opening and closing throughout the building. However, no one was out back, which suited us well. The rest of our crew had ingested invisibility spells and had spread out, taking their positions throughout the city. Rover and Hundurr stayed close, using the forest surrounding the city on all levels of the mountain as cover.

But Jax and I were visible, donning the funeral garb and porcelain masks that Aymon had procured for us. The ceremony for Vincent and Amalia was important and was going to unfold with much more pomp than the last funeral we'd attended in Azure Heights. According to Aymon, the procession was set to start from the sixth level, where the Lords' funeral house was. The masked clerics and Correction Officers were then going to lead both coffins down the main road all the way to the ground level, then to the burial ground.

The Imen were usually buried, but all Maras were cremated. After the funeral, we knew for a fact that the Lords were going to meet with Shaytan, and that was when all hell would break loose, one way or another.

Our cloaks were black and made of velvet, smoothly concealing our weapons and supply belts. They weren't loose enough for us to inconspicuously carry our shields, too, but that was something we had to work with. Blending in was more important. The large hoods and porcelain masks made us disappear in the crowd, as the similarly dressed Exiled Maras and Imen gathered on the sixth level.

As expected, Emilian, Rowan, and Farrah were present. They wore gold-threaded cloaks with intricate gemstone patterns embroidered around the head and shoulders. Their masks were painted red, and they wore red velvet gloves. Everybody else—with the exception of the clerics, who wore white robes—was dressed in black. Clearly, Mara nobles had different funeral ceremonies, as opposed to the commoners. I could easily spot the differences from Minah's burial.

All three Lords stood by the main entrance to the funeral home. All of their family members were here, from what I could tell. They were all waiting for Vincent and Amalia's caskets to be brought out.

Gasps erupted from the crowd by the main road. Soon enough, Jax and I understood what the fuss was all about, as people made room for Shaytan to come through, accompanied by three of his sons. I recognized Abeles, Garros, and Mammon. Behind them were ten other daemons—large ones, with meranium armor and extra-long rapiers. They looked like they meant business. Their expressions were firm, but clear: make one wrong move against the king or his sons, and your head will fall.

I could almost see the sudden tension gathering in Emilian's, Rowan's, and Farrah's shoulders, especially when Darius emerged from behind Shaytan. He wore his regular bourgeois outfit, all dark green velvet and gold thread beneath a flimsy black hood that shielded him from the sun. But what really caught my eye was the pair of charmed cuffs keeping his hands together.

"I take it Shaytan's being extra cautious," I muttered.

Emilian scoffed, then motioned for an Iman servant. "Someone get Lord Xunn his funeral coat!"

His tone was clipped. It quickly put the fear in an Iman maid, who rushed up to the seventh level and came back, two minutes later, with Darius's special cloak and red mask. The maid helped Darius put them on, as he briefly hissed from the direct sunlight, in the temporary absence of the black hood. Shaytan offered the Lords a polite bow.

"Please accept my sincerest condolences, on behalf of the entire daemon nation," Shaytan said.

Rowan shook her head slowly. "What is the meaning of this, Your Grace?" she asked the daemon king, pointing at Darius.

Shaytan smirked. "Precautions, milady. These are difficult times, and I completely understand that, but I am no fool. Let us proceed with your funeral ceremony, then discuss the matter of Lord Xunn's... repatriation."

The daemon princes snickered behind him but instantly stilled when he gave them a brief over-the-shoulder glance. Shaytan was not to be toyed with—not even by his sons.

My hand instinctively found Jax's, and we slowly inched closer and settled in the second row of the crowd, with a good view of both the Lords and the daemon king. We were much safer under these cloaks than we would be if we were wearing invisibility spells, since all the daemons on Shaytan's envoy wore a red garnet lens, and there were plenty of Correction Officers also equipped to spot any unseen hostiles. Shaytan's scepter also carried its large red garnet gem. However, we'd prepared for this.

Our team knew what positions to take in order to stay out of sight.

The clerics finally emerged with the caskets, which were both beautifully sculpted, their lids loaded with flowers. The message didn't escape me: while life is beautiful, it is fleeting, and it eventually ends. No matter how long different creatures live, the end is still a possibility, and when it comes, it is cause for misery and grief.

Sculptors had worked hard for those caskets, and they were going to watch them burn.

We followed the procession down the main road, keeping an adequate distance from the Correction Officers, the Lords, and the daemons. Two of the clerics played wooden instruments through which they blew, producing a soft but heartbreaking melody.

Emilian and Rowan led the funeral, while Farrah stayed back with Shaytan, his sons, and Darius. The latter kept looking around. "Where's Rewa?" he asked.

Only then did I understand that she wasn't with the rest of the noble families, beneath one of the masks. She would've been the first to try to get close to Darius, perhaps even protesting a little louder over the charmed cuffs that Shaytan had made him wear. Jax and I looked at each other.

"Do you think something might've happened?" I asked him, keeping my voice low.

"I wouldn't be surprised if she got on the dragon's wrong side," Jax muttered. "Let's not forget she's had quite the obsession brewing for Blaze."

I stifled a chuckle as we passed by the fifth level. Looking around, and knowing where we'd assigned key positions, I caught glimpses of air rippling. I put my red lens on, beneath the mask, and was relieved to see our people on top of buildings, peeking from behind chimneys and small towers.

"Our people are all in position," I whispered just as we made it to the ground level, the green fields stretching out before us.

"Good. It's safe to assume those aren't the only daemons that Shaytan has brought with him," Jax replied, nodding at the guards.

"Speaking of which, he's got three sons with him here. Where would the other two from his Council be?"

"They're most likely somewhere close and out of sight," Jax muttered. "I can't see any through my lens. Did you spot them?"

I shook my head. "They're probably well-hidden and ready to intervene if things go south."

"And with plenty of soldiers to back them," he said. "Either way, we have to stay on course, no matter what. We also have to assume that the other two sons could be trying to get the swamp witch out, for their father's gain. That means Caspian and the others will have their work cut out for them in the Palisades."

The crowd gathered around the funeral ground, where thousands of headstones poked out from the dark earth. The clerics positioned the caskets on their platforms, surrounded by large copper bowls filled with what looked like dry wood and oil. They lit them up, and orange flames were soon bursting and licking at the clear sky.

Emilian and Rowan took their positions in front of Amalia and Vincent's caskets, while the others stayed back. I understood the grief of the parents—even though I detested them both, and their offspring had been just as bad and toxic, I could feel their pain. It was sharp, and it cut through me like a hot knife. I'd buried not one, but six daughters. However, my girls were noble warriors. They never would've committed the atrocities Amalia and Vincent had.

It hurt, but there were plenty of creatures in this world who didn't deserve the gift of life, for they had squandered and soiled it. I blamed the parents here. They'd raised their young to think that the weak deserved to be tortured and killed for no reason. They'd raised Vincent and Amalia to have zero respect for life, so why should they be granted theirs?

"I'm not too worried about Caspian," I murmured, trying to get my mind off the concept of grief before it closed my throat up. "No one can stand between him and Harper."

"You're right about that," Jax replied. "Caspian's been a bundle of rage and darkness since Harper was taken. He will destroy everything in his path if that's what it takes to get her back."

Emilian cleared his throat, demanding the mumbling crowd's attention.

"Amalia was a piece of my soul," he said. I found that to be a little on the nose, given their depravity in eating souls. "The day she was born was the single most important moment in the universe for me. She was so tiny and pale, but her grip on my finger was strong, and... well, she had a pair of lungs on her." He chuckled softly as he reminisced.

We're all born innocent.

"Vincent was so soft and chubby," Rowan chimed in. I understood then that they were doing a joint eulogy. I'd never listened to one like this before, and thus found myself immersed in their stories about Vincent and Amalia. Had we not known the monsters that they really were, I would've felt sorrier for Emilian and Rowan. "He was quiet for the first two years of his life. But once he learned to speak, it became impossible to shut him up."

The crowd murmured softly, amused and charmed by the idea that Vincent and Amalia had been sweet, perfectly normal little Maras. Half of the people in attendance were mind-bent, anyway, and the other half were as savage and as evil as the ones they were about to cremate.

"Today, we lay our children to rest," Emilian continued, his voice trembling. "Today, we say goodbye to pieces of our souls. Today, we set our very hearts on fire and hope that there's an after-life waiting for them, filled with nothing but joy, bliss, and peace. They deserve it."

I scoffed, crossing my arms beneath my velvet cloak. They were either in denial or just playing a part, though for whom, I wasn't entirely sure. The jig was up a long time ago. There was no one left for them to impress. It made more sense to assume that Emilian, Rowan, and the rest of their wretched kind genuinely thought they were the actual victims. That they'd done nothing wrong. That their children were epitomes of greatness and perfection.

"Farewell, my beloved Amalia," Emilian said. "May you join your mother in eternal beauty."

"Goodbye, my darling Vincent," Rowan said through a sob. "May your soul be free and roam through the world."

With their parting words uttered, they both stepped away from the caskets. The clerics came around with torches and set the wooden boxes on fire. The flames swallowed them whole, instantly consuming the flowers and outer layers. The wood crackled as it gave way. Bright orange flames erupted and reached for the sky, their tips extending into swirling threads of black smoke.

The flute-like instruments resumed their mournful songs.

Emilian put his arm around Rowan as they both cried and watched Amalia's and Vincent's bodies devoured by fire. Farrah's shoulders shuddered as she, too, cried for the loss of the Lords' children. They were literally watching the future of the Exiled Maras going up in flames.

With Sienna and Caspian on our side, all they had were Farrah's sons, who were too young to rule anything. It dawned on me then, the magnitude of our actions. By killing Vincent and Amalia, we'd crippled the Lords of Azure Heights. What came next was going to obliterate them altogether.

I caught a glimpse of Shaytan, quiet and somber as he watched the funeral ceremony. Yet there was a discreet flicker of amusement in his red eyes—deeply unsettling. That was either his pleasure in watching the Exiled Maras suffer, or a foreshadowing snicker of some kind. Like he had something more in store for them.

It troubled me. But Jax was right. We had to stick to the plan, no matter what.

9

JAX

We followed the procession back into the city, once again keeping a reasonable distance from our key foes. I noticed Shaytan exchanging muttered words with his sons, and it confirmed what we'd been thinking, even though they used code words.

"I see the sun is out. It's nice today," Shaytan muttered to Abeles.

The Mara Lords were leading the crowd, and there were more than twenty feet between them and the daemons, but Shaytan didn't seem to want to risk being overheard. After all, we were known for our heightened senses.

"It feels warm," Abeles replied. "The birds are singing, but I'm sure that at the first sign of rain they'll fly to cover."

"There's no stopping the rain, is there, my son?"

"Never, Father. And there is only so much a little bird can do to shield itself from its drops," Abeles murmured.

To anyone else, it would've sounded like small talk, at best. To me, however, it was a troubling conversation. The daemons were forged in the heat of battle. They were a warlike nation, and they'd built their kingdom on top of the bones of their enemies. Concealing their true intentions in front of their so-called allies was a necessity, especially since tensions were so high between them and the Maras.

Shaytan was, in fact, demanding confirmation that their troops were in position. The Maras were the little birds. The raindrops were daemons. Once their exchange was translated, it drew a grim picture for me. There were soldiers nearby, ready to strike as soon as Shaytan gave his signal.

"I didn't peg you daemons for poets." Darius scoffed, walking just a couple of feet ahead of Shaytan. He kept looking around for Rewa. "And where the hell is my daughter?"

"Pipe down, Lord Xunn," Shaytan shot back, his tone flat. "You'll see your little birdy soon enough, I presume."

I found Shaytan's choice of words when describing Rewa to be a testament to his sadism. Referring to her as a little bird while conversing in code with his sons was, however, typical of his complex of superiority. After all, the daemons did consider themselves the supreme species of Neraka. Judging by Darius's inability to spot the hidden language, I couldn't help but think the daemons did have an edge on the Maras, where intellect was concerned.

On one hand, yes, the Maras were cunning. They'd fooled us well enough. But the daemons were vicious and led by an extremely intelligent Shaytan. I was convinced that a clash was imminent at this point.

I glanced over my shoulder, catching a glimpse of the Valley of Screams, its dark gorges rising in the distance and riddled with our allied troops. Whatever Shaytan had to bring in against the Maras didn't include hordes of Manticores, Dhaxanians, Adlets, and rebel Imen coming for their heads.

There was no trace of daemons in the fields, either. Whatever troops Shaytan had brought over were most likely hidden in the city.

"He's definitely got back up around here," I whispered to Hansa.

"Do we know how many?"

"No, but there aren't any in the field below," I replied. "I'm thinking dozens, at most. It wouldn't take much to overtake the Maras, if they're caught off guard."

"What if the Lords are prepared, though?" she asked.

I shrugged in response. "We'll have to wait and see. Either way, we're still doing this."

"Absolutely. We need to get out of this place."

On the sixth level, we split from the thinning crowd and made our way through the narrow back alleys behind the cafes and shops. We tossed our cloaks and masks behind a potted tree, then ingested a scoop of invisibility paste each. I could breathe a little easier without the layer of velvet, as I already had my gear on, mask, hood, and goggles included. We vanished and went deeper into the city, keeping out of sight.

There were Correction Officers patrolling the main streets, and one in three was wearing a red garnet lens. We climbed up the walls of the tallest building, then rushed and jumped across the roofs until we reached the far corner of the level, on the eastern side. From there, we had a quick climb on the mountain wall to the seventh level, with thick woods to hide in, if needed.

We made it to the top level almost effortlessly, then stopped to check our surroundings. I caught a glimpse of Hundurr and Rover in the woods to our right. As big as they were, they still managed to keep a low profile. They were, by all possible definitions, highly evolved predators, after all.

We snuck around the outer edge of the Lords' mansions to the back, then stopped behind House Obara's stables. Correction Officers moved around the buildings, never staying in one spot for longer than five minutes. They were on high alert.

"Let's go," I whispered, then ran to the back entrance of the Obara mansion, closely followed by Hansa. We had only a minute's worth of free movement before other Correction Officers came around.

We slipped through the door and took refuge beneath the service staircase. Imen servants buzzed around, visibly alarmed. No one was comfortable with daemons in the house, it seemed. I could hear Shaytan talking just outside in the front courtyard. They were about to come in.

Hansa and I snuck through the hallway and took separate positions in the living room. She settled behind a large, dark red velvet curtain, while I found a good spot in the corner, behind an armchair.

My heart was thumping. I hadn't engaged with an enemy like this in a while. With Azazel, things had been relatively straightforward. He knew we were there, and we knew what he was capable of. With the daemons and Exiled Maras, however, we didn't have all the information—specifically, we didn't know how much swamp witch magic they'd managed to get out of Lumi.

The main door swung open as Emilian, Rowan, and Farrah came in, followed by Darius, Shaytan, and his three sons—Abeles, Garros and Mammon—then five of his guards. The other five were ordered to stay outside.

Correction Officers came into the living room first, assuming positions against each of the four walls. My stomach tightened itself into a painful marble at the sight of just five feet between Hansa's hiding place and one of the COs. The closest ones to me were ten feet away, on both sides. Nevertheless, we were here. *No turning back now.*

Besides, Hansa would've slapped me silly for worrying about her like this. Tribe chief warrior queen and whatnot.

Emilian, Rowan, and Farrah each took a seat on one of the sofas. Shaytan occupied the other in front of them, while Darius sat in a chair nearby. The princes stood back, their red eyes narrowed and constantly scanning their surroundings. The daemon guards were a tad oversized for the space, despite its tall ceiling and ample room.

There was a brief moment of awkward silence before Shaytan spoke.

"You Maras can still have more children, you know," he offered, like the tone-deaf sociopath that he was, despite his high degree of intelligence.

Emilian scoffed and shook his head with contempt. "My Amalia is irreplaceable. Don't be ridiculous," he retorted, then nodded at Darius. "Why is Lord Xunn in cuffs?"

Shaytan looked at Darius for a brief moment, then chuckled. "Contingency, my friend. One can never be too careful, especially in this day and age."

"That's insulting, considering we're allies," Rowan hissed, crossing her arms.

"There's something about these cuffs," Darius replied with a frown. From my position, I could see the etched symbols glowing amber. "They're doing something to me... Where's Rewa?"

Emilian glanced around, snapping his finger at a Correction Officer. "You. Go find Rewa," he said, then shifted his focus back to Darius. "What do you mean, they're doing something to you?"

Shaytan chuckled softly. "As you remember, Darius came to Infernis while you skilled thespians were staging your play for the outsiders. You were supposed to catch them. Instead, you let them loose and put my kingdom at risk," he replied.

"What does that have to do with Lord Xunn's cuffs?" Emilian retorted.

"I'm getting there!" Shaytan shot back. "Now. After their attack on my palace, I had to take a better look at you, at Azure Heights, and at how this simple project turned into such a nightmare. Frankly, I had my doubts about you, Lord Obara. So, like the good king that I am, I figured I might as well ask Darius here, since he was in town. But then," he added, laughing, "I found him trying to sneak out without so much as a goodbye. Obviously, I took offense.

Then I took *precautions*," he said, pointing at the cuffs. "And oh, did the birdy sing!"

Darius sighed. "It's worse than mind-bending," he muttered. "I'm extremely dumbed down. I don't even remember what I told him. I can't recall what I said five minutes ago, either."

"This is preposterous," Emilian barked, banging his fist onto the coffee table in front of him. The glass top cracked. One more blow, and it would shatter.

"It's called critical thinking," Shaytan replied dryly. "You see, Lord Xunn, in his current state, is a bumbling imbecile with a loose tongue, while I am a wiser daemon for keeping him around."

"You must release him," Farrah demanded. "This is not part of any agreement, and certainly not in line with our alliance!"

Shaytan gave her a contemptuous smirk. "You should've thought of that when you bloodsucking fiends decided to band together and try to usurp me."

The Lords froze. Shaytan laughed.

"What are you talking about?" Emilian asked slowly.

Suddenly, Shaytan's humor went right out the window. Almost instinctively, my whole body bucked, tension gathering between my shoulder blades. There was a storm coming, and it was going to rattle the entire living room.

"You've been conspiring to knock me off the food chain for quite some time now," Shaytan replied. "I know all about your plans to cut off my access to the swamp witch. To sabotage my cities. To assassinate me. Who did you have in mind for the job, though? I doubt either of you could pull it off. You'd need someone capable of getting close enough to deliver a blow."

The Lords were silent. This was probably one of those precious nuggets of information only circulated between the Houses, and the only Lord we had to tell us about it couldn't, given his blood oath.

"I told you, these cuffs make me say things," Darius mumbled, visibly ashamed.

"But I appreciated your honesty, Lord Xunn. It's why you're still breathing," Shaytan said, a grin slitting his face. He then scowled at Emilian, Rowan, and Farrah. "So, who did you want to do the dirty job, huh? Lord Kifo? I'd bet my money on him. Despite his idealistic faults, he is a worthy opponent. I must give credit where it's due."

Emilian shook his head, then exhaled sharply. "I think we're getting off on the wrong foot here."

"I think you twisted your ankle altogether when you started believing you were in any way superior to the daemons," Shaytan replied. "Do not underestimate me, Lord Obara. Remember, you've got a mountain. I've got tens of thousands of grunts, ready to obliterate you. I've been courteous for the past millennia, simply to express my gratitude for your swamp witch's tricks. But you are all bugs to me. My right foot alone is big enough to squish you all."

A minute went by in deafening silence as they all assessed one another. From my experience, the Lords were either looking for weak spots to attack or excuses to avoid a bloodbath. If they had any sense left in them, they were bound to go for the latter.

"Perhaps it's time for us to address our alliance and strengthen our friendship," Farrah proposed, motioning for one of the Correction Officers. "Bring our guests down, please."

Emilian gave her a deadly scowl. "What are you doing?" he muttered.

"Possibly saving our lives," Farrah shot back, smiling at Shaytan.

Two Correction Officers left the room. I heard their boots rumbling up the stairs.

"I'm not thrilled about the current state of this alliance," Shaytan said, crossing his arms and pursing his lips. His sons didn't look too happy either.

"Your Grace, let us talk about this," Farrah replied calmly, while Emilian and Rowan stared at her in disbelief. It didn't take

Harper's sentry abilities to tell that they were feeling betrayed, that this conversation wasn't going where they'd originally planned. But Farrah seemed smarter, invulnerable to emotions. After all, Houses Roho and Obara had suffered a devastating loss. Their judgment was clouded.

"I'm listening." Shaytan sighed, feigning boredom. His face lit up when the Correction Officers returned with Blaze and Caia, their wrists bound by charmed cuffs and their expressions vacant, as if mind-bent. "Ah, yes, my future snacks!"

I knew they were still wearing their contact lenses and found myself in awe of their theatrical performance. Deep down, I was also thrilled and relieved to see them both alive and well. On top of that, I was becoming more and more certain that they had something to do with Rewa's absence.

Emilian and Rowan were seething. Darius was somewhat numbed by his charmed cuffs. All he could do was ask again: "Where's my daughter?"

They all looked at Caia and Blaze, as if they had the answer. Caia shrugged.

"I don't know," she murmured, staring blankly at the floor.

"What about you, little dragon?" Shaytan asked. "Do you know where Darius's precious daughter went? I'm afraid I'll sew his mouth shut if he asks the same question again, at this point."

"I don't know," Blaze replied, appearing equally dazed. "She came to the room to see me. She kissed me and promised Caia a world of pain. Then she left. I don't know where she went. She promised to come back and love me forever. I look forward to it, because I love her, too. I don't know where she went."

Well, the dragon could definitely play the mind-bent part. He came across as a bit of a fool, but, based on the Lords' expressions, he'd sold the story and they'd gobbled it up, down to the last word.

"There you go," Shaytan said, clapping his hands once. "They're mind-bent, I presume, and telling the truth," he added, then frowned at Darius. "Now, shut up. I've got some business to attend to here. Be a good bloodsucker and keep those lips tight."

Farrah rolled her eyes, sighing. "Your Grace, here's what I offer, on behalf of the Lords."

"Farrah, what are you doing?" Emilian said, gritting his teeth. "You can't—"

"Shut up, Lord Obara." Farrah cut him off. "I've had enough of your half-witted solutions. We have an alliance here that is in desperate need of repairs, before we all get our heads cut off. It's time we bring everything back under one treaty, once more," she said, and looked at Shaytan. "Your Grace, let us give you the dragon, the fae, and Miss Hellswan, the latter of whom we're keeping separately and extra secure, since she cannot be mind-bent. In return, we only ask that you release Lord Xunn. Rest assured that no one will make any attempts on your life."

Shaytan thought about it for a few moments, his gaze gliding around the room from one creature to another. He briefly looked at Abeles, who smirked and offered him a faint nod in return. Shaytan then clicked his teeth and focused his full attention on Farrah.

I had to give her credit. Though I hadn't spoken much to Farrah, and I'd seen Emilian and Rowan leading most of the governing-related conversations, I was somewhat impressed by her. She struck me as a devious survivor, ready to talk her way through any arrangement. I was also convinced that she was equally capable of stabbing and poisoning whoever got between her and her prime objective—and that included the other Lords.

However, I wasn't sure she'd survive Shaytan, in any shape or form.

"I see," the daemon king muttered. "I appreciate the offer, milady. However, I think it's time we shake things in this place up a little bit. It's getting too stale for my taste."

"What do you mean, Your Grace?" Farrah replied, her brow furrowed.

"You've had equal standing in this world for thousands of years," Shaytan said. "Yet all you've managed to do was to accelerate the depletion of our soul food sources."

"But the outsiders... It's why we brought them here, to gradually replenish the food population," Farrah breathed, visibly alarmed. "We're extremely close to getting this done, despite the minor hiccups."

"Minor hiccups?!" Shaytan shot back, then burst into laughter. "They destroyed my prison city. They tore down Ragnar Peak! You must be struggling with semantics, my dear, because those are not minor hiccups. They're major screw-ups. No, no, no. I think I'm done here."

The Lords held their collective breath.

"What do you mean?" Emilian asked. The look on his face, however, told me he already knew what was coming. His worst-case scenario was most likely about to unfold.

Shaytan sneered at them.

"We need a change in the power structure here, Lord Obara. I've had enough of your amateurish shenanigans," he said. "The daemons are the supreme species of Neraka, and I've grown tired of sharing the spoils with your kind."

My fingers gripped my sword handles, and I slowly shifted my weight onto my left foot. My blood pumped faster, heat spreading through my body. I knew exactly what was going to happen next, and I wanted to be ready to ruin it for them.

10

CAIA

E milian was the first to stand, his hands balled into fists.
    "What are you trying to say?" he asked, his tone flat
and cold.

"You keep asking like you don't understand what's going on,"
Shaytan replied, still casually sitting on the couch. "What is it that
you fail to comprehend, Lord Obara?"

"We had a deal!" Rowan shot to her feet.

Farrah gripped her hand in a bid to calm her down, but the
fear on her face told me she was starting to realize that no deal
would save them from what was about to unfold. Blaze and I
briefly exchanged glances. We knew we wouldn't kick things off.
Not yet, anyway. The scene had yet to build up to the maximum
boiling point.

"That deal went out the window the moment you decided to
conspire against me," Shaytan said. "I thought I'd made that clear
already. Has grief made you both stupid or what?"

I caught a glimmer of air rippling and the faintest flicker of
jade eyes, slowly moving from the corner toward one of the

Correction Officers. I discreetly nudged Blaze. He followed my gaze and spotted him, too. Caspian was most likely down in the Palisade, working to get Lumi and Harper out. We were both looking at either Jax or Heron. Chances were that he wasn't alone.

With the Lords busy arguing with Shaytan, no one spotted the intruders. Blaze and I continued to play our mind-bent parts in the meantime. We were still waiting for that pinnacle, the catalyst that would trigger our deadly surprise.

"Your Grace, surely we can talk about this," Farrah said, her voice trembling as she stood up. "Despite our shortcomings, we've had a good relationship with your kingdom over the millennia. There must be a way for us to get past this... unpleasant bump in the road."

Shaytan grinned. "This is no longer an equal agreement between daemons and Exiled Maras, milady. You tossed that aside when you went for my throat."

"I didn't—" Farrah stopped herself, then took a deep breath. "Granted, there were some discussions, but nothing was ever truly carved in stone. You must understand, we have to protect ourselves, too."

"You can protect yourselves as much as you want, just not at the expense of the daemon king's life," Abeles shot back. His expression was dark and firm. He was no longer interested in what they had to say, and neither were Garros and Mammon.

"This is preposterous! I will not stand here and—" Emilian said, but got cut off by a thump coming from upstairs, muffled by a scream.

They all froze. Shaytan didn't move but was visibly confused.

An Iman servant ran downstairs, crying and stricken with horror.

"Milords! Milords! There's a pile of ashes in the cupboard... There were charred fingers in it! And teeth! I saw teeth!" She sobbed, then raised a Lordship ring for everyone to see, her hand shaking.

Darius gasped. Emilian moved to take the ring from the Iman girl, who'd stopped in the living room archway, but the daemons instantly drew their swords. The COs reacted, taking out their blades as well. Every fiber in my body beckoned me to grab the nearest knife or sword and do something, but Blaze and I stood still. The perfect moment was just around the corner.

"Enough!" Emilian barked, scowling at the daemons, then at Shaytan.

The daemon king exhaled sharply and motioned for his guards to let Emilian move. The Mara Lord took the Lordship ring from the Iman girl's hand and carefully examined it before giving Darius a sorrowful look.

"It's Rewa's. She started wearing it in your absence," Emilian said, his voice trembling.

"No... No... No!" Darius cried out, stricken with grief. He slid off the couch and dropped to his knees. I felt a little sorry for him, but not enough to warrant any kind of mercy.

"Who... Who did this?" Rowan murmured, looking around the room.

The Iman girl sniffed and wiped her tears. "I found it in the room upstairs, where you keep your... guests," she said.

Suddenly, all eyes were on us. We kept our game faces on, though. They had no idea we were wearing protective contacts. They wouldn't figure it out unless we told them, anyway.

"You! Did you do this?" Emilian hissed, coming back to us.

"Do what?" I asked, playing exceptionally dumb.

"This!" he replied, lifting the Lordship ring for me to see. "Did you kill Rewa?"

I blinked several times. "No."

"Did you?" Emilian then asked Blaze, who looked equally befuddled.

"They're mind-bent by Rewa! How could they?" Farrah scoffed.

"Well, someone did!" Emilian shot back.

Darius was on the floor, completely broken down. He was

bawling like a little boy—the third Lord to have lost a child since we'd arrived on Neraka. Taken out of context, it would've made us look like monsters. But knowing what they'd done and planned to keep doing, I could only breathe a sigh of relief, knowing that Sienna, at least, was on our side, and that Farrah's kids were too young to get involved in their parents' mess.

"I didn't do anything," Blaze muttered. He'd gotten even better at playing his part. For a second there, I thought he'd picked the wrong career. The dragon could've very well belonged on stage.

"We saw Rewa leave our room. We don't remember anything else," I added.

"What if they were mind-bent by Rewa's killer?" Rowan asked, looking at Emilian and Farrah.

"You mean a Mara did this?" Emilian replied.

"Maybe Caspian!" Rowan offered, then frowned. "Or maybe the king here had something to do with it. He's got plenty of Mara prisoners in his... dessert cages."

The attention in the room shifted to Shaytan. His eyebrows popped up with surprise. I slipped the key into my cuffs, then discreetly passed it on to Blaze.

"You're joking," Shaytan muttered. "I've got better things to do with my time than stage an elaborate murder. If I want to kill any of you, I'll make a damn good statement of it, too."

Just then, as the Maras and daemons sneered at each other, I saw Jax and Hansa appearing behind two Correction Officers. Their invisibility spells had worn off. They'd timed this incredibly well. With or without the discovery of Rewa's charred remains, this was our moment of revelation.

Our cuffs dropped to the floor with a disruptive rattle. The Correction Officers in front of Hansa and Jax collapsed, their heads cut off. Gasps erupted around the room, and Blaze and I took a couple of steps back. Jax tossed one of his spare lighters my way—I caught it, flicked it open, and assumed an attack position.

Both the Lords and the daemon king were taken by surprise. Shaytan stood up, towering over everyone.

"The jig is up," I said, wearing a confident smirk.

"How... How can this be?" Emilian was baffled.

Rowan was burning with rage. Farrah was stunned, as were Abeles, Garros, and Mammon. Darius was lost for a second, before it all came back into focus and he rose to his feet.

"You... You killed my baby," he murmured, eerily calm. There was a storm coming. I could feel it in my bones.

"How? How?" Emilian still couldn't wrap his head around it. "You were mind-bent."

"We were never mind-bent," I replied. "We took precautions prior to coming here. Boy, you really underestimated our ability to adapt."

"Aren't you a fiery little thing?" Shaytan chuckled, genuinely impressed. "So, you've been playing these bloodsuckers since they first slapped the cuffs on you, huh?"

Blaze and I nodded. Shaytan then glanced over at Hansa and Jax, who'd been surrounded by several daemons and COs.

"And your friends came to rescue you," he added.

"Nope," Hansa shot back, then took out her Adlet flare, held it up, and winked at me. "We came here to terminate you all."

I produced a small fireball, which I threw at the flare. It ignited with a bright red flash, blinding everyone temporarily. I looked away but heard the ensuing bang. The Adlet flare was not made to burn indoors. It shot toward the sky, making a hole through the ceiling, the upper floors, and eventually the roof, before it reached the optimum altitude and exploded in its typical fashion.

Shaytan growled, baring his fangs at Hansa.

"If you think a little flare will save you, you're in for an ugly surprise," he said.

"Oh, that wasn't for me," Hansa replied, a grin stretching her lips. "That was for our allies."

"Allies?" Emilian scoffed. "What allies? The Dhaxanians, the

Adlets, the Manticores, they're all coming to sign an agreement with us. What allies? Ten rebel Imen and Lord Kifo? Don't be ridiculous!"

The entrance door burst open, and several Correction Officers came in, looking pale and sweaty. They were baffled at first by the frozen standoff between us, the daemons, and the Maras, but they had to tell the Lords what was happening outside.

"Milord," one of the COs said, "there are troops coming out of the gorges. Hundreds of them. Fights are breaking out in the city. There's something going on."

"Damn straight there's something going on," I replied, producing a large fireball with my lighter.

All of a sudden, the atmosphere changed in the room. The Maras and the daemons became aware of the ensuing battle. The Dhaxanians, the Adlets, and the Manticores were on our side. We had rebel Imen, daemons and Maras fighting for us.

"If you thought anyone would be foolish enough or suicidal enough to trust you, Emilian, then you're a lot dumber than I gave you credit for," Hansa said, raising her sword, ready to fight.

Shaytan checked each of us out, then narrowed his eyes at me.

"I take it you want a war, then," he muttered.

"Time's up," I said.

They couldn't believe it, but they couldn't deny it, either. We'd made good use of our element of surprise. Within minutes, more of our fighters were going to storm this place. All we had to do was fight, tooth and nail, until the protective shield around Neraka came down.

I mentally braced myself for what came next. After all, we were in the same room as Shaytan and three of his sons. The Mara Lords were equally vicious and dangerous. But I had no intention of dying in this place. None whatsoever.

11

FIONA

This time around, we decided to change things up a little, taking advantage of the funeral. After our previous incursion into the Palisade, odds were that the Exiled Maras would be extra vigilant and would be wearing their red lenses. Going invisible wasn't our best way in.

Instead, we secured some funeral capes and masks from Aymon. We'd stayed close to the funeral procession, but we were at the back, as far away from the Lords, the daemons, and even Hansa and Jax as possible. Once we came back up, we split away from the crowd and casually made our way toward the sixth level, black velvet hoods and porcelain masks still on.

Zane was the only one who made use of the invisibility spell, and for good reason, too. I could only imagine the anger and anguish in his heart at the sight of his brothers and evil father. He stayed out of sight, but close, and joined us outside the Palisade.

The townspeople were slowly going back to their homes and businesses. It was an eerie picture to watch unfold, as they all wore the same funeral garb. I caught faint ripples of air here and there. Our teammates and allies were close by. However, their main focus was providing backup to Hansa, Jax, Caia, and Blaze. We had to make do with our ensemble, but I was certain we'd pull it off.

Zane went ahead, as planned, and snuck into the building to prepare our access into the basement. That included diverting or disabling any Correction Officer that might wonder what we were doing down there.

Caspian, Heron, Avril, and I entered the spacious lobby area, then casually passed by the reception desk and headed for the secluded corridor. I led the team as we moved slowly, flowing with the rest of the Maras and Imen on the ground floor. We occasionally stopped and pretended to talk, while I kept an eye on the nearby corridor.

I got a glimpse of a CO being dragged out of sight by an invisible force—Zane. He killed every Mara in our path and discreetly shoved them inside vacant rooms and closets. He was fast and effective. I was impressed, though it didn't come as a surprise. I'd already seen what he could do, but I couldn't really get enough of it.

"Okay, coast is clear," I muttered, then walked toward the corridor, with the others right behind me.

We all came to a sudden halt when two Correction Officers emerged from a chamber to our right. They both seemed relaxed and amused, sipping blood from crystal chalices.

"I tell you, they were—" one of them said, stopping when he spotted us. He smiled. "How was the funeral?"

Dammit. Now I have to play along.

I shrugged. "Sad," I replied.

We had no choice but to talk our way out, before we could sneak through the corridor, which was literally just a few feet away. I briefly glanced around, noticing only a handful of Imen servants in the chamber. We were in a relatively quiet part of the ground floor, as most of the guests were buzzing around the reception area, along with the private quarters on the other side of the grand staircase.

"At least they did a joint funeral," the other CO said. "Imagine going through the same ordeal twice."

The first CO chuckled. The rest of us mirrored their demeanor.

"You weren't too fond of Amalia and Vincent, huh?" Heron asked from behind me.

"Amalia was a freakin' psycho!" the first CO replied. "I can't even count the times I've had to clean up her messes. That wench had a thing for draining the blood out of Imen children. It was disturbing."

"I mean, at least we drink from the adults," the other CO added. "We let the kids be kids, you know?"

I found that infuriating. Letting Imen children grow up into this nightmare, to then snuff the life out of them for pleasure. It was equally deplorable.

"Yeah, the kids need to grow before we can drink them dry, right?" I replied dryly. I instantly felt Avril discreetly nudging me.

The COs didn't catch my sarcastic tone, though. Instead, they laughed lightly and nodded. As if any of this was funny. My hand was itching for my sword.

"As for Vincent... Just no," the first CO said, while the other chortled, scratching the back of his head. "He was simply useless and pathetic. The upside is he's no longer here to order us around."

"Let's just say the city hasn't suffered too great a loss," the second CO said, and nodded at me. "You can take those masks off, though. This is a pleasure house. No one cares how hard you grieve."

I chuckled softly, moving to leave them behind. "It's fine, it's fine," I said. "We need to get a room and change altogether."

The first officer caught my arm, frowning. "What have you got to hide?" he asked. Then he grinned. "Are you that ugly? Let me see—"

He tried to grab my mask, but Zane had already snuck up on him. Zane stabbed his neck with a poisoned arrow, then disabled the other CO. Before they even hit the floor, we caught them, held them up as they lost consciousness, and followed Zane into the nearest room, farther down the narrow corridor.

We stashed them inside a closet, then made our way to the secret door at the end of the hallway.

"Thanks," Heron muttered.

Zane gave him a brief nod, then opened the secret door and rushed down the basement stairs. We went after him and stopped at the bottom. We all put our red lenses on underneath our masks, just in case there were any invisible fiends around. Wearing our hoods and masks was going to get us deeper into the underground level.

"Hold on," Zane whispered. He went ahead, checking the walls and ceiling for hidden traps. He passed his fingers over a small hole in the ceiling. "Aha." He grumbled, using his claws to disable it. It was a misting device, from the looks of it. It would've revealed any creature using the invisibility spell.

We followed him through another hallway, where he broke two other traps—one devised to deploy water mist, and the other meant to trap an intruder between two sheets of charmed, unbreakable glass. We'd learned some lessons from our previous visit, for sure.

We had one more corner to turn before we'd see Lumi's room straight ahead. It was as far as the cloaks were going to get us. From what I'd spotted along the way, only uniformed COs had access to these parts of the basement. We dropped our cloaks and masks, then ingested invisibility paste. Less than a minute later, we'd all vanished.

I peeked around the corner, spotting the two daemon guards and two COs posted outside Lumi's room. Harper was also in there, according to Aymon. *Two birds, one stone.*

"Okay, same deal as last time," I whispered. "We split up."

"Heron, Zane," Caspian replied, "can you two draw the guards out on both sides, so we can enter directly through the front?"

Both Heron and Zane nodded. "Yeah, the layout works," Heron muttered. "They'll have to chase us around the perimeter from both ends of that corridor, while you three go in perpendicularly."

That said, Heron and Zane darted off in opposite directions, while Caspian, Avril, and I waited around the corner, quietly watching Lumi's door. About twenty seconds later, two distinct noises drew the guards' attention. They all frowned, then looked at each other, briefly nodded, and went after the noise sources. A daemon and CO took the left, while a CO took the right. They left a daemon behind, but one was three times easier than all four of them put together.

I shot through the corridor at high speed. He spotted the air ripples, but it was too late. I rammed into his stomach before he had a chance to react. The impact was strong enough to throw him against the door and knock the air out of his lungs.

"Duck!" Caspian said behind me.

I instantly dropped to the floor, and Caspian cut the daemon's head off. I unlocked the door using a skeleton key that Laughlan had crafted for this mission, and then Caspian dragged the daemon inside, while Avril brought his head in with a disgusted expression.

"Ew, ew, ew!" She groaned, then tossed the daemon head into the corner.

I closed the door behind us and stayed close to it, listening to the noise coming from outside. Just as Aymon had said, both Lumi and Harper were in the room. Its walls had swamp witch symbols scrawled all over them, as did Lumi's and Harper's cuffs and restraints.

Lumi was gagged and frozen, watching us with wide, strangely white eyes. She could see me without a red garnet lens, despite my invisibility spell. She was beautiful but... different. Her hair was a bright orange, tamed into a luscious bun. She'd been stuffed into a black, conservative dress, which contrasted with the tattoos on her neck, cheeks, and temples.

Harper smirked, catching the air ripples and instantly figuring out what was going on. Caspian rushed to get her out. I tossed him the key and gave Harper a wink as soon as he put a red lens over her eye.

"Your escape service has arrived," I said, wearing a devious smirk.

12

HARPER

My heart soared at the sight of Caspian, Fiona, and Avril. As soon as I was free of my charmed cuffs, I wrapped my arms around Caspian, and he covered my face with feverish kisses. I'd heard the noises outside. Part of me had already known what was happening before the door even opened.

I shot to my feet, stretching with delight as Caspian handed me a sword. Mine had been taken away, along with the rest of my gear. I took the key from him and used it to remove Lumi's cuffs, then took the gag off. The swamp witch was in shock, hope glimmering blue around her for the first time.

"Where are the others?" I asked as I tossed the chains and cuffs aside, resting my hands on Lumi's thighs and giving her a warm smile.

"Zane and Heron are outside, giving the guards a run for their money," Avril replied, settling by the door, next to Fiona. "The rest of the team is in position."

"You're... You're all from Calliope." Lumi finally spoke, for the first time in millennia. Her voice was faint and raspy, her vocal cords weakened. She took several deep breaths, smiling at the sound of it.

"And The Shade," I said. "I told you, we're getting you out of this place."

"After all this time... I didn't think I'd ever utter a word again," she whispered, tearing up. "I'm so weak."

"I know," I replied gently. "I'm... We're not going to let anyone hurt you again, I promise. I've said it before, and I will say it again. You're one of us, Lumi. We don't leave our people behind."

"How come you can see us, even though we're invisible?" Fiona asked.

"Swamp witches can see the magic of the Word, even when it's cast. Invisible spells, cloaking shields, hidden charms, everything. It all glows gold for us," Lumi explained. "I cannot see you like I see Harper, for example, but I can make out your figures and most of your facial expressions. It's difficult to explain right now."

Avril stilled and sniffed the air. "Hold on. There's a sudden mixture of scents coming from above. From outside, specifically. I think the Adlet flare was launched."

Fiona gasped. "Oh, hell, it's showtime. It's about to get busy in here, for sure," she added, and looked at Lumi. "Lumi, what spells have you given them so far?"

Lumi sighed, then nodded at Caspian. "Can you scratch off as many of the symbols on these walls as you can? They're holding me down, physically and spiritually."

Caspian immediately took out a pocket knife and started breaking the seals. His skin started to burn, as he was going against his blood oath. Avril took over from him, while I helped Lumi stand up. Her knees were weak. She gripped my shoulders, giving me a frightened look. I responded with an encouraging smile.

"I gave them plenty of spells," she said. "Invisibility, fertility, defense, and attack. Warfare magic. Poisons and scrying potions. Cloaking shields of various dimensions."

"Including one big enough to hide the entire planet, right?" I asked.

"Yes," she said.

She regretted each spell she'd given, but we already knew she'd had no choice.

"You did what you had to in order to survive, and that's a good thing," I replied. "If you'd gotten yourself killed, our chances of going home would've dropped to zero the moment we set foot on Neraka."

"They tortured me," Lumi murmured, taking a few steps as she held on to me for stability. We had to get her in better shape, and fast, so I cut my palm and offered her my blood to drink. "They nipped at my soul."

"I know," I said. "Drink some of my blood. It'll help you heal faster, at least enough for you to replenish some of your strength, because we're about to bust out of this joint."

Lumi nodded again, then consumed some of my blood. I could see the color gradually returning to her cheeks. Her gaze looked sharper, slightly more focused than before.

"What do you need in order to take down the shield they put around Neraka?" Fiona asked.

"A safe space and about half an hour," Lumi replied. "I don't need much else. The one thing I never told anyone, including the Exiled Maras, is the fact that I can break any swamp witch spell with just a few ounces of my blood."

"Smart witch," Caspian muttered.

"I think I know where we can go," Fiona said. She was about to continue, when the door burst open, prompting all of us to step back and draw our weapons.

Standing in the doorway, accompanied by two daemon guards, was Adaris, one of Shaytan's sons—the sixth on the Council, before Zane. He looked surprised, wearing a red lens and perfectly aware of our presence.

My heart jumped in my throat. We had been bound to get

company, sooner or later, only I'd hoped it wouldn't be one of the princes. They were vicious bastards and very difficult to kill. Time wasn't on our side, this time. We had to get Lumi out before more hostiles converged on our location.

"What are you ladies doing here?" Adaris muttered, drawing his humongous, bejeweled broadsword. That seem to be a common denominator for Shaytan's sons—big bodies, big egos, big weapons.

"Waiting for you," I replied.

I stepped in front of Lumi and raised my sword, its tip pointed at him. The bigger they were, the harder they fell. And I was not leaving this place without my swamp witch.

13

FIONA

For a second there, I felt like a guilty little schoolgirl caught doing something that was against the rules. Technically speaking, the last part was true, but we were fighting to save thousands of innocent creatures.

It was time to kick things up a notch. We had Lumi now. We just had to get her out of this place. Adaris stepped into the room, leaving his two guards in the doorway. Avril and I looked at each other, then went straight for their throats, leaving Harper, Caspian, and Lumi to deal with the prince.

I took on one of the daemons, dodging his rapier as it swung left and right, its blade thirsty for my blood. I swerved around and slashed his back, then severed the tendons behind his right knee. He growled from the pain, but I didn't give him the time to react.

I drove my sword through the back of his neck, then twisted with all my strength. He croaked, then choked and gurgled as blood ran down my blade, poking out at the front. I pushed him down, pulling my sword back in the process.

Avril's daemon was also down.

Harper showed no mercy toward Adaris, either. We dragged the daemons' bodies inside and closed the door again, as Harper fought the daemon prince. Caspian secured a position in the corner with Lumi, who watched as Harper dodged Adaris's broadsword, then hit back with decisive swings of her blade.

I noticed Lumi muttering something, her lips moving rapidly as she slowly lifted a hand, wiggling her fingers. Their tips took on an incandescent hue, then sent out a pulse through the air. It smacked Adaris between his shoulder blades. He stiffened, suddenly out of air. Lumi had just cast a spell on the daemon.

It gave Harper the window of opportunity she needed, and she drove her sword through his chest. Adaris collapsed, bleeding out, as Harper stared at Lumi.

"I didn't know you could perform spells with just... words," she breathed.

"What we wrote down in the triple tome is barely a fraction of what we can do," Lumi said, leaning against Caspian, her legs still weak. "Those are just what we selected to pass down to generations of non-witches, in case we were ever destroyed. The power of the Word goes well beyond that, and it's too dangerous for just anyone to wield such magic."

"So, it's true. Non-witches can become swamp witches?" Harper replied.

Lumi nodded. "Yes. We're not born but made. However, it's not an easy path. It is a complicated and lengthy process. It requires plenty of self-sacrifice."

"I get it," Avril said. "Lumi's got the real magic going on, the heavyweight stuff that daemons and Maras don't even know about. She's been stringing them along with spells that require potions and charms and all kinds of symbols. It's why they've kept her gagged all this time. They probably suspected she would eventually get herself out of here just by uttering her magic."

"That is correct," Lumi replied, then froze in sheer horror.

Adaris wasn't dead yet. He got up and raised his sword at

Harper—too fast for any of us to react. He was right behind Harper, and by the time she'd turn to stop him, there was a high chance he'd get her.

My stomach tightened. Lumi quickly whispered a spell, then flicked her wrist.

Adaris's head was instantly thrown to the side. We all heard the horrific crack of his spine breaking. He dropped dead, and Harper exhaled sharply.

"Oh, wow," she murmured.

Lumi's eyes rolled in her head. She passed out. Caspian caught her and sat her in the chair, while Harper produced a small bottle with a special elixir that Patrik had cooked for all of us, to help jolt any of us back to consciousness. It was a powerful smell, enough to make Lumi's eyes pop open.

She squirmed and pushed the bottle away, visibly disgusted.

"Good grief, I haven't smelled a Druid potion in ages," she muttered, then rubbed her face with her palms, regaining full awareness of her environment.

"Sorry, but we need you awake," Harper replied, putting the bottle away.

"I'm still weak," Lumi said. "That kill-spell took its toll on me."

Harper smiled. "Thank you for that. But we need you to stay awake and capable of taking down the shield. It is the single most important thing you can do for us right now."

"Harper, just so you know, we've got confirmation that our people in GASP are waiting outside the shield," I said. It was finally an appropriate time to brief her on this. "The Exiled Maras spotted them on one of the moons. They plan to attack them, but Aymon and several of our crew are taking care of that. Point is, our people are here. All we need to do is take down the damn spell."

Harper stared at me for a couple of seconds, before she lit up like a Christmas tree. "Hell, yeah!" She stood, then helped Lumi up as well. "Wait, who's Aymon?"

"A Correction Officer who switched sides," Avril explained.

"He's the one who helped us prepare for all this. He's somewhere in the Palisade, I think, disabling whatever the Exiled Maras plan to use against GASP."

"I can take care of that, too," Lumi interjected. "Just get me somewhere safe so I can sit down, break all the charms they've put in place, and disable their attack spells."

"Holy moly, you can do all that?" I breathed, in awe of her.

"It took us thousands of years to master the art of the Word," Lumi replied, wearing a sad smile. "My sisters and I were always aware that everything we could do needed a way of being undone, as well, to preserve the balance in the world, if it ever got out of hand."

Avril sniffed the air, frowning. "Guys, it's getting hot in here. There are more daemons coming to our location," she said, then narrowed her eyes at Lumi. "We need a fresh take on this," she added.

"What are you suggesting?" Harper asked, somewhat confused. "I thought we were just going to sneak out of here."

"I've got a better idea. You might not like it," she replied, then shifted her focus back to Lumi. "I'm going to need your help with this, if you can."

Lumi raised her eyebrows, curious, like the rest of us.

14

SCARLETT

W e waited until the funeral procession returned and began to scatter before we abandoned our hiding spots and made our way into the fourth level. Aymon had left to find out where they were planning to launch the attack on our moon-based crew, and we'd agreed to meet behind Marlowe's Tavern to join him in thwarting that endeavor.

We found him waiting just around the corner, wearing his daytime uniform. He wore a red lens and was able to see us as soon as we emerged from the shadows.

"This way," he muttered, then guided us through the back alleys of the fourth level.

"I thought they would be launching from the Palisade," I said, looking over my shoulder. Patrik, Sienna, Tobiah, Pheng-Pheng, and Cadmus were close behind me as we snuck past unsuspecting Imen. Aymon's presence worked in our favor, as the townspeople were fearful of him and kept their distance.

"I thought the same thing, but my source said they moved. Apparently, they've got a better angle from down here," Aymon said, pointing at a stone tower rising far back, close to the mountain wall. "That's the spot."

Patrik scoffed. "This is going to be easy, then."

"Thank the stars," I replied, knowing exactly what he meant.

"What do you mean?" Aymon asked, looking straight ahead and pretending there wasn't a string of invisible rebels behind him as we turned right and got closer to the tower.

"We'll just rig the base with explosives and tear it down in one go," Patrik replied. "As soon as the Adlet flare goes up, we'll—"

A loud pop erupted from the top level. We all froze and looked up. The Adlet flare had just been launched, shooting into the sky and exploding into a bright, hovering red orb. The signal was up. War had begun.

"I think we need to hurry," Aymon breathed.

He sped up, while we spread out behind him. Fifty yards ahead, where the tower was, we could see that six COs had been assigned to protect it. We needed to take them all down fast. Aymon went up and greeted them with a military salute. They all looked nervous, glancing at the flare in the sky.

"What's going on up there?" Aymon asked, pointing at it.

The Correction Officers shrugged.

"I don't know, it just—" One of them tried to reply but found himself stung by Pheng-Pheng's scorpion tail.

Before the others could react, Tobiah, Sienna, and Cadmus moved in and delivered the fatal blows. Patrik set the fifth guy on fire. I swooped in and cut his head off. Aymon drove his sword through the sixth Mara's chest, then withdrew it and decapitated him in a flash. Two seconds later, they were all on the ground, lifeless.

The city rumbled as the townspeople became agitated at the sight of the flare. A war siren rang loudly, blaring through all the city levels, announcing an impending attack. We didn't have a view of the Valley of Screams from our position, but it was safe to assume that the allied forces had come out and were advancing toward the mountain.

"I'll keep a lookout in case there are more COs in the tower," Aymon said, settling by the ground floor entrance. "You do your thing."

Patrik handed each of us a handful of explosive sticks, which he'd crafted from a combination of manure, crystals, and highly flammable powders. We spread around the tower and attached every bundle to the wall, connecting the wires and rolling them out, back to Patrik.

I looked up and spotted a cannon coming out from the top window, pointed at the sky. That was the weapon they were going to use against our people. It was powered by swamp witch magic.

"Hurry, Patrik, they're getting ready to fire," I murmured as we all stepped back.

Patrik rolled the wires farther, leaving a distance of twenty yards between us and the tower. He gripped them tightly between his hands, then muttered a spell under his breath.

My heart skipped a beat as I watched a flurry of glowing yellow veins spread across the length of the cannon. Whatever that spell was, it was revving up and preparing to launch a potentially devastating attack on our people. I glanced up, following its aim, and saw one of Neraka's moons—one narrow side of it, anyway— barely visible in the clear blue sky.

"Everybody, find cover!" Patrik said, then finished his incantation.

His hands lit up in a bright blue glow, which extended into the wires, all the way to the explosive charges. Light burst through it, then split into multiple sparks and darted into the charges. They were all instantly detonated, an eardrum-shattering bang ripping through the entire neighborhood. The blast radius was contained to about thirty yards, knocking us off our feet as we ran back.

Dust and smoke billowed out in suffocating rolls. We all got back on our feet and kept running away from the hot point. The ground shook. The tower structure groaned and rumbled. Once we got far enough away, we turned around, just in time to watch it all go down like a house of cards. With its base destroyed, the tower didn't stand a chance. It went down fast, the screams of the Maras caught inside reaching our ears.

With one tragedy averted, Patrik and I gave each other a brief nod, then headed back to the main road leading to the second level.

"Come on!" I said, motioning for the rest of our team, along with Aymon, to follow us. "We've got a prison to sabotage!"

Pheng-Pheng chuckled as she ran right behind me. "Not my first one!"

We left the devastation behind as concerned Imen and stunned Correction Officers on that level rushed toward it. This was only the beginning. By the time we were done with them, the Exiled Maras wouldn't even know where they were or what they were anymore.

Correction Officers were pouring out of the prison and from the darkest nooks of each city level, rushing to the mountain base to take their defensive positions. They were so anxious and preoccupied with the incoming allied forces that they didn't even notice us as we slipped through one of the second-level doors into the prison.

The alarms inside were ringing as well, a bell repeatedly tormented at high speed by a small hammer. It scratched my brain, but I had to push the annoyance back, as we followed Aymon through the main corridor into the prison block.

"Get your skeleton keys and explosive pods ready," Patrik said to us.

Laughlan had made skeleton keys to open every single cell in here, while Ryker had prepared a special batch of explosives— extremely potent and concentrated quantities inside palm-sized wax pods with long fuses. The best part about these pods was that we could time their explosions, from one minute to ten seconds, depending on how short the fuse would be cut.

"So, what's the timing on the pod fuses?" I asked as Aymon opened the large iron door leading into the cylindrical hall of the prison.

"It's a second per centimeter," Patrik replied.

Aymon took his first step inside, then stilled. A puff of yellow dust was blown in his face. He passed out and fell backward, flat on his back.

"Crap," I said under my breath, then pulled my mask on. "They've gotten extra vicious this time around."

Tobiah darted forward, growling as he rammed into the two Correction Officers who were waiting by the door and who were responsible for Aymon's current state. He ripped the head off one in a single, decisive move, then slashed the other's throat with his bare claws.

Sienna came from behind and removed the head from the Mara's shoulders altogether.

We made it inside the prison, still baffled by the ambush, as more Correction Officers came at us. We fought tooth and nail, struggling to keep our distance, since they'd all brought the swamp witch knockout powders.

"How did they see us coming?" I croaked, then slashed at a CO's chest. Blood sprayed out. I stepped back, making sure I didn't get any of it on me. I didn't want to lose my invisibility advantage, since not all of the COs were wearing red lenses.

Pheng-Pheng drove her tail spike into another Mara's throat. Cadmus cut off his head to finish her job. But it wasn't enough. It was only a matter of time before they knocked one of us out, weakening our defenses.

A bloodcurdling roar cut through the prison.

We all froze for a split second. Velnias emerged from an open cell with two swords and started cutting down Correction Officers left and right, ruthless and chillingly efficient. His intervention gave us the boost we needed to take the others out.

A minute later, headless bodies littered the ground floor of the prison, blood pooling beneath them. It made my stomach churn, but this was war, and the Exiled Maras were determined to do whatever they could to keep their reign of terror going.

"Good to see you're still here," Patrik said to Velnias, the corner of his mouth twitching.

Velnias grinned. "I figured I'd stay back, watch what these suckers were up to, and prep the scene for you," he replied.

"We thought you were dead," I retorted, my tone reprimanding.

"I was worried about you, too," Velnias shot back with amusement, making me smile.

"They saw us coming," Pheng-Pheng said.

Tobiah and Sienna rushed back to get Aymon. They used smelling salts to force him to wake up, then helped him stand as he shook his head and regained full consciousness. I passed the water around, so we could all reveal ourselves to the prisoners. There was no longer a need for us to hide.

"They had mirrors installed in every corridor after you kids left yesterday," Velnias replied. "They're small and angled to reflect into that big one over there," he added, pointing at a large round mirror mounted on the wall perpendicular to the door.

"And the knockout powders," Tobiah muttered. "I've never seen Maras use them before."

Velnias shrugged. "They're the stuff of swamp witches, but these pompous bastards thought they were above them." He scoffed. "Until they realized they were actually useful and were desperate to catch you all at any cost."

"Okay, let's move. War's about to break out, and we need to free all the prisoners," Patrik said, looking up and around at the cells.

Creatures watched us from behind bars, a mixture of fear and curiosity imprinted on their faces. We spread out and worked our way through the ground-floor cages first, then moved on to the upper floors.

One by one, Imen and rebel Maras were set free. Sienna guided them to a clear space near one of the daemon tunnels, motioning for them to split up. "Those of you who think you can put up a fight, move to the left. Those in need of rest, medical attention, and assistance, stay where you are," she said.

More creatures came down from the upper cells as Patrik, Tobiah, Pheng-Pheng, Velnias, and I unlocked more cages and solitary units. I stilled at the sight of a creature that wasn't quite like the others. She didn't look like an Iman, and she certainly didn't bear any Mara characteristics. I slid the cell door open, then offered her a hand.

She seemed weak as she stood up and leaned against the wall.

"I'm Scarlett," I said softly. "We're here to help you. It's time you all go free."

She looked at me, a sparkle of curiosity lighting up her turquoise eyes.

"You're not from around here," she murmured. "You're not a Mara."

"No, I'm a vampire. I come from another world," I replied, smiling. "You're not from around here, either, are you?"

There was an eerie glow about her that seemed somewhat familiar, but I just couldn't put my finger on it, until she told me.

"I'm Tisha," she said. "I'm a fae."

"Whoa, how'd you get *here*?" I asked, while the prison murmured in the background. "Were you on the Druid delegation?"

She shook her head. "No, I was on a travel mission from Youna. It's a star system not far from here. I was meant to deliver some rare crystals to the fae king in the Mandris system," she explained. "The Maras here used a beacon to draw my pod. Once I entered their atmosphere, I couldn't pull back. I crashed, and they captured me."

"You've got space travel pods?" I replied, raising my eyebrows.

"On Youna we do, yes. The crystals I was delivering to Mandris make travel through this universe possible," she said. "It's why I was out here, to share our technology with other fae planets. It's easier than relying on any form of magic, and our solar system is rich in stysis crystals."

"I take it those are the crystals that power your pods?" I asked. She nodded. "When did you get here, Tisha?"

She sighed, then pointed at the wall behind her, which was covered in scratches. She'd been counting the days, etching a small line for each. At first glance, I counted approximately five Nerakian years.

"You said they used a beacon," I said, then walked over and put her arm over my shoulders. I helped her walk out of the cell and guided her down the metal staircase.

"Yes. It was a thin beam of light, flashing out from the mountain. I could see it from space. It had a deliberate sequence of short and long flashes. I thought it was a distress signal or something, so I steered my pod toward it. As soon as I entered the atmosphere, however, I was shot down by a bright ball of fire."

Around us, the last top-level prisoners were coming out and making their way to the ground floor. We all gathered at the bottom, where Patrik smiled at the sight of us.

"Ah, I see you found another non-Nerakian up there," he said lightly, then respectfully bowed before Tisha. "I'm Patrik, Druid of Eritopia."

The fae lit up like the morning sun. "Eritopia! I'm from Youna!"

Patrik nodded, clearly thrilled to meet her, while I watched the exchange with great interest. "Youna is a system known for its technological advancements," he briefly explained to me. "They've got incredible resources out there, minerals you won't find anywhere else. Merchants used to come in from there before Azazel's reign, trading their goods for ours. I haven't seen a Younan for a very long time."

"She crash-landed here," I replied, frowning and unable to hide my concern. "The Maras used a beacon to draw her pod into the Nerakian atmosphere, then shot her down and captured her."

Patrik nodded, then sighed and pointed at five other creatures —two males and three females. They didn't seem local either. "Fae from Mandris, and two Druids from Persea," he said lowly. "Also drawn in by a beacon and shot down. They were all on different travel missions when they were lured onto Neraka. The Druids used interplanetary spells, but they didn't have swamp witches on board with them. Thank the stars."

I scoffed. "Yeah, last thing we need right now is to try to get more of them out."

"The Mandrisians used their proprietary transport methods, combinations of local magic and technology," Patrik added. "They were headed to the Youna system, looking to purchase stysis crystals."

"And Tish here was on her way to Mandris to deliver stysis crystals," I grumbled.

"The Exiled Maras have been using the beacon over the past century or so," Aymon interjected, nodding at Tish and the other outsiders. "They were hoping they would capture and feed on random travelers, when the Imen population first started dropping."

"Then they reached out to us, looking to bring in more of our kind so they could force us into camps, right?" Patrik asked.

"Pretty much, yes," Aymon replied. "The idea, like you probably already know, was to get the outsiders to reproduce and repopulate Neraka as the Maras' and daemons' main soul food source."

"This is disgusting and wrong on so many levels," I muttered, crossing my arms and shaking my head.

"I know. It's one of the reasons why I could no longer—Ouch!" Sienna tried to say something, but her blood oath spell took over, burning her face. My heart broke to see her like this. Even though the red blotches were already healing, it must've been torture to not be able to speak openly.

"It's okay," I replied gently. "I know. It's why they branded you with that blood oath."

"As bad as it sounds, I'm glad we found them here," Patrik said, nodding at the Druids, Tish, and the Mandrisians. "We need all the help we can get right now."

"What's the plan?" one of the Druids asked.

"Our crew is rescuing the swamp witch from the Palisade as we speak. Once she's in a safe place, she'll take down the shield that blocks Neraka from the outside world," I explained. "We've got a fleet of Eritopians and our own warriors waiting on one of the moons. As soon as that damn thing comes down, it'll be over for both the Maras and the daemons."

They all nodded slowly. Velnias pointed at the two groups of prisoners. Tobiah stood by the wounded and weak ones. I counted over eighty of them. Pheng-Pheng was with the able-bodied ones, the majority of whom were Imen. There were two hundred of them, plus another sixty Maras. Those were good numbers to work with—good enough to make my heart skip a beat, animated by an extra dose of hope.

"We need as many fighters on our side as possible. There's a war coming to the surface," Patrik said. "Cadmus will get the others out of here through one of the daemon tunnels. That way, they won't need to use any invisibility paste and risk an exit through the city."

"I'll go raise one of the gates," Velnias chimed in, then rushed across the hall, where all the mechanical controls were.

Less than a minute later, the alarms went off, and the southern gate went up with a loud, metallic screech. Velnias then came back out, while Tobiah pointed to the tunnel.

"Go through, straight ahead," Tobiah said to Cadmus. "At the four-mile marker, you'll see a set of circular stairs leading up to the surface. Go up. It will take you to the field south of here, approximately fifty yards from the gorges. You'll be safe there."

Cadmus nodded, then went in first, followed by the prisoners. The weaker ones went through, leaving the rest of us to prepare for the battle upstairs. Velnias scratched the back of his head, looking down at the dead Correction Officers.

"Okay, so who's up for killing some more of these bloodsuckers?" he asked, then looked at the rebel Maras. "No offense, fellas."

One of the freed Maras shrugged. "None taken. It's literally what we are."

I couldn't help but chuckle.

"Thank you all in advance for everything that you're about to do," I said. "Now, everybody, grab a weapon. It's about to get crazy up there, and once it does, it's up to us to wreak a little extra havoc. Whatever it takes to keep the Maras and potential daemon hostiles busy while our friends get the swamp witch to take the shield down."

They all nodded, then picked swords and knives off the ground, relieving the fallen COs of all their weapons.

"Grab those powder pouches, too," Aymon said, pointing at the COs' belts. "Just don't sniff them; they'll knock you out in a second."

"How do we know when it's the right time for us to go up?" Tish asked, getting herself acquainted to a longsword's ivory grip.

"There's another set of mirrors mounted in a small vertical duct that connects the office ceiling to the second level," Velnias said. "I'll give you the green light once I see allies breaching the first-level defenses. The COs angled the mirrors at the top to give them a full view of the mountain base."

I sighed, bracing myself for that moment. "The Adlet flare was launched. I'm guessing it'll be another ten or twenty minutes before we go up."

"Good. In the meantime, our friends here can drink some

water and feed on some blood," Velnias replied, then went back across the hall and opened a refrigerated storage room.

It looked dark and spacious, filled with tin pots and glass jars. The COs had used swamp witch magic to preserve the food supplies in there—both blood and actual food for the Imen. They needed them fed and hydrated if they wanted to consume their souls long-term. The idea sent shivers down my spine, but that storage came in handy now.

We needed our fighters in good condition—or as decent as possible, given the short notice they had prior to going to actual war.

One by one, the able-bodied prisoners had their previous mind-bending marks removed by Sienna. We needed their heads clear for this. They then retrieved nourishing portions from the storage room. Velnias brought the south gate down. If there were daemons coming through, we certainly weren't going to make it easy for them. My only hope was that the other prisoners would get out before the daemons made their way toward the city. Their chances of survival were high at this point, since most daemon hunters were out after dark. Even with a war coming, hunters didn't stop doing their jobs. Their people needed to be fed.

"Alrighty then," I muttered, taking a deep breath.

Patrik gave me a soft, loving smile, then closed the distance between us and kissed me. The feel of his soft lips against mine instantly reinvigorated me. There was something about him that just pumped me full of energy, and I needed plenty of that for what lay ahead.

"We'll get through this," he murmured in my ear.

I dropped a kiss on his cheek, then grinned, brimming with confidence.

"We'd better! You need to take me out on a date or two. Or ten," I replied.

"Would a thousand work?"

"An eternity?" I asked, raising an eyebrow.

He chuckled. "Even better."

Provided we survived this, we were looking at an eternity together—also provided, of course, that Patrik would choose to turn vampire. The thought of watching him die of old age made my heart bleed. Sure, Druids had a ridiculously long lifespan, but he was my forever guy.

First things first, Scarlett.

With that in mind, I looked at the rest of our crew as they got ready for the fight. We were lucky to see so many of them still able to fight. At least half had been down here for decades, confined to their cells and cages.

Soon enough, they would see the outside world again. They would join us in our fight for freedom.

15

HANSA

As soon as the Exiled Maras and the daemons realized what was going on, we made our move. I whistled once, sharp and loud. Hundurr and Rover burst through the back door of the mansion and tore into the guards in the hallway. They then smashed the front door, wreaking bloody havoc outside. No daemon or Correction Officer could stand in their way. Their instructions had been clear before we'd come here.

Emilian scowled at me, baring his fangs.

"You've made the biggest mistake of your life, you silver-blooded wench!" he said, hissing.

I darted forward to attack but came to a screeching halt as Emilian snapped his fingers. The Iman girl standing in the doorway rushed to his side. He brought a knife up to her throat, sneering at us.

"Stay back!" Emilian commanded, then looked at one of his COs. "Ring the bell."

The Correction Officer nodded and took out a small bell from his coat pocket. The rest of us were stuck in a tense standoff, weapons pointed at one another, while the pit wolves mauled the guards left outside.

More COs were bound to come up, but so was the rest of our crew. Our focus was the room we were in.

The Correction Officer rang the bell. Emilian sneered, pressing the blade against the Iman girl's neck. He drew a droplet of blood, which he licked off. Footsteps rumbled through the house.

I froze at the sight of fifty Imen of different ages, both males and females. They came in from all over the mansion, entered the living room, and lined the walls, like obedient little animals. They'd been mind-bent into submission, and I feared the extent of their manipulation was going to get them killed in the middle of all this.

"What did you do?" I asked Emilian, menacingly raising my blade another inch, gripping it firmly with both hands as I pointed the tip at his head.

"Precautions, Hansa. How many innocent creatures will you allow to die here today?" Emilian grinned.

I scoffed. "Obviously, you've never been at war with a succubus," I replied dryly. "You think using Imen as living shields will save you?"

Caia was the closest to the Imen on her side. She took a couple of slow, calm steps to her left and reached out to a young Iman. He looked pale and blank and was covered in a sheet of sweat.

"Don't let them break you like this," she said gently, trying the impossible. I couldn't fault her for hoping she might get him to overcome his mind-bending. The fire fae was ambitious and relentless, just like her sister, Vita.

Emilian chuckled, then snapped his fingers.

The young Iman moaned, then produced a small blade from his pocket and slit his own throat. He collapsed to the floor and bled out in seconds.

Caia screamed with horror. Blaze pulled her back, growling at the Correction Officers and daemons who tried to make their move. Caia quickly snapped out of it and shifted her focus back to the hostiles. At least she'd let go of the idea of swaying the Imen out of their mind-traps. That wasn't going to happen.

But something else about this situation had caught my attention.

"You can mind-bend without words," Jax said, almost reading my mind. He narrowed his eyes at Emilian. The Lord bared his fangs once more.

"I'm a Lord for a reason, you pompous fraud!" Emilian spat. "You think you're superior to us in any way, Lord of White City?" he added mockingly.

This was one of the moments when I truly regretted the absence of Jax's wards. Even with one or two of them on his side, Jax would've broken any mind-bending influence that Emilian had on his Imen, without uttering a single word.

"Okay, so basically, you're all cowards, hiding behind innocent Imen instead of coming out and facing us like the all-powerful champions that you claim to be," I shot back.

"All is fair in war," Rowan replied with a smirk, producing a short sword from a hidden crease in her dress.

"We'll do whatever it takes to protect and preserve our way of life," Farrah added, then put her hands out to her sides, allowing two long knives to slip out from her sleeves.

"Hm. I like this side of you," Shaytan chimed in, crossing his arms. His sons had drawn their weapons, and so had his five guards, but he didn't seem at all bothered or threatened. In fact, he looked entertained. We were putting on a good show for him. "I forgot you Maras could hold your own in a fight."

"Oh, you haven't seen anything yet, Your Grace," Emilian replied, gritting his teeth.

I chuckled. "At least we agree on that," I shot back. "Jax, you know what you have to do."

Jax nodded, then looked at the Iman girl, his jade eyes flickering gold. "Free yourself."

The Iman girl sucked in a breath, then elbowed Emilian in the ribs. The Lord doubled over from the pain, giving her the momentum she needed to get away from him and take several steps back. Rowan and Farrah were baffled.

"How did you—" Rowan tried to ask, but Jax cut her off.

"You thought you were the only capable Maras in this room?" He scoffed. "Hubris will be your downfall."

It had taken a lot of mental strength for him to do what he'd done without his wards, but Jax could still override another Mara's mind-bending, even though it was a short-term fix.

I didn't wait another second. I went straight for Emilian's head. He registered my move and brought out a second knife to cross with his first and block my broadsword from coming down hard. I kicked him in the stomach, then went at it again. Rage surged through me as I relentlessly attacked him.

The fight finally broke out and unraveled in the room, as Caia, Blaze, and Jax took on the others. I caught a glimpse of Shaytan slipping out of the room, along with Abeles. The other two, Garros and Mammon, stayed behind and went for Blaze—but the dragon's fire breath was not to be toyed with.

I heard the pit wolves growling outside. Correction Officers screaming. Swords clashing.

Jax fought Rowan and Farrah as they tried to come at him from different angles. He was agile and light on his feet, blocking one's hits while slashing at the other. I didn't have the time to watch him in action, but I'd seen him many times before. Jax was the very definition of a graceful swordsman. Those two bloodsuckers didn't stand a chance against him.

Emilian came at me, slashing at me with his knives in fast, repetitive motions, trying to cut me. I blocked every hit, taking several steps back in the process. The Correction Officers, along with Mammon, Garros, and their five daemons, closed the circle around us.

Blaze blew out a curtain of fire, aided by Caia. Several COs went down in flames, wailing and rolling on the floor in a desperate attempt to save themselves.

Caia produced her fire sword and went straight for the daemons. The little fae had gathered plenty of heat since she'd come to Neraka. This was the perfect time to let it all out.

The windows were smashed simultaneously as the rest of our crew forced their way into the mansion. Idris, Rayna, Wyrran and his Imen, Peyton and his Maras—they were all pouring into the mansion. Emilian, Rowan, and Farrah were stunned but couldn't stop. They kept fighting back.

"Get them!" Emilian snarled.

The remaining Correction Officers moved to attack the newcomers. The Imen servants jumped in as well, but they were quickly disabled and rendered unconscious by Peyton's Maras.

"Boy, am I glad to see you all!" I called out.

"The allies are coming!" Wyrran replied, blocking a hit. He swerved to the right and slashed at the CO's side. Blood sprayed out, drenching him. More followed, as Wyrran delivered the final blow. "They're less than a mile away!"

"Good," I said, then launched another attack on Emilian.

He was quite spry for his age. More than twelve thousand years in this world had certainly worked to his advantage, as far as combat experience was concerned. I ducked to avoid one of his knives, then shot my leg out and crashed it into the side of his knee. I heard a bone break.

Emilian brought his other blade down. I faltered for a split second. It cost me. The knife cut into my forearm. I hissed from the pain, then jumped back up and delivered an upward blow with my sword.

"I'll chop your head off for this!" Emilian hissed. "You continue to underestimate me! I've fought hundreds of thousands... millions of fiends! You're just another scratch on the wall for me!"

I slashed at him again. I missed, but quickly spun into a 360-degree turn at a descending angle and caught him by surprise. My blade sliced through his thigh. He cried out from the pain and took a couple of steps back. Blood dripped from his wound, staining the wooden floor. Around us, swords continued to clash. Daemons and Correction Officers' heads kept falling.

"And you really need to understand that experience with a million of your previous opponents mean nothing against a freakin' succubus!" I growled, then moved in for the kill.

He blocked my hit, but my sword came down hard enough to crack his joints. I only had a few moments before his elbows and wrists would heal. I had to move fast.

Whatever happened, I couldn't stop.

We all had to hold out and fight, tooth and nail, until the shield came down.

Whatever it takes.

16

HARPER

After Zane and Heron came back, we replenished our invisibility spells and gave a scoop to Lumi, as well. The guys had gotten rid of the COs and remaining daemon guard the old-fashioned way—their blood was spattered all over the walls, their heads decorating the corridors.

We made our way out of the basement, steering clear of potential red lenses. We'd all put on black capes, just in case we had to go visible and get lost in a crowd again. It also helped with our extraction plan.

As soon as we reached the ground floor, we realized the war had begun. The alarms were ringing throughout the building. Battle sirens blared outside. The Adlet flare had been launched.

The resident Maras rushed down the stairs from the upper floors, grabbing swords and spears that the receptionists handed out. They'd gone from pleasure workers to soldiers in what seemed like a split second. They mind-bent the Imen into joining them outside, and they all proceeded to go down the mountain and join the defense lines.

"Good grief, the Imen don't even want to fight," I murmured, watching the servants run out with blank expressions, clutching knives and short swords, clubs and hammers.

"They don't have a choice," Fiona replied.

"Intruders!" one of the receptionists screamed.

I didn't even spot her red lens, but she'd seen us, and she was pointing a finger at us. We'd stopped at the end of the corridor, where we'd disabled the two Correction Officers prior to sneaking downstairs.

"Crap," I muttered, gripping my swords.

Both receptionists came out from behind their desk, accompanied by several COs and a handful of Imen. I dashed forward and threw out a barrier. The pulse knocked them backward. They all landed on their backs, the air knocked out of their lungs.

Caspian handled the Imen, mind-bending them and over-riding their previous commands.

"Lumi, stay back!" I said. "We need you to preserve your energy. We can handle these fools."

Fiona, Zane, Avril, Heron, and I fought the others, hacking and slashing until not a single fiend was left standing. Lumi stayed back, like I'd asked. Once they were all down, we looked around and noticed the Palisade was empty. They'd all gone to war.

There was a doubtful pang troubling my stomach.

"This feels a little too easy," I breathed, putting my swords away.

"I think we deserve some 'easy' today, babe," Fiona replied.

"Let's go," Zane said.

He took the lead. We followed. I looked over my shoulder and scanned the interior of the Palisade once more, using my True Sight. Some Imen had been left behind in the rooms, most of them females, and most of them not moving. They'd been drained and killed.

Rage flowed through my veins, red hot. I looked forward to tearing down this entire city, brick by brick, and erasing all traces of the Exiled Maras. Neraka had been cursed with the worst of plagues.

I put on my mask and goggles, ready for the sun.

I didn't even realize that Zane had stopped in the doorway until I bumped into him.

"Dude, keep—" I wanted to say "keep moving," but then I saw what had brought him to such a sudden halt.

We had company. The worst kind of company.

Shaytan and one of his sons, Abeles, stood outside, red lenses on. Behind them, lined up in a semicircle, were over two dozen daemon soldiers—the bigger ones, with meranium armor and extra-large blades. Boots thundered up the stairs.

For a moment there, I noticed the frown on Shaytan's face. He hadn't been expecting company.

Correction Officers came up, their swords out and their red lenses on. They surrounded us and the daemons. They all looked at each other, equally displeased to share this space and, most likely, the swamp witch we were trying to sneak out.

"I take it you were going to snatch Lumi for yourself?" I asked Shaytan, my hands gripping my sword handles. My palms were already sweating.

I'd dreaded this moment, but, at the same time, part of me had hoped I'd get to keep my promise to Shaytan. Maybe this was my chance, after all. Shaytan grinned.

"You know me so well, darling," he replied dryly.

One of the COs stepped forward, his expression firm, his brow furrowed. "Your Grace, I know our people have some issues to resolve, but please, let's work together on this one. We cannot let the swamp witch escape."

Shaytan rolled his eyes, then let out an exhausted sigh.

"Heron, go," I whispered. "Back door."

Two of us were supposed to get away if we ran into trouble. This was trouble multiplied by a thousand. They took advantage of Zane's large figure still standing in the doorway and rushed back inside. There was a service door that had yet to be covered by the enemy, given that they were all gathered out front. *Perfect.*

"You know you're not walking out of here with the witch, right?" Shaytan said, giving me a lazy grin. He then shifted his focus to Zane. His smile faded, replaced by a contemptuous sneer. "I should've killed you when you first helped these wretched fiends."

"We both know you should've killed me long ago," Zane replied, a muscle ticking in his jaw as he stepped forward.

Fiona, Caspian, and I kept our precious "asset" back. I quickly scanned the area; these were the only hostiles we were dealing with. Though they clearly outnumbered us, at least they were a finite quantity. Everybody else was rushing down to the ground level. From what I could see, the allied forces were yards away from the base of the mountain.

In a matter of minutes, they were going to tear through Azure Heights's defenses, then work their way up to the top.

"That's fine," Shaytan shot back. "I'll just kill you now, with the rest of them. I was going to keep you all as my midnight snacks, but you've really ruined your chances this time."

I stifled a chuckle. "Oh, no! Whatever will we do?" I mockingly retorted. "Wait. I know. I'll chop your head off and get this over with."

Shaytan's deadly scowl made my blood freeze for a moment, but I refused to let him see his effect on me. He was twice my height, massive, his muscles bulging, his veins throbbing all over. His gold-threaded horns were sharp and begging to rip me apart. I had my work cut out for me.

"I'll go the extra mile and carve what you just said into your headstone," Shaytan replied dryly.

"The city is under siege," Zane cut in. "You're not going to win this time, Father. You should start considering a truce."

Shaytan let out a roaring laugh, then pointed his thumb over his shoulder. "You think a handful of Dhaxanians, mutts, and poisonous bugs will be the end of the daemon kingdom? My boy, I thought you were smarter than this."

"It's not just—" Zane started his reply, but stopped himself, as a nasty realization dawned on him. "You didn't come here with just a squadron of daemons, did you?"

Shaytan smirked, his confidence setting me on fire.

"I didn't come here to attend a funeral. I didn't even come here to listen to the Lords scramble for excuses and then beg me to renegotiate our agreement," the daemon king said. "I came here to conquer the mountain and establish my unbreakable supremacy."

I used my True Sight to see past him.

Our allies were, indeed, coming in hot on the ground level. The Exiled Maras were dropping in a devastating combination of Dhaxanian frost, Adlet ferocity, and Manticore venom.

But farther back, across the field, hordes of daemons were pouring out of the gorges. Thousands of them.

My heart stopped for a split second.

They marched toward Azure Heights. Their drums of war echoed louder through the early afternoon. They'd started a few hours earlier, albeit muffled by the distance. But they were getting closer now. Their meranium shields glistened in the sunlight. They had catapults and ballistae, throngs of pit wolves and dark clouds of Death Claws.

Dread poisoned my resolve.

All we were left with was a small window of time. Our only hope was in Lumi's ability to take down the protective shield. In less than half an hour, the daemon armies would reach the mountain, and all hell would break loose.

"I summoned all my armies from across the kingdom the moment you bastards destroyed my beautiful Draconis," Shaytan added. "It took a while to get them all to move, but... there they are."

"You never intended to continue your alliance with the Exiled Maras," I breathed, my heart struggling against my chest. I gave

Caspian a sideways glance and nearly unraveled. He was stunned, his chest moving with every tortured breath that he took, as he understood exactly what our circumstances were.

Shaytan shook his head, mildly amused. He took a couple of steps forward. His daemons moved as well, but he motioned for them to stand back.

"I'll be honest. Last night, I *was* still thinking about giving them another chance," he replied. "But then, I had an epiphany of sorts. I simply asked myself: Why should I? Wouldn't it be easier if I just wiped them off the face of Neraka?" He clicked his teeth. "The Maras are emotional and greedy, Miss Hellswan. They're partially responsible for the impending extinction of the Imen. We're much more conservative with our soul food. We keep ourselves under control. We ration our portions. These idiots will wipe all the Imen out if I let them live. The Maras are pests, and it's time I start treating them as such."

I scoffed. "I can't believe I'm agreeing with you on this, but you do realize you're just as bad, right? You're killing Imen slowly and painfully, just so you can add more years to your ridiculously-long lifespan. They're already stuck with just a hundred, maybe a hundred and twenty if they stay healthy and spry. And you're taking that away from them, too. You think the Maras are the only pests soiling this beautiful world? No, Shaytan. You're just as bad. Screw your so-called conservative eating habits. That's a load of crap. It's still murder. It's genocide. And you will pay for this."

Shaytan sucked in a breath, narrowing his eyes at me. "I see why my wayward son likes you and your soon-to-be-dead friends. You're all a bunch of naïve idealists," he replied, then bared his fangs at me. "This is a wild world, Miss Hellswan. It's the survival of the fittest. Only the strong get to live forever! And we're the true Lords of Neraka!"

The drums of war grew louder in the distance. The siege on Azure Heights unfolded below, with swords clashing, fiends screaming and wailing, and Adlets roaring as they tore into the ground-floor defenses.

There wasn't much we could do up here, given the circumstances, but I was sure as hell not going to let Shaytan stop us. Our mission objective was clear. No exception. No derailment. No turning back.

"You see, you say that," I retorted sarcastically, "but you've yet to see what we can do for the wellbeing of *all* Nerakians."

"I have to admit, I will enjoy draining the life out of your smart, plump little mouth," Shaytan said in his most serious tone.

Chills ran down my spine.

I dry-swallowed, then took a deep breath, looking for that internal balance I desperately needed to get through this in one piece. Our allies were screwed down there if we didn't take the shield down. We would all die within the hour if we failed in our mission.

We were smack in the middle of a perfect storm.

17

CAIA

We couldn't exactly unleash our fire powers, given that the ground floor of Emilian's mansion was lined with Imen. But the least we could do was deliver targeted attacks against our enemies. Jax had his hands full with Rowan and Farrah, while Hansa held her own and then some against Emilian.

It got worse when Karellen, one of the other daemon princes, made his way into the mansion and grinned at the sight of Blaze. We hadn't seen him with Shaytan before, and it left me wondering where Adaris, the last of the daemon king's Council, was lurking. Blaze, however, didn't seem too affected. My dragon had taken on plenty of Karellen's kind already.

I took on Shaytan's son, Mammon, the biggest of the hostiles left in the room. Broken glass crackled beneath my boots as I used my flaming sword to protect myself from Mammon's attacks. He defended himself remarkably well with his broadsword, but my fire was starting to heat his blade, gradually chipping away at its integrity.

The rest of our allies handled Garros, the remaining Correction Officers and two daemon guards, while the mind-bent Imen left standing tried to intervene. Peyton and two of his Maras overrode their previous commands, forcing them to retreat into a corner with the others. We couldn't let them go outside, where more of our rebel allies were fighting the Mara townspeople.

Despite their animosity and the cancellation of their truce, the Maras and the daemons were working together against their common enemy—us. Unfortunately for them, we'd come to win, and we would stop at nothing until they were dead or until they surrendered.

"I'm going to eat your fiery little soul." Mammon sneered at me, then brought his sword down with considerable force. I blocked it with my fire blade, but the impact still took its toll on my joints.

"Careful not to get burned," I shot back.

I brought my right leg out in a powerful side-kick. It was nowhere near enough to cripple him, but it did cause him pain. I followed it up with a sword slash, making sure I hit the same spot on his blade. I could see the meranium steel alloy blade starting to crack, almost imperceptibly. A couple more blows, and his sword would be rendered useless.

He came at me, vicious and determined to deliver the deadly blow. However, I ducked, then slashed at his abdomen. It drew blood, making him hiss. I shot back up and went for the sword again. This time, I launched a flurry of hits, until I heard the satisfying clang of his blade breaking.

Mammon froze, staring at me, wide-eyed. "How did you..."

"Nothing beats fire," I replied, then went after him even harder.

With less than half the sword left, Mammon found it harder to defend himself from my strikes. Despite his considerable size and intimidating muscle mass, he could still go down, if I knew where to strike. I'd fought him for long enough to register his weak spots.

My own body was hurting, worn out by the exertion of each sword hit, but I wasn't ready to give up. On the contrary, this was my moment. I swerved to his left, then stopped halfway and quickly slipped to his right. He'd already begun turning in the opposite direction to block a left side attack. I stabbed him with my fire sword.

The red-hot blade went in deep. Mammon cried out in agony. I withdrew my weapon, then jumped and cut off his head. The smell of burning flesh invaded my nostrils. His head rolled onto the floor. Then his body collapsed.

"This is to thank you for your 'hospitality' back in Infernis," I muttered.

I was panting, but I was nowhere near done. I caught a glimpse of Blaze, who was seconds away from obliterating Karellen. The daemon prince was strong and resilient, and he'd managed to avoid most of the dragon's fire attacks, but he could only keep it up for so long. Blaze got his hands on a bigger sword from one of the fallen Maras, then proceeded to combine his fire breath with ample sword hits.

Before I could witness the conclusion of that fight, I was confronted by a new opponent. This time, a Correction Officer had taken it upon himself to try to take me down. I smirked, then produced a fireball from my lighter and threw it in his face. He'd probably expected me to attack him with my flaming sword, so he didn't register the fireball until it engulfed his head.

He ran around screaming and flaming, until Idris decapitated him and put him out of his misery. Across the room from us, Hansa had just dodged one of Emilian's long knife hits. She brought her broadsword up in an ample slash, leaving him with another deep cut across the chest. The Mara Lord has seen enough fights in his lifetime to make it difficult for the succubus to kill him quickly.

"It's a good thing that you're taking care of Shaytan's sons for us," Emilian hissed, then launched another offensive against Hansa. He couldn't do much with those two knives. Hansa blocked his every attempt, then came back with heavy, joint-shattering blows.

"You're next, Emilian," Hansa replied. "Your arrogance, your greed, and this fracture between your species and the daemons are going to be your downfall. Just give it another minute. I'm almost done with you."

"Don't be foolish, succubus! Look around you! There's only so much you can do without your dragon at full force," Emilian shot back.

Hansa didn't have a single moment to spare, but I looked around and found myself concerned. We were losing plenty of our own. The bodies of rebel Imen and Maras were starting to pile up on the bloody floor. Peyton and Wyrran were still hard at work, hacking and slashing left and right against the Correction Officers. The enemy was losing fighters as well, but there were plenty more where those had come from. Our advantage was not in numbers.

However, we'd never really relied on that. Our main objective was to keep the fight going and the Lords busy, while Harper and her team got Lumi to bring down the shield and let our people in.

I tackled another Mara, while Idris and Rayna handled the remaining daemons. A loud thump caught my attention. I looked to my left, then breathed a sigh of relief at the sight of Karellen lying flat on the floor, blood pooling beneath him. Blaze gave me a passing smile as he advanced through the room and joined the fight against the daemons.

Just then, I saw Scarlett coming in through the front door, accompanied by Patrik, Pheng-Pheng, Cadmus, Aymon, Velnias, and several other supernaturals. I assumed the latter had been released from prison, though I had yet to hear the story of how they'd ended up on Neraka in the first place.

They didn't waste a single minute. They jumped right in,

taking on the Correction Officers that were left inside the mansion, as well as Garros and the others that started coming in after them and through the back door. We fought together, keeping an eye on each other and providing backup wherever the extra hand or flame was needed.

"Arrah and the rest of her crew are outside," Scarlett breathed, once she ended up by my side. "We stopped the moon attack. All we need is that shield to come down."

"I take it there are plenty more of these bastards outside, right?" I asked, watching another Mara headed my way. I brought my flaming sword up, and genuine fear made him break into a cold sweat. Nevertheless, he didn't have a choice. He had to fight me.

"She's been working her way up from the sixth level. She's looking to square things off with Rowan," Scarlett replied, then moved back into the center of the living room, where a Correction Officer was about to kill Peyton. She drove her sword through his back, giving Peyton the second he needed to cut his head off.

"There you are!" Arrah's voice boomed through the mansion.

For a split second, everyone paused. Arrah had just come in, carrying two swords and a furious scowl aimed at Rowan. The Mara Lady stepped away from Farrah, leaving her to deal with Jax by herself. She sneered at Arrah, bearing her pearly white fangs.

"I was wondering how long it would take you to find me," Rowan muttered, then licked the blood off her blade. She'd managed to wound Jax, it seemed.

"It ends here, you vicious, heartless, insufferable bloodsucker," Arrah shot back.

There wasn't enough swamp witch magic and brute force among the Correction Officers and the one remaining daemon in that place to stop us. This sudden increase in our numbers, caused by Scarlett and her team's arrival, was the boost we desperately needed to get one step closer to victory.

I could hear the entire city rumbling outside. Our allies had reached the base of the mountain and were working their way up through the levels. War was progressing at a frightening speed, and all I could think of was to hold on and take as many of our enemies down as possible.

Soon enough, this would all be over. Or so I hoped.

18

HANSA

E milian managed to cut me, leaving a deep gash across my abdomen. I sucked in a breath, keeping my focus on his movements. I didn't have a Mara's healing abilities, but I couldn't afford a single moment's worth of hesitation—it could get me killed.

Instead, I took the sharp pain and used it to fuel my anger at seeing him still standing. I retaliated with multiple heavy blows, one after another, until I managed to knock one of the knives from his hands. It didn't take him long to grab a sword from the many left on the floor by their dead owners, but it was a sign that I was starting to get to him.

I just hoped my stamina would outlast his.

Rover hurled into the room and attacked one of the last daemons standing. The armored fiend was pinned down, struggling to reach for his knife. Rover snapped his fangs at him, eager to rip his throat out. The daemon stabbed the pit wolf repeatedly in the side. My stomach churned as I could almost feel the pain he'd inflicted on the creature, as it whimpered and collapsed. The daemon crawled out from under Rover and managed to get back up on his feet.

He froze at the sight of Hundurr in the wide doorway, his red eyes flaring with rage. The pit wolf was too big for the already-crowded living room, but I couldn't get him out, either. The daemon had committed the unpardonable sin of killing one of our own. It hurt me deeply, but I couldn't even take a second to mourn, as Emilian came after me again.

"Give up, Hansa!" he snarled. "You'll never win! There are too many of us!"

I'd heard Scarlett's brief update regarding the tower. Holding on to the hope that Harper was going to get Lumi out and bring the shield down, I grinned.

"Not sure you knew, but your little plan to attack our people on one of Neraka's moons has been thwarted," I retorted. "The shield will be coming down any minute now, and you will all feel the rage of GASP and Eritopia combined. You will all pay for your crimes!"

I didn't give him a chance to respond, just darted forward and brought my sword down once more, then followed up with a frontal kick. I knocked the air out of his lungs, but I still couldn't get close enough to finish him off. I had no choice but to keep fighting, until I wore him out properly.

I caught a glimpse of Hundurr tearing the last daemon to literal pieces. Blood sprayed all over the room, dousing us in crimson. The rest of our crew were remarkable in their fights and perseverance. That surge of pride animated me further, giving me the energy I needed to withstand Emilian's attacks. Whether I was going to live through this or not no longer mattered. What did matter was securing the freedom of my group and the Nerakian people. But if I was going to go down in this war, I sure as hell planned to take Emilian down with me.

Emilian dodged one of my hits, then took several steps back, breathing heavily. He was stalling. I was about to move in for another attack, when I heard Rowan's voice again.

"I should've killed you when your mother plopped you out!" she growled, then ran across the room and engaged Arrah in combat.

The Iman girl was fast and agile, but Rowan was better. She slipped to Arrah's right and drove her short sword through her chest.

"No!" Scarlett screamed, unable to go help her, as she was busy fighting off another Correction Officer.

My stomach churned as I watched the tragedy unfold, almost in slow motion. Arrah stilled, blood spreading out from her wound. Rowan pulled her sword back, grinning. She watched as Arrah dropped to her knees, then fell backward, giving her last breath.

Scarlett whimpered as she cut off the Correction Officer's head and went straight for Rowan.

Jax was still struggling with Farrah. And Emilian didn't look ready to engage me again.

I still had a shot to bring him down, sooner rather than later.

Just as I took the first step forward, Patrik's voice rose above the others.

"Everybody, step away from the front wall!" he shouted.

His hands lit up blue as he sent out a pulse that shattered the walls. I glanced down at his feet, where he'd drawn a slew of swamp witch symbols in blood to perform that spell. The mansion split open, and the fight spilled outside.

It gave us some much-needed room, as Scarlett and the others pushed the hostiles out. Hundurr howled, then proceeded to tear into some of the Correction Officers that had surrounded Idris and Rayna. He jumped over several bodies and snapped his jaws over a Mara's head, dragging him outside.

I spotted another CO sneaking up on Caia.

"Caia! Behind you!" I shouted.

I didn't get to see whether she got him before he got her, as Emilian charged at me, roaring with rage. I dodged his knife and sword but missed the lateral kick. His leg hit my side, cracking several ribs. I grunted and fell, landing on my shoulder.

"Tell you what." Emilian chuckled. "I shouldn't be the one to kill you. I'll let one of these weaklings you're so desperate to protect finish you off," he added, then snapped his fingers.

Two of the Imen who had hidden beneath a nearby table came out, instantly and fully mind-bent. Peyton had missed them in his endeavor to override the Lords' hypnotic powers. They picked up the swords of fallen COs and headed straight for me.

I was losing blood from my abdomen wound, and my ribs hurt too much for me to move straight away. I had to think fast. Emilian watched the Imen he'd mind-bent come toward me. The smirk on his face made my blood boil.

Only then did I notice I'd fallen next to Garros's body. Whomever in our group had done it, I owed them a big "Thank you!". We'd all been busy fighting, making it impossible for any of us to keep track of the bodies dropping, but it didn't matter. All that mattered was that he was dead, too.

I briefly scanned his belt and found a small leather pouch. I reached out, struggling to ignore the burning pain spreading through my torso, and retrieved the pouch. The Imen reached me and raised their swords, their expressions blank. I managed to open the small bag and found yellow dust inside.

I scooped out a handful and blew it at them. They both stilled and wheezed as they inhaled the yellow cloud. Their eyes rolled into their heads. They fell backward, their swords clanging as they landed on the floor.

Emilian cursed under his breath and rushed to kill me himself, but I managed to scoop out some more of the yellow powder and blew it at him. He yelped as he came to a grinding halt, then took several steps back. He didn't inhale enough to knock him out, but I could tell from the way he started shaking his head that he was having some trouble.

"This is it," I muttered to myself.

I pushed myself up, crying out from the pain, but managed to stand, once again.

Retrieving my broadsword from the floor, I raised it before me, seeing my reflection in its blade.

"You've served me well," I whispered. I sometimes felt like my weapon had a heart of its own in some ways, enduring and gracious, deadly and purifying, like a dragon's fire. "Serve me once more."

Drawing from the energy I'd felt when I killed Goren back on Calliope, I took deep, albeit painful breaths, and went for Emilian's head. He was blinking rapidly, trying to counteract the dazing effects of the powder. He managed to block several hits, but I roared and slashed even harder.

First, he lost his sword.

Then he lost his left arm. He screamed as blood spurted out in thick jets from his elbow.

I swung my bejeweled sword as if it were an extension of my very soul, and—swish.

Emilian's head came clean off his shoulders.

Rowan and Farrah both howled, temporarily distraught, giving both Jax and Scarlett the windows they needed to gain the advantage.

I stood there, with Emilian's body at my feet, watching as Scarlett cut through Rowan's defenses. The young vampire was ruthless and incredibly fast. She flashed around Rowan, delivering a flurry of cuts all over the Mara Lady's face and body. Rowan cried out in pain, overwhelmed by the increasing speed and depth of Scarlett's attacks.

She dropped to her knees. The trouble with Maras' healing abilities was that they needed a breather here and there for the body to get to work and start closing up the wounds. What Scarlett had done was overload Rowan's natural system, repeatedly cutting into her so many times that the Mara's mental state was dismantled.

Scarlett stopped in front of Rowan and put the tip of her sword against her throat.

"You have two choices here," Scarlett declared. "You live, or you die. I'm fine with either."

A couple of seconds passed as Rowan considered her options, then lowered her head in simmering shame. I had a feeling she'd try something stupid, but Scarlett would have none of it. Whatever came next, Rowan was royally screwed.

Farrah had some fight still left in her. Jax leaned backward to avoid her blade, then came back with both swords in an ample, downward move. He put all his strength in that blow, and it showed. One of the blades cut halfway through her forearm.

She cried out and moved back, keeping her distance as Jax slowly circled in, ready to deliver another hit.

"Give up, Farrah," Jax said.

Around us, the fight was gradually thinning. Our crew was taking the Correction Officers down, one by one. Arrah lay on the ground, pale and lifeless, just ten feet away from Rowan and Scarlett.

Farrah, however, wasn't ready to call it quits just yet. She grinned, then produced a small whistle from a secret dress pocket. She blew it; a faint hiss came out. The sound was released at a different frequency that only the Maras seemed to react to, as Jax cringed, visibly uncomfortable.

Within seconds, more Correction Officers emerged from the other Lords' mansions.

I counted fifty of them as they gathered around us with their weapons drawn.

"I've always had my little faction ready, scattered across the Houses, ready to serve me when the time was right," Farrah replied.

Rowan gave her a confused sideways glance, which prompted Farrah to scoff, no longer hiding her contempt.

"You've been planning to overthrow the Lords, haven't you?" Jax asked, slightly amused.

Farrah shrugged. "A Lady must look after herself. It was only going to be a matter of time before I'd have to take matters into my own hands, or before we all got ourselves killed by the daemons. Had you fools not intervened, I would've had my COs come in and stop that circus."

"You bitch," Rowan muttered, a muscle ticking in her jaw.

"No hard feelings, darling," Farrah retorted. "I wasn't going to kill you or the others. But with all your bickering, I knew I'd have to be the level-headed one and take over before you all lost it!" she added. "Darius was a greedy bastard. Emilian's conceit... Well, see for yourself," she said, pointing at his corpse. "You were too busy coddling Vincent, the city's most obnoxious coward! And don't even get me started on Caspian. He was the worst of you all!"

"So, what, you thought you'd just overthrow the Lordships and rule over Azure Heights, all by yourself?" I interjected, moving closer to Jax as my gaze wandered around us.

The Correction Officers were ready to fight, but I was more interested in seeing what was going on behind them—specifically, on the lower levels. I got closer to Jax and the edge of the seventh level platform, then craned my neck, and smiled before shifting my focus back to Farrah.

She narrowed her eyes at me. "Obviously," she replied. "This city needs a level-headed ruler. But first, I need to wipe you idiots off the face of this planet."

I chuckled. "Your efforts and acolytes will be wasted," I shot back. "Our allies are making their way up here. You're done for."

We could hear the swords clashing. The screams. The roars and the cries for help.

The temperature started to drop, as well. The Dhaxanians were getting closer.

But then I registered another sound, one that sent shivers

down my spine. I'd heard it before, during the war against Azazel and, most recently, on Ragnar Peak.

Farrah looked to her left, then burst into hysterical laughter. It wasn't a symptom of joy, but rather one of madness, a maniacal cackle of the overly ambitious fiend who had gotten a glimpse of her own demise.

I followed her gaze and felt my muscles stiffen at once.

"We're all screwed, darling," Farrah murmured, suddenly and eerily calm.

"Daemons," I croaked.

Thousands of them, coming in dark, square patches across the two-mile fields between the Valley of Screams and the mountain. Those were drums of war I was hearing. Above them, dark clouds of Death Claws swarmed, flying toward the mountain base.

Our allies had breached the city, but, soon enough, the daemon armies were going to hit them hard from the back. Our only hope was with Lumi.

"It doesn't matter," Farrah then said. "I'll kill you all before they get here."

I felt my lips stretch into a grin. After Emilian, despite the blaring pain in my side, I looked forward to taking Farrah down, as well. Jax and I briefly glanced at each other—a silent moment, a mutual, unspoken agreement. We both raised our blades once again and looked at Farrah.

This is it.

Just a little while longer.

19

HARPER

Zane took several steps forward, leaving us behind.

He drew his rapier, ready to square off with his father. I looked around, watching the daemons and Correction Officers move in.

"I told you all to stay back!" Shaytan snarled, his voice thundering throughout the entire neighborhood.

They all froze, while we held our positions, our faces partially obscured by our cloaks.

"Father, don't be foolish. Stop this before it's too late," Zane said.

Shaytan scoffed, then took out a handful of blue powder from a small satchel tied to his massive gold belt. "First of all, let's cut this invisibility crap. It's annoying," he replied, then blew the dust out.

It scattered into a bluish cloud that engulfed us. Within seconds, our invisibility spells were broken, and we were once again visible. That must have been some kind of water-related swamp witch magic, as I could feel the moist particles tickling my skin.

"Second, let's cut the 'give up' crap, too," Shaytan added. "It's unbecoming. I didn't raise you to be a coward. You've gone against your own father and kingdom, and that takes balls, my son. Don't make a fool of yourself now that this whole debacle is coming to an end."

Zane and Shaytan faced each other, with just five feet of super-charged space between them. The tension oozing from their standoff was starting to weigh us all down, in a way. The daemon king, the most feared of all the hostile creatures on Neraka, stood tall and proud, holding his bejeweled staff. His son, the rebel daemon that had come to our side in favor of a free Neraka, faced him with his chin up and his sword ready.

"You're right about one thing," Zane replied. "It all ends here. Now."

Shaytan took a deep breath, exhaling slowly as he measured his son from head to toe. "I will rule Neraka forever, Zane. And there is nothing you can do about that."

Zane cocked his head to one side. "I can try."

"Tell you what. Defeat your brothers," Shaytan replied, slightly amused. "Kill them, and then I'll consider fighting you."

"Are you afraid?" Zane shot back.

Shaytan chuckled, his contempt obvious. "Don't insult me, you little brat. I just want to see if you're worth my time. Last time we sparred, I beat the living daylights out of you and your mother begged me to spare you."

The daemon king didn't give Zane the opportunity to reply. Instead, he stepped back, allowing Abeles and another daemon warrior to come in. Both drew their swords and came at Zane, roaring. Fiona groaned.

"Oh, hell no! You don't get to have all the fun, Zane!" she shouted.

Fiona darted from our side and joined Zane in the fight. The daemon guards moved to intervene, as did the COs, but Shaytan's hand shot out to the side.

"Don't!" he ordered them, then smirked, watching Fiona and Zane against Abeles and the daemon warrior. "I want to see how this plays out."

I had to give Shaytan a mental thank you. By keeping the fighters back, he was inadvertently giving me the precious minutes I needed to devise an attack plan. While he enjoyed the theatricality and the showmanship of a good old-fashioned fight to the death between his own sons, I carefully analyzed every daemon and Mara stationed outside the Palisade.

Fiona's strength gave her a tremendous advantage against the daemon warrior, who was basically three times her size. She dodged his attacks and returned with hard offensive moves. Her short sword was made of an extremely light alloy, allowing her to deliver multiple hits in the span of seconds.

Zane, on the other hand, had his work cut out for him with Abeles, who was noticeably larger. But Zane had his speed and agility working for him; he moved around his brother and slashed at his sides before withdrawing and shifting his position again. He didn't give Abeles the opportunity to strike back, since he refused to stand still.

Shaytan shifted his focus to me, his red eyes burning holes through my very soul.

"Come on, Miss Hellswan. It's time to surrender the witch," he said.

I briefly used my True Sight to check out the mountain base again. Our allies had breached the first level and were working their way to the top. The Maras didn't stand much of a chance at this point. But the incoming hordes of daemons made my throat close up. All we had to do was get Lumi to take down the shield, then hold out against the thousands of horned fiends headed our way.

I exhaled, then raised an eyebrow at Shaytan.

"Now, why would I ever do that?" I asked.

My sarcasm didn't escape him. "Because I'll kill you quickly if you do," he replied. "Otherwise, I'll take my sweet time with you."

Abeles was the first to drop, his throat ripped out. Shaytan frowned, watching his son give out his last breath, blood pouring out of him and glazing the cobblestones. Zane gave his father a sideways glance.

"Don't make me do this," Zane said, his voice trembling. "Stop this nonsense."

"It's too late to stop," Shaytan replied, then walked toward us. I instinctively reached behind me and gripped Lumi's wrist.

Caspian stepped in front of us, drawing his sword and shaking his head.

"You're not taking her anywhere," he said, gritting his teeth.

Fiona was having a little trouble with the daemon warrior. He'd managed to pin her beneath him and was about to bring his sword down. Zane rammed into him and knocked him over, and Fiona panted and moved back, looking for her sword. They continued fighting, as the warrior wasn't going to let Zane get anywhere near Shaytan.

"What are you going to do?" Shaytan replied, smirking at Caspian. "Scowl at me? Poke me with that toothpick?"

My heart jumped in my throat as Caspian rushed forward and brought his sword out in a diagonal slash. Shaytan raised his arm. The blade hit the daemon king's wrist cuff with a loud clang. Sparks flew. In the next fraction of a second, Shaytan formed a fist with his other hand and drove it into Caspian's jaw.

The blow was incredibly powerful. I heard Caspian's jaw break, then watched him fly backward and land on his side with a painful thud. He was unconscious. A gasp slipped out of my throat, and I looked at Shaytan with genuine shock. I hadn't thought he'd be able to cause that much damage with a single punch.

Shaytan took another step in my direction.

I instinctively moved back. I'd thought about fighting him before, but now I was beginning to question that endeavor.

The daemon warrior came down with a thud, prompting Shaytan to look over his shoulder and curse under his breath. He'd lost another fighter.

"You're taking this a lot better than I'd thought," Fiona muttered.

Zane retrieved his rapier, which he'd lodged into the daemon warrior's throat, and came toward Shaytan with a murderous look on his face. I knew the daemon prince hated hurting his own family, and the fact that Shaytan had forced him to do just that had clearly made something snap inside Zane.

"Plenty more where they came from," Shaytan replied dryly. "I just don't like losing prime fighters in the middle of a war."

"Nice to know we're of *some* value to you, Father," Zane growled and charged at Shaytan.

The daemon king raised his staff and whispered a spell. The bejeweled instrument trembled and morphed into a massive sword, with a mixture of meranium and gold swirls decorating the blade.

Zane hit first, but Shaytan used his right arm cuff to block the attack, then brought his newly formed sword in a lateral swing and cut deep into Zane's hip.

"Zane!" Fiona croaked.

Shaytan kicked him in the gut, forcing him back several feet. Zane fell backward. Blood poured out of the gaping gash in his side. Fiona ran to him, slid down on her knees and immediately applied some of her healing paste to his wound. She then bit into her wrist and pressed it against his lips, forcing him to drink.

This wasn't going in the direction I'd wanted. My heart started beating faster as Shaytan resumed his mission to take Lumi away from me.

He sauntered toward us, a confident grin cutting across his

face. I could hear the golden marbles braided into his beard jingle as he got closer.

"Come on, little bloodsucker." Shaytan sneered. "Hand the witch over."

"Screw you!" I shot back, then put my hand out and released the most powerful barrier I could muster. I felt my entire body instantly drain as the pulse went out. It was strong—remarkably so. It was probably the biggest one to come out of me yet.

It knocked most of the daemon soldiers and Correction Officers back, but, most importantly, it smacked into Shaytan with enough strength to take him down. He fell flat on his back with a pained grunt. Rumbles emerged from the level above—it was definitely going down in Emilian's mansion! I briefly looked back up and watched the fight spill onto the open terrace.

Shaytan chuckled, then got back up. My blood ran cold. It took him very little time to recover. That didn't bode well for future efforts to destroy him.

This time, however, he didn't walk. He darted toward me.

I drew both my swords, but his punch found my face first. The impact made time stand still for a split second. He hit me so hard, I felt my bones break—my cheeks, my nose... even my forehead. Pain spread through my skull like hot lava.

Everything went white. I lost my balance.

I heard him laugh again. Then I heard the sharp clang of my swords hitting the ground.

Then I heard Lumi's gut-wrenching whimpers.

My eyes peeled open. I could see through the smoky glasses. The sky was beautifully blue and clear. Within the hour, the suns would begin their slow descent into the horizon.

"Let me go!" Lumi screamed.

Shaytan laughed even harder, as if he were having more fun than ever.

My whole face hurt. It would require a few minutes for the bones and crushed tissues to repair themselves. Nevertheless, I needed to see what happened next. I groaned from the pain as I sat up, leaning onto my shaking arms.

Shaytan had grabbed Lumi, his large hand gripping her upper arm.

He tore her black cloak off, delighted to have her in his possession. The satisfaction on his face was too much to bear, but not in a negative way. It hurt like crazy, but I couldn't help it—I grinned, watching his satisfied expression as he looked Lumi over from head to toe.

He gave me a quick glance, his bright white fangs still bared. Nothing could wipe that smirk off his face. Except what came next, of course.

"What are you grinning about, toothless?" He scoffed.

I ran my tongue over my upper teeth and felt the gap where an incisor had been until a minute earlier. I licked the bleeding gums, feeling another tooth coming out already. I shuddered from the incoming wave of laughter. On one hand, I would've loved to see myself in a mirror in that moment; on the other, I would've killed to have a camera handy, so I could capture his expression as he followed my gaze and glared at Lumi.

Something was awfully wrong, he must've thought, as Lumi's skin began to ripple all over.

She gave him a broad grin, then started to laugh.

As expected, Shaytan's amusement abandoned the mountain altogether in the following second.

He let go of Lumi—only to realize that she wasn't Lumi at all.

As her skin trembled and twitched, Avril regained her natural form. She'd swapped places with Lumi via the swamp witch's proprietary magic. Heron had been against it for a minute, until he'd understood the genius behind it.

"What the hell?" Shaytan murmured, his eyes wide with shock.

"Dude, you really underestimated our ability to pull one over on you," I replied, running my tongue over my teeth again. They were all back and healthy, despite the taste of blood in my mouth.

"You... Where is she?" he growled.

Avril took a couple of steps back, in case he sought to take it out on her first. I got back on my feet again, picking my swords up in the process.

"Not here, obviously," I replied with a smirk.

"Where is she?!" he shouted, downright livid and unhinged.

Fear tickled my throat. I was about to witness the full extent of his wrath.

"What part of 'not here' didn't you understand?" I shot back, then assumed my attack stance and brought my swords up.

Lumi was with Heron. With a little bit of luck, she was already doing what she was supposed to do. All I had to do now was try to stay alive. That was, by far, the greatest challenge I'd ever faced.

The king of daemons had his sights set on me.

His blazing red eyes promised me a world of pain.

20

HERON

I hated leaving Avril behind with Shaytan the evil overlord and his fiendish hordes, but she'd made a good point back in the basement of the Palisade—none of us were going to survive this if we didn't get Lumi to safety.

I was also thankful to have Zane take the lead once we reached the main doors. His large figure had kept Lumi and me out of sight. Even though we were invisible, and she was disguised as Avril, we still couldn't risk being spotted. At first, we'd thought we'd just take one of the many alternative routes to the second level, rather than the main road. But then Shaytan showed up with his daemons, and, well, we had to improvise.

Fortunately, the Palisade still had a functional back door, and the COs were too dazed by the Adlet flare and incoming allies to consider the possibility that there were others coming out of the building—besides the ones they'd already seen, of course, whom we'd left behind.

I took Lumi's hand and slipped through the service entrance. I helped her walk for a while, as we snuck through the back alleys of the sixth level, as far away from the Palisade as possible. A few minutes later, I decided we were better off if I carried her.

She climbed onto my back, and I continued my trek down the mountain, jumping from rooftop to rooftop and generally staying out of sight. We could both see the daemon armies pouring out of the gorges and coming toward the city.

"How long will it take your people to leave the moon and come down here once the shield is down?" Lumi asked.

I slid down the side of a building, then rushed through the crowded street. Imen who had yet to be mind-bent into joining the fight below were running in the opposite direction, seeking shelter in the buildings at the back of the third level. The COs were too busy moving to defend the city and could not come after these innocents.

"Probably minutes," I replied. "I imagine they're all waiting on the edges of their seats right now, constantly watching over us."

"They can't see us. They can't see the planet at all. Not until the shield comes down. It's how the spell works," she replied.

"Oh. Great. They'll definitely be coming in blind, then. Good thing we've got a crew out in the field to intercept them. We'll probably have Telluris back up and running, but if there's one thing I've learned in this place, it's that we should never rely on just one option..."

I made my way through the thinning crowd with Lumi on my back, then hid behind a small pottery store—just in time, as I would've bumped into a squadron of Maras running down to the first level.

"Should we try this area for a safe place?" Lumi asked.

I shook my head. "No, we're going down to the second level. The allies are in the area. They can help protect us. I know a good spot."

We reached the top of the stairs leading down to the infirmary, then stopped. Dhaxanian frost was spreading across the cobblestone. Nevis's archers were shooting hundreds of arrows at once, all of them dipped in Manticore venom. I watched dozens of Maras collapse as the poison worked its way through their bloodstreams.

Manticores and Adlets ripped through the Correction Officers' flanks, while three dozen rebel Maras worked around the mindbent Imen defending the city. They overrode their previous commands and ordered them to get off the mountain. The Maras used swamp witch warfare spells to take down the allied troops, casting fires and electromagnetic pulses that crippled the fighters.

Still, the locals didn't stand much of a chance and were forced to pull back.

I jumped over the banister and landed on the infirmary roof with a thud. Tiles cracked under my boots. I watched the rebels roar and slash at the Correction Officers with their swords, as they pushed them farther up the mountain.

"This is our chance," I breathed, then jumped down and went around the infirmary, looking for the back door.

It was open. Lumi got off my back, then followed me inside. I locked the door behind her. She muttered a spell under her breath, and the doorknob glowed white before it was magically sealed.

I crossed the back room and walked into the front one, where we'd first cared for Patrik and Minah during the daemon attacks. *Boy, were we young and clueless back then.* It felt like ages ago.

There were two Mara nurses hiding in here. They'd huddled under the bed, whimpering and covering their heads, as the war intensified outside in a variety of bangs and clangs. They couldn't see us, but they did notice the side door opening and the air rippling around us.

"Get the lens. Get the lens!" one of the nurses barked, keeping her eyes on our general area. The other nurse fumbled through her dress pockets.

"Dammit, it's not here... I think I lost it."

"You idiot," the first nurse muttered.

She scoffed, then came out and stood up straight, holding a sharp glass shard in her hand. The other followed, then broke the leg off the bed. They didn't even have weapons on them. It almost didn't seem like it would be fair to fight them, until I remembered their habit of draining the life out of the Imen who came to them for help.

I stalked across the room and cut the head off the first nurse. Blood sprayed out and doused the other in crimson. She started screaming. My blade took care of her next. Her head dropped to the floor, closely followed by her body.

"I'm not one to enjoy watching others die," Lumi murmured, watching me, "but I must admit, it does feel a little better to know there are two fewer of... these." She gestured to the dead nurses.

"I can't blame you. Especially after everything they did to you," I replied, then put my sword away and pointed at the front door. "Do you mind?"

Lumi shook her head and used the same glow spell to permanently lock that one, too. I pulled all the blinds down, in the meantime.

"What do we need to secure this perimeter for as long as you need?" I asked, looking around for any kind of spell paraphernalia that we could possibly use, besides what I always carried in my satchels and slim backpack.

Lumi frowned, as if trying to remember. "Chalk. A piece of red garnet. And my blood," she said. "I can cook something up with that."

I fumbled through my pouches and offered a piece of chalk and one of my lenses.

"These good?" I asked.

She motioned around the room, then took the red garnet lens and sat on the floor. "Draw a line along the walls, uninterrupted. Do it on both the floor and the ceiling."

I did as instructed, while she crushed the red garnet into a fine powder with her bare hands. Lumi lived and breathed swamp witch magic. Even Viola, who'd mastered most of the three-book spells, didn't hold a candle to her. It was mind-blowing just to watch her perform the simplest of tasks.

A thud made me jump out of my skin, just as I finished the ceiling line. Lumi had cut her thumb and was dripping a thin red circle around the garnet. She, too, stilled and looked up at the main door. Another bang followed. Then a third.

"Oh, crap," I muttered.

Lumi sighed, then proceeded to whisper a spell.

"Open up, Heron. I can smell you in there!" Velnias shouted.

"Lumi, stop," I breathed. "Hold on."

I rushed to the door, my heart jumping out of my chest. I tried to open it but quickly remembered she'd sealed it shut. I gave her a brief glance, and she murmured something. Two seconds later, I was able to turn the knob again.

Standing in front of me, measuring a glorious ten feet, was Velnias, accompanied by the equally large Tobiah and his pixie-sized soulmate, Sienna. Velnias chuckled, looking me up and down through his red lens.

"What are you guys doing here?" I asked, then looked behind them. Several Maras were still fighting against the rebels, but the others had already left the second level.

"I spotted you carrying Avril on your back," Velnias replied. "I could see you from the edge of the seventh level, and it struck me as odd that you'd have to carry your lady out of the Palisade, until it hit me that that might not be Avril." He glanced over my shoulder, his red eyes lighting up at the sight of Lumi. "I see I was right."

"Yeah, small artifices," I said. "What are you guys doing here? What's happening upstairs?"

Velnias scoffed, then nodded at Tobiah and Sienna. "You kids stay here," he said. He pushed me out of the way and came inside the infirmary. "Lock the door again."

I did, and then Lumi sealed it once more, looking at the both of us with confusion.

Velnias stopped, then bowed before her. "I cannot express what an honor and relief it is to see you," he said gently. "Velnias, traitor to my people, at your service."

"Dude, what's happening out there?" I asked, slightly irritated.

"What's happening is that whatever you kids were trying to pull, it worked. But Shaytan's pissed and sent daemons through the city to look for you and Lumi. They'll be here soon, no doubt. I watched them deploy from the Palisade, and I thought I'd be more useful down here than up on the seventh," Velnias replied.

Lumi gave him a shy smile, nodded, then resumed her incantation. The blood circle lit up white. The red garnet dust ignited in a bright flash. Light spread through the room and washed over us. It hit the walls and expanded into a glowing membrane that covered the entire room, from top to bottom, before it faded and vanished.

"Thank you, Velnias," she said, then looked at me. "The room is safe, for the time being. It will wear off soon, though I'm not sure when. I'm saving most of my energy for the shield. I need more chalk now."

I gave her another piece from my satchel, then leaned against the door and watched her get to work. She drew a variety of symbols all over the floor and the walls.

"What's going on up on the seventh level, then?" I asked Velnias, who peeked outside through the blinds, watching Sienna and Tobiah as they fought aimless fiends and kept our area clear.

"The Lords are down," Velnias replied. "But Shaytan is nowhere near done, my friend. Daemon armies are coming. We're screwed every other way if our little witch here doesn't take the shield down."

"I'm working on it," Lumi muttered, and pointed at the ceiling. "I can't reach it."

"Say no more," Velnias said with a half-smile. He gently picked her up and sat her on his shoulder. He moved around with her as she kept drawing symbols across the ceiling.

"Harper is back at the Palisade, with Avril, Caspian, Fiona, and

Zane," I replied, crossing my arms. "They're doing everything they can to keep Shaytan busy."

"Well, I think he knows it's a ruse, which is why he sent his daemons out to find you," Velnias said. "Provided they put up a good fight, the kids might actually keep that bastard busy long enough for Lumi here to do her thing. But, Heron... you should know... I've rarely seen Shaytan this furious. Losing the swamp witch will make him livid. There will be blood."

My stomach tightened into a crippling black hole as my mind instantly flashed back to Avril. As long as she stayed out of his attack range, she was probably going to be okay. *Just a little while longer, babe. Hang in there.*

"I see a glimmer of hope in your eyes," Velnias added, watching me intently. "I hate to be a spoiler of such thinking, but you should know that Shaytan knows plenty of the swamp witch spells they've pulled out of Lumi. Most are attacks and curses. The stuff of nightmares, really."

"Dude, enough. Seriously. You're bumming me out," I groaned, rubbing my face with my hands and struggling to keep my cool.

Every atom in my body begged me to go back and get Avril, but I knew, deep down, that I couldn't. I had to protect Lumi with everything at my disposal. Even with Velnias, Tobiah, and Sienna around, we were still vulnerable. The protection she'd cast around the room was only temporary.

I took several deep breaths, mentally bracing myself for what came next.

"I'm just being realistic here," Velnias replied with an innocent shrug, nearly losing Lumi from his shoulder. His hand came up and held her in place, and he gave her a sheepish smile. "Sorry."

She frowned at him, then continued drawing her symbols.

"It's taking a little longer than usual because my incantation symbol knowledge is a tad rusty," she muttered. "I haven't undone a spell in thousands of years."

"It's cool, Lumi," I replied. "It's more important that you get it right. We are here to keep you safe and make sure you can do it."

Sooner or later, this place was going to be crawling with daemon soldiers. I instinctively gripped my sword handle. I was ready.

One glance at Velnias was enough to tell me that he was ready, too.

No matter what they throw at us, we're doing this.

21

VESTA

We had a good spot in the field, perched on the thick branches of a tree, on the edge of a small forest patch. I could see the Adlet flare burning bright above the mountain. Our allies were laying siege on the city. Azure Heights was being conquered, one level at a time.

Fires burned here and there, with columns of black smoke billowing and reaching for the sky. We could all hear the roars, the bangs, the spine-tingling screeches of swords clashing, even from afar.

But the worst was yet to come. The drums of war grew louder as the daemon army crossed the two-mile field and headed for the city. Our patch was at a reasonably safe distance from their path, but my nerves were still stretched to the point of snapping. We were on the edge and could not, under any circumstances, reveal our presence here.

Laughlan passed around his satchel of invisibility paste. "Take the equivalent of a fingertip," he whispered. Rush and Amina were the first to ingest it. "We only need it while these mongrels pass us by."

Rush then passed the satchel over. I scooped out a small amount, then gave it back to Laughlan, who tied it back around his belt. We all looked out at the daemon army—their boots stomping on the ground, their swords hitting their shields. They aimed to make as much noise as possible. Just like before, the daemons relied on being loud and intimidating, on top of their increased numbers. They were looking to inspire dread—and they were certainly succeeding.

"Oh, great, Death Claws, too," I murmured, staring at the dark cloud flying over the army.

"There are hundreds of them," Amina breathed, her eyes wide with horror.

Laughlan scoffed, scratching the back of his head. "They had better hurry up with Lumi," he said. "If those daemons hit the city before the shield comes down, we are absolutely screwed."

The army was now just two hundred feet away and moving at a rapid pace. They were going to pass by our patch within the next ten minutes, based on their speed. My blood boiled, thinking of all the innocents still stuck in Azure Heights. I worried about Harper and the others, as well. They had a lot on their plates, dealing with the likes of Shaytan and the Lords.

I'd seen the atrocities that those creatures were willing to commit, just so they could continue tormenting and draining the life out of us. They were vicious and always had dirty tricks up their sleeves.

"What if something went wrong?" I asked, suddenly animated by a sense of alarm. "What if they're having trouble? Maybe I should go help..."

"Don't even think about it!" Laughlan replied, his tone clipped. His reprimanding gaze kept me in place. I clutched my branch.

"I just hate sitting here. I'm useless," I muttered.

"Nonsense!" Laughlan shot back, while Rush and Amina

nodded in agreement. "You are essential to this part of the mission. What if GASP can't steer their interplanetary spell and land right in the middle of that mayhem? I need you here more than they need you out there, Vesta," he added. "Besides, I promised your parents I'd make sure you're safe when all this is over. I don't plan on breaking my word."

"Well, they promised they'd stay alive, too, so... whatever." I scoffed, crossing my arms.

He had a point, though. Once the shield came down, we had to keep an eye out for the big ball of light coming down from the sky. I'd learned to manipulate the winds quite well over the past couple of years. Water had always come naturally to me. According to Mom, that applied to my pre-amnesia years, too.

However, as soon as I'd figured out that I could manipulate the other elements as well, I'd started training. With all the moving around I did in my adoptive tribe, I knew I wouldn't always have water around to help me. But there was always dirt or stone. There was always air. Sometimes, a fire could do the trick.

The war drums grew louder, making me cringe. They brought back flashbacks from Ragnar Peak, sending shivers down my back. Chills rushed through me at the sight of pit wolves running ahead of the daemon squadrons and slightly spreading out.

"Uh-oh," I murmured. "I don't like that."

"They might catch our scent," Rush added.

"No worries," Laughlan replied, then put his palms together, closed his eyes, and muttered a spell. By the time he was done, a circle had formed in the grass around our tiny forest patch. It lit up red for a split second, then faded away in a puff of smoke.

By the time the pit wolves reached our area, the fumes had spread out.

"Everybody, stay calm and quiet," Laughlan whispered.

I watched one of the beasts casually come closer. It was huge, its skin black, its eyes bright red, and its tongue hanging from the side of its ginormous mouth. It sniffed the air, then shook its head with what looked like disgust and rushed back to the pack. They thundered past our patch and rumbled toward the city. There was less than a mile left before they'd reach it. Maybe twenty minutes before the daemons would hit the first level.

"What did you do?" I asked Laughlan. He looked at me and put on a satisfied grin.

"A little trick I used to employ when my teacher's crops on Persea were targeted by pests," he replied. "The smell is nasty to pretty much any animal. Thankfully, it applies to pit wolves, too."

"Your Druid teachers had crops?" Rush asked, slightly confused.

"Of course. Our herbs had to come from somewhere, right? So did our food. The Druid Temple was always self-sufficient. It was part of our apprenticeship to look after our fields. We're naturally bound to the environment that we inhabit, after all," he replied, then stilled as the daemons finally started coming through.

We all turned into living statues. I held my breath for a while, my muscles tight and burning with a mixture of fear and anger. I couldn't wait to see them all go down for their crimes.

"Don't move," Laughlan mumbled. "Don't make a sound."

We didn't.

Death Claws flew across the field in front of us, cawing and screeching. The flapping of their leathery wings sent currents of warm air outward, making the leaves in our forest patch rustle.

The daemons followed, grunting and smacking their swords against their meranium shields. The drums thundered on the edges of this first squadron. The others were farther away, as the army advanced in a horizontal line against the city. We were right on the edge, and, fortunately, only had to put up with the blood-curdling ruckus for about three minutes before they were all gone.

They'd brought catapults and ballistae. I could hear their giant wooden and iron structures moaning and grumbling as they were pushed through the tall grass. Daemon Legions, the oversized generals I'd learned to steer clear of, whipped the weaker soldiers around, forcing them to stay in line as they advanced toward the city.

"Oh, man, they're in a heap of trouble," Laughlan murmured, watching them go.

He took a lens out from his pocket, along with two small vials of what looked like colored oil. He proceeded to spread both liquids over the lens, making it shimmer in a pale shade of blue.

"Worst part is that there are so many innocent Imen stuck up there," I replied, finally able to breathe again, since the daemons were out of our range.

"The Exiled Maras are the worst," Rush said, gritting his teeth. "Absolute cowards, hiding behind defenseless creatures like that."

"It's despicable," Amina added. "You know, my mother was part of the council that banished them, along with House Dorchadas. I remember my father vehemently protesting the decision to exile them, instead of wiping them all out. Gah... If only they'd known."

I exhaled sharply. "Unfortunately, we can't go back and change history," I muttered. "But we can sure as hell fix as much of the damage they've done here as possible."

"Which is why it's imperative that we intercept GASP when they come down," Laughlan said. "They need to know who the innocents and the rebels are. I'm guessing they've brought more dragons with them. They can't just let them loose on Azure Heights."

I shook my head slowly. "We'll make sure they don't just blitz the place. Though I would *love* to see dragon fire swallow that entire mountain in one breath."

"What are you doing?" Rush asked Laughlan, who kept looking through the blue lens, then added more colored oils to its surface.

"We don't have a sentry's vision, but I do remember some tricks to help us see better," Laughlan replied, then put the lens against his lips and muttered a spell. "There... This should be good to go in a few minutes, once the oil dries."

I looked up at the mountain, wondering where Harper and Lumi were in particular. My heart swelled with hope as I thought about a future where Neraka would be free, where the Imen, who had taken me in and loved me unconditionally, would get to rebuild their world and their cities. I longed to see this world ridded of the crippling fear of going out at night and getting your soul eaten, of leaving your house and having your blood drained by a hungry Mara.

Enough is enough.

Our fates were now in Lumi's hands.

I closed my eyes, and, for the first time since I'd first heard the rumors about the Hermessi, the elemental spirits that fueled this world and the other, I prayed to them. I prayed to the wind, the seas, the deserts and the limestone, the lightning and the fire, the rivers and the mountain springs.

I prayed to every natural element that resonated with my fae nature that we'd get the much-needed break to tip the scales on Neraka. I prayed for peace.

22

HANSA

Farrah's Correction Officers went straight on the offense, but we rose to the occasion—and then some. Jax and I went against Farrah at the same time, while Caia, Blaze, and the others fought her guards.

"Come on, Jax, let's take these vermin down and go lend Harper a hand. I have a feeling Shaytan's after her," I said, then brought my sword down on Farrah.

She dodged my hit and took a couple of steps back. Jax moved in for his chance, but she muttered a quick spell and sent out a pulse that knocked him back. Farrah had learned some swamp witch magic, it seemed.

"Hah!" she exclaimed, grinning from ear to ear. "I've never expelled one so fast before."

That little moment of truth told me a lot about her. It also gave me an idea, as Jax took several steps forward, shaking his head and blinking rapidly. The pulse had dazed him a bit.

"The sides, Jax," I muttered.

He heard me and replied with a brief nod. We moved around her and attacked her simultaneously. She muttered another spell and sent out a second pulse, but she could only aim it at one of us. She chose me this time but couldn't push Jax away.

He slashed at her with both his swords. I had to give her credit, though: she was fast and light on her feet. I felt blood dripping from my nose. That pulse packed a punch, after all. I wiped my nostril and checked my hand. There was a silvery smudge that confirmed the tickling sensation. As a Mara, Jax took that spell in differently. I didn't want to give her the chance to launch another swamp witch magic attack, though.

I quietly moved around and stayed out of her sight, watching her as she fought Jax.

Growls erupted from below. Adlets climbed up the stairs. My heart soared at the sight of those magnificent beasts with luscious red fur and large, sharp fangs. They spared none of the fiends as they tore through the CO's.

It got so bloody so fast that Caia, Blaze, Scarlett, Patrik, and the rest of our crew had to pull back, just to make room for the Adlets. One by one, Farrah's Correction Officers dropped dead—most of them mangled and dismembered.

I recognized Colton as he killed one of the last remaining Maras, then stood on his hind legs and shifted back to his humanoid form. Hundurr growled as he tackled another CO behind him.

"The daemons are coming," Colton said, panting. "We made it up to the third level, but they hit us hard. I left Nevis and Neha with the others down there."

A nightmare unfolded below on the lower levels. I looked over the edge and broke into a sudden, cold sweat. Dhaxanian frost exploded all over the third level, as hordes of daemons fought their way up. Blood sprayed all over. Our allies struggled to keep the enemy at bay. We had already known it would come to this, sooner or later, but it still made my stomach churn as I watched the horror transpire.

"I came up to help you guys," Colton added. "I heard the screams and the walls coming down."

I gave him a brief and thankful nod, then looked at Blaze, who had just torched another Mara—whom Caia then decapitated with one swift blow.

"Blaze! I think it's time you go dragon, kiddo!" I said. "Daemons galore."

Blaze smirked. "I thought you'd never ask," he replied, then ran to the edge of the terrace and jumped. He burst into his full dragon form in midair and flew down the mountain. A literal hell was about to swallow the daemons.

I watched him fly for a second, until movement to my left caught my eye.

Several Correction Officers ambushed Colton. He didn't have time to turn back into his Adlet form, but his pack mates were quick to intervene. He got cut by a Mara's blade in the process but managed to take a couple of steps back.

"Colton, watch out!" I cried out, as Farrah was just a couple of feet away and headed toward him.

She'd kicked Jax away and had caught a window of opportunity to sneak up on Colton. She moved faster than he could turn around and rammed her sword into his back.

"Colton, no!" I screamed.

The Adlets roared and rushed to finish off the other Correction Officers, while the rest of our crew stayed back, unable to advance because of the bloody and somewhat confusing scuffle.

Colton collapsed to the ground. Farrah pulled her blade back, then turned around to block one of Jax's retaliating blows. He growled furiously as he struck again and again, moving to her side and forcing her to turn her back to me.

Perfect timing.

Hundurr's wail made my heart twist itself into a painful knot.

I dashed forward and drove my broadsword through her spine at the same time that Jax moved away. I heard the blade shatter her vertebrae as she froze.

A split second later, Hundurr reached her and snapped his jaws into her shoulder, ripping her entire left arm off in one devastating bite. Farrah screamed in agony and dropped her blade. I withdrew mine, then came around and pointed it at her throat.

Her legs gave out. She dropped to her knees, coughing and groaning from the pain. Blood gushed out from her shoulder, pooling beneath her.

Jax put his swords away and immobilized her, pinning her down with his body weight. Caia rushed to her side and pressed the tip of her flaming sword against her wound. Her shrieks tore through the air itself, as her flesh simmered until it was cauterized, and the amputation was complete. She cried out, covered in sweat and blood.

Hundurr spat her arm out, then sat next to Colton's body. He whimpered and licked the Adlet pack leader's face as Colton gave his last breath. The other Adlets finished the last COs off, then gathered around Colton. Together with Hundurr, they howled from the bottom of their lungs.

I could hear their grief. It gave me goosebumps and brought tears to my eyes. I breathed deeply, then looked at Farrah.

"Darius is dead. Emilian is dead. Rowan is down," I said, gritting my teeth. "It'll take a while before you regain the feeling in your legs, Farrah."

"You'll never get that arm back, either," Ryker added, moving closer and pointing at her shoulder. "A pit wolf's bite is permanent. The wound will heal, eventually, but the arm won't grow again. There's something in the perverted swamp witch charm that forces Adlets into pit wolves. It amplifies the damage that they can do. Their saliva is so toxic, it counteracts any growth enzyme, natural or otherwise."

"Concede now, and I will make sure you get a fair trial," I continued.

In any other circumstance, I would've felt a sliver of mercy for someone like her. But Farrah, just like the other Lords, had proven herself to be the worst of her kind. No moral compass, no intention of ever redeeming herself. She was done for.

She sobbed, overwhelmed by the circumstances—not just her physical injuries. Farrah was helpless and at our mercy. She'd played fast and loose with morality, and she was paying a steep price for what she'd done already. She knew, deep down, that this wasn't the end of her punishment.

On the contrary, it was only getting started. She and Rowan were the only Mara leaders left alive at this point. Someone had to answer for all the crimes committed. Of course, there would be individual trials. But Farrah and Rowan were going to receive the harshest punishments, as they were entirely responsible for all the policies and actions that had led to the enslavement of the Imen and the deaths of many innocent creatures.

Jax gave me some of his blood and spread some healing paste on my more serious wounds, giving me a couple of minutes to recover. My body had taken quite the beating, but, with a little bit of care, I could go on and chop off more enemy heads.

The battle continued to ravage the lower levels, but our mission on the seventh had come to an end. I walked over to Hundurr and the other Adlets as they sat around Colton's body and whimpered, overcome with grief.

I rested my hand on Hundurr's back and stroked him, gently.

"I'm sorry for your loss," I whispered. "We wouldn't be here if it weren't for Colton. He fought well. He'll always be remembered as a hero."

Hundurr shuddered, then slowly raised his head to look at me, tears glazing his big red eyes. I understood then, effortlessly, that he wouldn't leave Colton's body until his funeral. Hundurr's fight was over, in a way. He'd lost enough as it was—his Adlet body, then Rover, and now Colton. I couldn't ask any more of him at this point.

"I get it," I said, then let out a heavy sigh. "Keep him safe, buddy," I added, shifting my attention to the dozen Adlets around us. "We're done here, but they need our help down at the Palisade. Are you still with us?"

The Adlets growled, then stood on all fours, lowering their heads as a means of telling me that, yes, they were most certainly still on board with kicking as many Mara and daemon asses as possible. My broadsword was already itching for more.

I nodded slowly, then walked back to our crew and quickly scanned the seventh level.

"Peyton, I need one of your guys to stay here and keep an eye on Farrah and Rowan," I said. "I wouldn't leave Farrah, in particular, alone with Hundurr. As little as I'd mind if he finished the job, we need her in one piece. Well, most of her, anyway," I added, chuckling softly. "For the trial. She will testify on the record, whether she wants to or not."

Peyton smirked and motioned for one of his rebels to assume a guard position next to Farrah. She was close to passing out anyway. I wasn't even sure she could hear us anymore. Her eyes kept rolling into her head, and she let out a moan, every now and then.

"Ready to go down there and take on the daemon king and his armies?" Jax asked, giving me his signature half smile. It filled me with the much-needed energy and confidence I needed to keep going.

"Oh, absolutely," I replied. "We're not done here."

We certainly weren't.

We regrouped and made our way down the main stairs toward the sixth level. Until the shield came down, we had no choice but to keep fighting. We'd lost valuable people along the way, but, in the end... I had known this would happen.

Nevertheless, I could almost taste freedom on the tip of my tongue.

As long as Lumi was kept out of Shaytan's reach so she could complete her part of the mission, we were going to be okay. We had to be okay.

We have to be.

23

HARPER

Shaytan was a freaking beast, and I was about to fight him. He'd sent some of his daemons down to look for Lumi, but there were still plenty left surrounding us, along with the Correction Officers. However, the drums of war had already reached the mountain base. We could all hear the battle thundering below.

Fiona left Zane to heal on the ground and got up. She brought her sword up, pointing it at the Correction Officers nearest to her. Avril joined her, wearing a confident smirk. They were both itching for a fight, even though they were outnumbered.

A massive shadow passed over our heads. We all looked up and saw Blaze in dragon form as he flew down to greet Shaytan's daemon armies. That only further aggravated the daemon king. He glanced at his soldiers, baring his fangs.

"Go down there and bring me the blasted dragon!" He barked his order.

"But, Your Grace, these—" One of his guards tried to speak, but Shaytan cut him off with a chilling snarl.

"Get me the dragon!"

They didn't wait for him to say it again. Within seconds, we were only left with Shaytan and the Correction Officers, who were starting to get restless. I could see the concern on their faces. They were most likely wondering what good it did for them to stick around, when Shaytan had already sent some of his daemons down the mountain to look for the witch.

"We have no use for these outsiders," one of them muttered. Judging by the insignia on his lapel, I pegged him for a lieutenant, like Cadmus. "We need to find the witch before the daemons!" he added, raising his voice.

They pulled back and followed the lieutenant down the stairs.

Shaytan looked at me, wearing his murderous grin. "Ah, now I have more room to spread your entrails around."

"I would normally say that I'd love to see you try, but you're a psychopath with too much power, so I'd rather not tempt fate," I shot back dryly. "However, that doesn't mean you're walking out of here alive."

I didn't give him a chance to reply. I couldn't prolong this anymore, either.

He brought his sword up and effortlessly blocked my first double hit. He then stepped back, smirked, and muttered something—a spell. I froze, unsure of what was going to happen next. He kissed his index and middle fingers, then pressed them against his blade. A nanosecond later, he attacked me.

I brought my swords out in an X to block his hit. His weapon came down so hard, my blades screeched. He grunted and released a pulse from his core. That was the spell. It slapped me hard and threw me backward.

My entire body hurt. I landed on my back.

Fiona and Avril came at him next, as I tried to pick myself off the ground. It was as if every bone in my body had been cracked. Shaytan had certainly learned to make the most of the swamp witch magic he'd collected from Lumi. I'd never seen anything like this, and it worried me.

I heard both girls whimper as they were thrown backward. They fell and rolled on the ground like broken ragdolls. My heart bled as I watched them, half-conscious and struggling to get back up.

Shaytan's booming laughter made my blood boil.

"What did I tell you, Miss Hellswan?" he said. "You have no chance of winning this. I'll get my witch back, and I'll run these streets red with your blood, before I redecorate Azure Heights as my new summer home."

I managed to get up on my knees, looking for my blades.

He guffawed, then dashed across the cobblestone, ready to take me out. Caspian cut him off with his sword.

I held my breath, watching him and Shaytan. The daemon king rolled his eyes as he blocked his blade, then punched him hard enough to break his jaw again and throw his head to the side. He pushed Caspian away, keeping his focus on me.

"I'll deal with you in a second, Kifo," he muttered. "I'm not done with this little bloodsucker yet."

"Too bad, because I'm not done with you yet, either," Caspian managed, despite his facial injury, then came back around and tried to slash him again.

To his credit, Caspian was fast and beautifully agile. But Shaytan was a freaking monster with a dangerously sharp instinct. He didn't even look at Caspian when he blocked his side hit with his wrist cuff.

He quickly followed his defense up with his massive sword, but Caspian ducked. The broad blade missed him by inches, but it managed to snip off a bit of his hair at the top. *Good grief.*

I had to get up. My body was healing already, just not fast enough. I reached for one sword, then the other, as I caught a glimpse of Caspian delivering yet another sword attack. Shaytan scoffed and swiped his arm out, knocking the blade out of Caspian's hands.

Half a second later, Shaytan grabbed Caspian by the throat, gripping him with enough strength to crush his windpipe. Caspian struggled against his hold but could do nothing as Shaytan lifted him a couple of inches in the air.

"Caspian," I whispered, finally finding the strength I needed to get up. "Let him go!" I shouted. "It's me you want!"

Shaytan gave me a sideways glance. The shadow of a smile passed over his face.

"It's true. It's you I want. But I can hurt you in more than one way," he muttered, then uttered another spell.

His whole arm lit up red, and flames burst through his skin, then spread up to his hand, and... swallowed Caspian whole.

Caspian was on fire.

"Caspian!" I screamed, as loud as my lungs could manage.

I heard him grunt and roar from the pain as the fire burned through him, consuming his skin.

My heart gave out. Desperation broke my brain.

I ran toward them as Caspian's arms and legs flailed. Shaytan held him firmly above the ground, laughing as he watched the love of my life *burn*.

Something snapped inside me.

I mustered every ounce of energy I could gather and pushed out a barrier. I didn't even realize I had any spark left, but the adrenaline managed to give me the push I urgently needed.

The pulse was concentrated and targeted.

It hit Shaytan in the solar plexus with such unexpected strength that it hurled him backward, throwing him up like he'd done with Fiona and Avril.

Caspian dropped to the ground, still burning.

Shaytan landed flat on his face fifty feet away. I came to a screeching halt in front of Caspian, shaking like a leaf. What could I do? He was literally burning up.

The only thing I could do was cover him with my body and roll us both until we put the flames out. I moved to do just that when Rayna's voice stopped me.

"Stay back, Harper!" she shouted as she rushed toward me.

I looked up and watched as she pulled out a water bladder she'd kept tied to her belt. She pulled the water out and sprayed it all over Caspian with her fae abilities. The flames died out, leaving Caspian severely burnt, his clothes charred, and his skin a painful combination of black and raw red that turned my stomach inside out.

I dropped to my knees and burst into tears, crying from both sorrow and relief.

Hansa, Jax, Patrik, Scarlett, and the rest of our crew came running down the alley just behind Rayna. Avril and Fiona were still struggling to get back on their feet. And I couldn't even touch Caspian. I didn't even know if he was still alive.

Worst of all, I didn't get the chance to check.

Shaytan came up behind Rayna in a flash.

I heard Hansa scream. "Rayna, watch out!"

Too late. Shaytan smacked her away as if she were a little nuisance. An insect.

He towered above me, panting and furious. His red eyes glowed with rage—and only then did I notice the tattoos gradually lighting up on his body. There were thousands of swamp symbols etched into his skin, and he'd just activated them.

How could he even do that?

There was still so much we didn't know about swamp witch magic. But I had no time to worry about it. All I could do was fight him and keep Caspian alive.

The others tried to come at Shaytan, but he let out a long, unsettling roar as a powerful golden light exploded from inside his body and spread outward like a glowing shockwave.

It knocked everybody back with the same effect that had

temporarily disabled Fiona and Avril, only on a much larger scale. He then scowled at me, a grin stretching his lips.

"Now, where were we?" he asked.

I was paralyzed by fear.

For the first time in my life, I had no idea what I could do next that could help me even stand a chance in a fight. He'd clearly kept the best for last, and he was ready to dish it all out on me.

I'm screwed.

24

HARPER

"How... How did you get this level of swamp witch magic?" I managed, my knees quaking. "The Lords—"

"The Lords never thought outside the box," Shaytan replied with a smirk. "They just took whatever little spells the witch dished out at face value. Not one of them thought to experiment, to combine, to edit the incantations where possible."

I took a couple of steps back, crossing my swords in front of me and keeping several feet of distance from Shaytan. He'd been holding back. Only now was I witnessing the true extent of his power. And based on his account, he'd successfully modified, combined, and upgraded swamp witch spells to bring himself to this horrifying level of strength.

It was bad enough that he was freakin' massive, three times my size. His swamp witch game was infinitely superior to everything I'd witnessed so far—with the exception of Lumi, of course. I couldn't help but thank the stars that Lumi had kept the heavier stuff to herself, despite the torture. That creature was truly the epitome of resilience.

"So, what? You started toying with the spells, mixing them around to better fit your purposes and to boost your combat abilities?" I asked, trying to stall while I figured out a way to either keep him busy or actually kill him, though the latter was starting to sound like an impossible feat.

I glanced around us. Caspian was down and horrifically burned. I couldn't even afford the luxury of crying at this point, as it would've affected my visibility. The last thing I needed was a hazy view of my mortal enemy, who was stalking toward me and grinning like the sum of all my fears crammed into a pile of muscles and cruelty.

Fiona, Zane, Avril, Caia, Hansa, Jax, Scarlett, Patrik... our Druid delegation allies... our rebel Imen and Maras... even the dozen Adlets... They were all down. I didn't see Hundurr or Rover anywhere... Arrah... Colton... I had to put them aside in my head, hoping they'd stayed behind to keep an eye on the Mara Lords— assuming they'd captured at least one or two of them alive, like we'd discussed.

I could hear the battle unfolding on the lower levels of the city. The screams. The bloody scuffles. The mayhem.

"Pretty much," Shaytan said, waving his massive bejeweled sword around, as if to get accustomed to its weight and swing. As if warming up for what came next. "You see, the regular spells are okay, but they're just little pulses, much like your weird ability, in fact," he added, smirking. "But the way I put them together? Miss Hellswan, I am the undefeated champion of the daemon kingdom. Thousands have challenged me, and thousands have died by my blade. I'm unbeatable."

"I don't know, man. I do like a good challenge once in a while. Mediocrity is deadlier than any horned megalomaniac out there," I shot back.

He chuckled. I darted around him and moved in to deliver multiple hits. He turned in a flash and blocked both my swords with his. The clang and the ensuing screeching of our blades pressing against each other almost made my ears bleed. Strange glimmers of light caught my eye—symbols engraved into his blade, lighting up brighter the longer our swords made contact.

For some reason, it snagged my breath.

Shaytan grinned. I kicked him in the gut, then jumped back.

My shoulders and arms felt weak. My swords were slightly heavier than they had been a few seconds earlier.

I swerved to his right and tried another attack. He brought his sword down in a counterattack. Sparks flew from our blades, the symbols on his lighting up again. It knocked the air out of my lungs this time. The impact of his hit pushed me back, as well, and my boots slid across the cobblestone.

He laughed with visible delight, further making my blood boil.

How am I already tired?

I must've drained myself with those barriers. I wasn't even sure I could get another one out. I couldn't get close enough to syphon any energy from him, to replenish what I'd lost. He wouldn't have allowed it, anyway. Mind control didn't work on daemons, either. It was just me, my swords, and this nightmare of a creature whose sole purpose was to give me misery prior to a slow and painful death. He definitely looked like he was enjoying it.

Hansa and Jax were the first to come to. They were still weakened and dazed, unable to get up. They watched, pale, helpless, and trembling with despair, as I squared off with the daemon king. At least they had the sense not to get up again. I would've hated to be on the receiving end of that golden pulse.

"You're enjoying this a little too much," I muttered, then charged him again.

He slashed his sword forward, catching my swing in midair. The symbols lit up. Bright amber sparks flew once more. And my arms got heavier. This time, however, he didn't give me a moment. He came at me and rammed his foot into my chest before I could even react.

I flew backward and landed with a heavy thud. Pain burned

through my ribcage, more than half of it fractured. Judging by my sudden difficulty in breathing, one of my ribs had punctured a lung. Everything hurt.

Was he really that fast? Or was I slowing down?

I rolled to the side, coughed, and spat some blood. That didn't feel right.

Nevertheless, I managed to pull myself back up, raising my swords and resuming an attack position. I dashed forward and ducked as soon as his blade came out to greet me. My left sword managed to slash a thin line across his abdomen, cutting through the leather vest. My right sword came up as I twisted and backed away. His blade nearly crushed it, but I managed to pull back before he could try again.

I was panting. The symbols on his sword kept glowing.

It was becoming harder for me to move. Despite my ribs already healing, I was still having trouble breathing, as if my lungs were close to giving out.

Something was horribly wrong here, and if I didn't figure out what, I was definitely going to die outside the Palisade. I frowned at his sword.

"That thing is doing something, isn't it?" I asked, my voice barely audible.

Shaytan whispered something against his finger, then licked it and swabbed it across his abdomen wound. I could see the bleeding stop and the cut close up. He then sneered at me.

"It took you a while to figure that one out, huh?" he replied. "I guess your brain is starting to slow down now. You're on the same level as an Iman at this point, Miss Hellswan. That's how weak you've become."

"Just because the Imen aren't as strong or as vicious as you are, it doesn't mean they're weak," I retorted. "They're a million times more resilient and more educated than you or anyone else in your species. With the exception of Zane and all the pacifists, of course.

They had the common sense to understand and oppose your insanity!"

Shaytan didn't like my response. He ran toward me, roaring.

I shuffled to my left and swung my right sword out. He hit it with his as he rushed past me. The impact broke my blade—and my arm. My bones cracked, and I cried out in pain. Whatever I did, things only got worse.

I tried to move away, but he came around and cut me across the chest.

Heat spread through every inch of my skin. I fell and hit the back of my head against the cobblestone. I wheezed and coughed, struggling to breathe. I could hear him laugh, but I couldn't see him. He was close, though.

"Harper!" Hansa cried out.

The others moaned as they started to come to.

I managed to look down and saw the gaping wound he'd inflicted. It stretched from my left hip to my right shoulder in a soft arch. It was wide open. Blood trickled out and pooled beneath me. I felt my back warm up.

"My blade eats souls, Miss Hellswan," Shaytan said. From the sound of his voice, I estimated ten feet between us. "With every hit, I drain the life out of you. Bit by bit, whenever our swords meet. But if I cut you, directly... Oh, darling, it's a motherlode!"

It all made sense. The weakness in my arms. The difficulty in breathing. The fact that I'd been slowed down to the point where he was able to cut me like this.

He'd been nipping at my soul from the moment our swords had first clashed.

I only had one blade left, but I refused to let go of it. I tried to take a deep breath, but a sharp pain choked me up and burned through my throat. My vision wasn't clear, either.

Wheezing, I glanced to my left.

The looks on my friends' faces broke my heart. Hansa was

horrified, struggling to get back up, desperate to get to Shaytan before he could do something worse to me. We all knew, by now, that it was only a matter of time before his charmed sword separated my head from my body.

Am I dying? Is this it?

I would've liked a little more time in this world. I would've loved to see Neraka free. Caspian smiling. My mom, my dad... Serena...

"I have to say, this isn't as much fun as I'd thought it would be," Shaytan muttered.

He'd gotten closer. His shadow enveloped me in cool darkness. Either that or I was already hallucinating.

"You're not going to win this," I croaked, barely sucking in half a breath.

Lying on the ground just twenty feet from me was Caspian. He wasn't moving.

I felt my heart swell—it hurt like crazy, but I could feel everything. I could feel my skin burning. That was Caspian. He was still feeling things. He was alive. I was still tied to him, body and soul. Our inner-sentries were connected. Shaytan hadn't cut us off yet.

Caspian's eyes popped open.

My stomach hurt. My breathing became shallow.

At least he's alive.

"You keep saying that, but you're the one dying out here, darling," Shaytan replied, snickering. I felt something sharp and cold on my throat. His sword. He was pressing it against my skin, teasing me, tormenting me.

I have to do something. I can't die here. I don't want to die here.

I heard wings flapping. I looked farther beyond Caspian. Up in a tree nearby, an Ekar settled on a branch. Its fiery red feathers looked familiar. Its beady eyes were fixed on mine. *Ramin...*

"Ramin," I whispered.

Time stood still—or, at least, that's what it felt like. A second became a minute as I thought about the Ekar bird and Neha's stories about the fire spirits. Were they true? Was a fire spirit watching me through Ramin's eyes?

What were the odds?

Shaytan chuckled, but he didn't sound that close anymore. The noise rather echoed around me, instead of reaching my ears.

"Any last words, Miss Hellswan? Lord Kifo's coming to, and he's about to watch you die," he said.

I wanted to kick him in the nuts and cut his head off. But I couldn't feel my body anymore. I wasn't even sure if I was still breathing. My soul hurt. There were gaps in it. It hurt so much...

All of a sudden, as I kept my gaze fixed on Ramin, I heard whispers.

They didn't come from the outside. They swirled inside my head, like distant memories, getting clearer and louder with each second that passed.

Let go, Harper.

I froze. That wasn't my thought. That was someone else's voice. A male timbre, soft as honey, but intense, like freshly brewed coffee. It set my soul on fire. Or was it just my body giving out, shutting down, one organ at a time?

Let go, Harper.

There it was again! I tried to move, but I felt as though I'd been separated from my body already. I looked up and found myself staring into Shaytan's blistering red eyes. His satisfied smirk made me want to wipe it off with my blade.

Let go, Harper. We need to talk.

"Who's this?" I whispered.

Shaytan frowned at me. But I wasn't talking to him.

The Hermessi have heard your thoughts, Harper. Let go.

What was this voice talking about? Let go of what? I wasn't ready to die, yet. I didn't want to. I vehemently refused it, in fact.

My head felt so heavy... I shook it, slowly.

Come, Harper. Let's talk.

"But I don't want to go..." I breathed.

I didn't hear the answer. Everything went white. Everything was gone.

25

CASPIAN

My body was frozen and burning at the same time.

I couldn't move. Every cell, every molecule that composed me, hurt. I wanted to move. I needed to say something, but... nothing functioned properly.

The sky above me was a pale shade of violet. The suns were going down.

How long has it been? Where am I?

Harper. I'd just seen her. Shaytan. Zane. Fiona. Avril.

The daemon king had caught me by the throat. He'd set me on fire, somehow.

He'd muttered a spell, and... I couldn't speak.

I wanted to cry out. My field of vision shifted as my head moved. Harper was on the ground. Her arms and legs were twitching. I could feel everything she was experiencing, and it tore me apart on the inside. Grief. Anger. Despair. The desire to live.

She was bleeding out. Her eyes rolled into her head.

Shaytan towered over her, chuckling. He had the tip of his blade against her throat.

I had to do something. He was going to kill her.

"Harper," I whispered.

No one could hear me. But I could hear Shaytan laughing.

"Any last words, Miss Hellswan?"

Darkness constricted around my heart. It squeezed and tightened around it.

I needed to get to her... To save her...

From the moment she'd walked into my life, I'd known... I'd known I was in deep trouble. The same heart that was caving in now had thumped and soared in my chest at the sight of her. I'd cursed my fate when she set foot on Neraka. I knew we'd end up somewhere like this.

But I couldn't let her suffer like the rest of us. She didn't belong here. She didn't deserve any of this. She was innocent.

Harper Hellswan was a force to be reckoned with. Before I could stop myself—not that I could've, but I might've tried—I was in love with her. Harper was stubborn and proud. Determined and lethal. Calm and yet... could turn into a veritable firestorm if challenged. I'd taken great pleasure in teasing her during the Spring Ball.

I would never forget the way her heart skipped a beat whenever I got close. Her scent. The way she looked at me when I refused to tell her the truth—when I couldn't tell her the truth, because of my blood oath.

Our souls had merged. We belonged together. We were going to set Neraka free and travel through the millions of stars out there. The universe was supposed to be our oyster.

She didn't deserve to die. Certainly not by Shaytan's blade.

I had to stop it.

Caspian. It's time to believe.

There it was again. I'd heard this voice before. Maybe in my dreams? I wasn't sure. But I recognized it. It felt familiar, and it was only in my head. I couldn't take my eyes off Harper. Tears welled up in my eyes. I couldn't see clearly anymore.

Caspian. Believe. Have faith in the fire spirit.

Was I losing my mind, perhaps?

I'd heard the old folk tales about the elemental spirits. The Hermessi. They fueled the stars. They flowed through the rivers. They settled in the stones. They flew with the winds. But they were just legends. No one had ever seen one. All we had were faded illustrations in the preserved books of ancient Imen.

Caspian. You have to believe.

How could I? I'd never seen any myself.

The fire could've killed you. Yet you're still alive, Caspian. I'm trying to come back to this world, but I need you to believe. Harper had a flicker of hope in my existence.

I couldn't take my eyes off her. Despite the pain, I was filled with love.

But I couldn't die just yet. I had to save her.

She saved you, Caspian, because she believed in me.

I tried to process what the voice was whispering to me, but I just couldn't connect the dots. It didn't make sense. Where were the Hermessi, if not in this world, already? How come I could hear one of them, after a lifetime of silence? What was happening to me?

Everything is connected, Caspian. The natural elements that feed into the fae, they're all gifts of ours. They're all threads of Hermessi. Every spark, every drop of dew, every salty breeze, and every grain of sand. It's all us, Caspian. You must believe.

What do you want from me? I asked, internally.

I want you to live, the whispering voice said. *I need you to live.*

I tried to move again, but my body didn't respond. My limbs were weak. My blood simmered. On top of it all, the only concept I could truly focus on was saving Harper. She needed me. I needed her.

Shaytan's laughter boomed across the entire sixth level.

He raised his sword high above his head, ready to deliver the final blow. Ready to destroy the creature I loved most in this world.

Believe in me, Caspian! Believe in me, and I will burn through the poison that has spread in this world.

"Will you save her?" I heard myself mumble, though I couldn't feel my lips move.

Do you believe in me?

"I believe... I believe."

The sword came down. Everything went white.

26

HERON

Lumi and Velnias kept moving around the room as she finished drawing the ceiling symbols. She'd done all the walls, and, as soon as she got off Velnias, she started writing on the floor. Velnias tossed the beds aside to give her room, breaking them and piling them on top of each other in a corner.

Outside, the fight was turning savage. I peeked through the blinds, watching Sienna and Tobiah as they fought against the incoming daemons. Soldiers were pouring in from both the first level and the third, the latter most likely the horde that Shaytan had sent to find us.

"How long do you think this protection charm will last?" I muttered, frowning at the sight of Tobiah as he took a tumble, then jumped back to his feet, roared ferociously, and rammed into a group of armed daemon soldiers.

He was fighting his own people, slashing and tearing them apart as he kept them from getting close to the infirmary building. Sienna was surprisingly fast. I'd never seen her in battle against so many enemies at once, but I was definitely impressed. I made a mental note never to cross her. She was as vicious as the daemons she was fighting.

"I'm not sure," Lumi murmured as she kept drawing.

A thud on the door made me stand back. The second made me draw my sword.

There were daemons out there, trying to get in. I looked at Lumi, then at Velnias, and shrugged. My nerves were stretched. I'd never been this nervous in my entire life. Not even when I told Avril how I felt.

Actually... That might've been worse.

I worried about her. I didn't know if she was okay. Shaytan was probably livid about the swap. I prayed to every single deity in all known pantheons that they look after her. I wasn't much into this kind of stuff, but, given our circumstances, I figured it was worth a shot. All Avril had to do was keep that bastard and his goons busy while we did our thing here.

"Dammit, Lumi, are you writing the book of life down there?" I groaned, increasingly anxious. The third thud made the door shudder.

More daemons gathered by the windows. They tried to smash them in, but the protection spell kept them from succeeding. Unfortunately, Tobiah and Sienna were outnumbered. I caught glimpses of them from one of the windows. Daemons had made it past the couple. Two of them were snarling and baring their fangs at me, our faces separated only by an inch of glass and Lumi's magic.

Behind them, Tobiah and Sienna were kicking major ass. I was so frustrated that I couldn't get out there to help, that I found myself smirking at the daemons in contempt as they struggled to break into the infirmary. They punched the glass. They tried to smash it with their sword handles. Nothing worked.

I couldn't help but snicker and offer them an obscene hand gesture I'd learned from Velnias the other day. It riled the daemons up. They roared and hit the window even harder.

"It's better if they give up, not if you make them try harder," Lumi replied, giving me a reprimanding frown.

"What? I didn't do anything," I replied with an innocent shrug.

Velnias chuckled. All three of us froze when the window in front of me started to crack.

"As I was saying," Lumi muttered, as she filled out the last corner of the room with chalk symbols, then walked into the middle and sat down, crossing her legs.

"Yeah, I see what you mean now," I replied dryly.

Chills ran down my spine. The thought of daemons breaking in made me break into a cold sweat. Tobiah and Sienna were holding their own out there, but Velnias and I were stuck in a room and were in charge of protecting the swamp witch.

The moment they'd figured out that the glass was unbreakable, the daemons must've known she was in here with us. I was also convinced they'd caught her scent. They were incredible hunters, after all.

I took several deep breaths, looking for the kind of internal balance that allowed me to go into war-mode. I was a soldier. I needed to fight like one. My brother had taught me everything he knew, and I'd taken all of that knowledge and turned myself into a veritable killing machine. I didn't need to brag about it, though. My body count said enough.

The daemons kept banging and ramming their shoulders into the door. The wood started to give out. The spell was wearing thin. *Only a matter of time.*

"Lumi, how much longer till you do this?" I asked, getting more anxious.

Velnias and I took our positions in front of her. I faced the door, while he faced the windows. He was big enough to handle two to three of his own kind at once. I was perfectly happy with one at a time. My pulse quickened. My vision came into crystal-clear focus.

"You'll know, trust me," Lumi replied, as she closed her eyes, resting her hands on her knees.

"I'd like to still be alive to know it!" I shot back.

"Just hold them back. I can't be interrupted," she muttered, then proceeded with her incantation. I didn't understand a single word coming out of her mouth, but I could see the symbols in the room light up, one at a time. It was a slow but fascinating process.

The door burst open. The windows broke. Shattered glass scattered across the floor.

The daemons poured into the room, their rapiers out, thirsty for blood. Velnias roared as he tackled a bunch of them, as expected. He used his sword and claws, his fangs and his horns, as he tore through the soldiers.

I handled my opponents in a slightly different fashion. I ducked, narrowly avoiding decapitation by rapier, then brought my sword out and cut off the first head.

The second daemon came at me with his massive frame. I counteracted his assault with my own body. I jumped and ripped his throat out with my fangs, then tossed him aside and drove my sword through the third one's neck.

I kicked him back, ready for the next one. I had the taste of daemon blood in my mouth, and, I had to admit, it was fantastic. Full-bodied and robust, just like the horned meat sack I'd taken it from.

The fourth daemon swerved to my left and headed straight for Lumi.

I kicked him in the gut and pushed him back, then cut off his head. I didn't spot the fifth one in time. He tackled me and knocked the air out of my lungs. I heard Lumi cry out.

It took me a few seconds to realize that the bastard had thrown me into her. I was literally on top of her.

"I can't stop! Get off!" Her voice was muffled beneath me, and she grunted.

I cursed under my breath, then rolled over and faced off with the fifth daemon again. He punched me. My head was thrown to the side. My jaw broke. I couldn't afford to even think about the pain. I punched him back.

The room was crawling with daemons. But I could hear Lumi muttering her incantation. I could see more symbols lighting up. I caught a glimpse of metal coming toward my head. I leaned backward in a flash. The rapier missed my face by half an inch.

Then I slipped.

I landed on the floor with a painful thud.

"What the—" I cried out, then stilled, as I registered the sudden temperature drop.

Dhaxanian frost had spread out across the wooden floor. Lumi's symbols kept lighting up beneath it, undisturbed. I looked up and sucked in a breath.

Relief washed over me at the sight of all daemons frozen like icicles. They were coated in Nevis's Dhaxanian frost. Velnias grunted as he got back to his feet, then looked around. Our eyes met. His eyebrows were up. He was as surprised as I was.

The ruckus had stopped outside the infirmary as well, but I could still hear the mayhem below. The war was still going, just not in or around our location. I exhaled sharply as Tobiah and Sienna proceeded to cut off the frozen daemons' heads.

"Good idea," Velnias murmured, and moved to do the same to the ones inside.

Before his blade could reach the first daemon, a swishing sound came across. The air fluttered over my face. Then all the daemon heads came off clean, as if sliced off with a single blade simultaneously. They shattered on the floor like broken crystal vases—only much gorier, as there was plenty of frozen daemon gunk scattered around.

Nevis stood in the splintered doorway with his hand out.

"I didn't think I'd say this so soon, but man, am I glad to see you!" I blurted out.

The Dhaxanian prince smirked, then put his hands behind his

back, assuming his usual posture. He wore his battle armor—splendid meranium plates with intricate designs and thousands of tiny diamonds encrusted into the pattern. They covered his chest, his shoulders, and his arms, as well as his legs. His feet were bare, and there were short pieces of white silk covering his hips. He wore a beautiful battle helmet made from the same material and covered in diamonds. His icy blue eyes filled me with a sense of determination.

"I have snowflakes all over the city," he replied. "I thought I'd pop by and check things out."

"Where are the others?" Velnias asked.

Lumi kept muttering her spell on the floor, with more symbols continuing to light up. Nevis watched her with keen interest, but I still caught the glimmer of sadness in his eyes.

"They're out there fighting and dying for freedom," he said, his voice low. "My people are giving the daemons frozen hell. The Manticores and the rebel Imen are helping. The dragon joined the fight and is currently dousing them in fire. But I'm not sure we'll last much longer. How are we doing here?"

"Almost there, I guess?" I replied, not really sure myself.

Nevis's expression changed, his eyes widening as he stared at Lumi. I glanced over my shoulder, realizing she'd stopped chanting, and instantly realized why he was stunned.

Lumi had lit up white from the inside, matching the glow of all the symbols in the room.

"I take it all back," she whispered, though I could no longer see her lips moving.

White light exploded from her and expanded outward.

It swallowed us all whole.

Everything turned white.

27

HARPER

The material world around me had vanished.

I was weightless, hovering in a vast, white emptiness.

Nothing hurt anymore.

Am I dead?

I heard water flowing nearby. I looked to my right and saw a stream flowing through the white void, snaking toward me.

The wind blew, brushing through my hair and whistling past my ears.

The small river passed by me, then around me, drawing a liquid circle.

In front of me, a tree grew from the water. It was all so strange, yet... so beautiful. I couldn't understand any of it, but still, it all made sense at the same time.

The tree groaned, then fell backward and scattered into moss. It was as if all matter in this emptiness were not tied to a single form or function. The moss moved around and drew another ring around the one of water.

Fire sparked out of nowhere and formed a third, larger ring

around the other two. Air flowed into the fourth. I could see it rippling softly. Then another water circle formed around it, followed by dirt and moss, then fire, then air again.

It went on like that for what seemed like an eternity.

The rings surrounding me changed their form once in a while, in no particular pattern. Water became ice, then water again. Moss became sand, then clusters of raw, precious gems, then splinters of wood, then dirt and moss once more. The air was stable, ever flowing between the layers. The fire crackled into lightning, then back into flames.

I was witnessing a superb spectacle of nature, as all the elements gathered around me in billions of circles, displaying the full power and beauty of the world and its elements of life. One didn't exist without the other. Not really.

The rings kept spinning around me, as if orbiting my body.

I gasped as I looked down. I'd lost my flesh. I was but a wisp of white light, much like the vast nothingness surrounding me.

"Is this real?" I heard myself ask, though I couldn't understand how I was able to speak with the absence of a mouth. I had no lips or tongue to enunciate my words, but I could still hear my voice.

Do you believe in the elements, Harper?

That voice! Ramin. The Ekar bird. My dying breath as Shaytan brought his sword down. I remembered everything. I recognized the voice. It had asked me to let go.

"Am I dead?"

No, Harper. We're just having a conversation, far from the outer world, the voice whispered. *Tell me, do you believe in the elements?*

"I think so... I can see them. Yes," I replied. There was no point in denying the only things that were now a part of my existence. Wherever this was, it made everything surprisingly clear and real. "The fae themselves are proof of the elements' existence, in a way."

The fae are mere conduits, Harper. They're not the elements. They're vessels designed to hold us, to connect us to the material world. We are the elements. We are energy, Harper, and the fae are just some of our tools. We give them the power, and we can also take it away.

"You're the Hermessi?" I asked.

I am a Hermessi, yes. That's what the Nerakians call us, anyway. The ancient Nerakians, that is. The ones who used to believe in us, who used to make us strong.

"How does that work? I'm not sure I understand."

We function on the energy of belief, Harper. The more you believe in us, the stronger we are. The fae are genetically engineered to be our conduits, but we cannot thrive on their life force alone. We require belief so we can make our rivers flow stronger. Make our winds blow harder. Make our fires burn brighter. Make our trees grow bigger. The world as you know it, Harper, is but a fraction of what the Hermessi can do.

I thought about that for a while, mentally rummaging through all the pages of folklore and mythology that I'd read over the years. Not once had I ever heard of Hermessi, but I could still distinctly remember even the humans back on Earth, who had once worshipped the natural elements.

"Would the world still function without people believing in you?"

I don't know, Harper. There are creatures who still believe in us somewhere, in this universe and the others. The more who are aware of our existence, however, the stronger we can become, the better we can manifest. Here, on Neraka, I am weak. Barely anyone still believes in me. On Zathura, some little planet a million years away from here, the Hermessi are strong and powerful, and are worshipped by the thousands.

A few seconds passed. I stared straight ahead, fixated on a black dot. I hadn't seen it before. It seemed as though it was moving. Getting closer.

"So, the more people believe in you—the more of us believe in you—the stronger you become?"

Yes, Harper.

"And what do the Hermessi do with such power? What's your end-game?"

The voice became clearer—soft, male, like drizzling honey melting into a pot of warm milk. He chuckled softly. It made me smile on the inside.

I have no end-game, Harper. I only want to thrive, to feed on your energy, to put the love you give me back into the world. To make things right again.

The black dot grew bigger. Only then did I realize it wasn't actually black, but red.

It had wings.

It was flying toward me.

Part of me already knew what it was.

"Ramin... You're Ramin."

"That is the name I was given most recently, yes," the voice replied, suddenly much clearer and louder, echoing through my very being.

The Ekar bird approached me in flight and burst into flames.

"Whoa," I murmured, staring at the creature that took shape before me.

The flames flickered and poured into a humanoid form, with a head, two arms, and two legs. It didn't have eyes or a mouth, but its voice—*his* voice was the one I'd been hearing. Ramin was a Hermessi, and he'd been talking to me.

He'd been asking me to believe in him.

The more I looked at him, the firmer my belief, the more sense I could make of this world, in a way. "This is so weird," I added.

"I know," Ramin replied. "It's been forever since I could manifest myself like this."

"But why the Ekar? Why were you a bird?" I asked.

"The Ekars, like the fae, are conduits," he explained. "But their consciousnesses are different. I, as a Hermessi, have never tried to speak through a fae. At least, not through the few I've come across on Neraka. But I've done my best to empower them, in the absence of belief."

"And the birds?"

"Their consciousnesses are different. They make it easier for me to settle inside them, to use their physical forms in order to manifest myself," Ramin explained. "I haven't truly felt the need to speak out before. But then I met you, Harper, and everything changed."

I was getting answers, but I was also getting more confused with each minute that went by.

"What do I have to do with anything?" I asked.

"You believed, Harper," Ramin said. "You didn't even know it! You believed before Neha even told you what a fire spirit was. Your energy, Harper, it's unique. Before I met you, I simply watched Neraka's tragedy unfold. It didn't matter to me whether the Imen, the Dhaxanians, the Maras, the Adlets, the Manticores, and all the other creatures lived or died. It didn't matter. The world would go on. The cycle of nature would continue. My fire would burn either way. The other Hermessi would continue to exist as well. Water, air, fire, and earth's destinies are infinite and not bound to the creatures that cannot live without them."

"So my belief gave you strength?"

"Yes, Harper. I do not need to feed on your soul like the daemons or the Maras do. That is perverse. I do not take anything. I feel, and I give back," he replied. "And I can feel your emotions. Your love, your hope, your joy and your grief. Your sorrow and despair. I do not like it when you're sad. I can't explain it, but... I just don't like it."

It hit me then. Ramin was somehow attuned to my soul. Whether that had something to do with my sentry nature was yet to be determined, but if he could feel what I felt, and if he drew power from my belief without draining me of anything... then he could even help me.

"Tell me, Harper, do you want to live?" he asked, as if reading my mind. He'd probably done just that.

"I do. So much, you have no idea."

"Would you give up your own life to save Caspian?" he replied.

"I would die if it saved everyone. Caspian would do the same," I said. If I'd still been in my body, anchored to reality, maybe my answer would've been different. But given my circumstances and unprecedented clarity, I stood by my words. "The daemons, the Maras, they cannot win. The Nerakians deserve freedom and peace. I will die for it. I will."

The fire figure cocked his head to the side. Had he had eyes, he probably would've narrowed them, watching me intently, filled with curiosity. I could feel it.

"You will die for Neraka's freedom, then?" he asked.

"Yes. Though I'd obviously rather not," I muttered.

I'd made my peace already, in a way. I wanted to live, but I couldn't live if I couldn't save this planet. If my death meant that Neraka would regain its freedom, that its people wouldn't suffer at the hands of daemons and Maras anymore, then yes. I was okay with dying. It wasn't my best-case scenario, but it wasn't my worst, either.

I couldn't take my gaze off Ramin. He was so beautiful, even though he was just a humanoid wisp of pure fire. His flames licked at the emptiness around him. His sparks reflected onto the surface of all the water rings around us.

"I understand," he said. "I'd like to offer you a deal, then, Harper. I will help you defeat Shaytan, if you grant me a favor."

"What favor?" I instantly replied. I wasn't accustomed to making deals in general, not to mention deals with fire entities from dimensions I'd never been to before.

"I will collect it later. It will be a favor of my choosing. I cannot tell you what it is because I do not yet know it myself," Ramin said. "But it is a risk you will have to take if you want my help. Consider it your sacrifice, Harper."

I thought about it for a few moments. "Can you really help me kill Shaytan? He's insanely powerful. You've seen it yourself."

"Harper, I am the raw force of nature. Fire destroys everything. Do not doubt me. You know what fire can do."

"Okay, then. Let's do this," I replied.

I had no choice but to accept, anyway. It was either this or useless death, since I had no guarantee that Lumi would finish the spell before Shaytan would find her—not without me wedging myself between them, of course.

I needed to be a good wedge for a little while longer.

Suddenly, everything vanished into blackness.

My eyes popped open.

I was outside the Palisade again. I was on the ground, bleeding. Everything hurt.

Caspian was wheezing, struggling to move and to breathe. Idris and Rayna were slowly moving toward him, their auras blazing red from their own injuries.

I looked up to find Shaytan holding his charmed sword over his head, ready to bring it down and split me open. This was it. The split second I'd missed while conversing with Ramin. Wherever it was that I'd been, time flowed differently there.

A bright flash made him freeze and squint.

The sky above us rippled.

Something was happening.

28

HARPER

Like a transparent sheet burning from the bottom to the top in bright sparks of yellow, the cloaking shield that had been covering Neraka for weeks disappeared. Lumi had done it!

"The shield is down," I heard Hansa murmur.

I could breathe and move again, though every atom in my body screamed from the pain. Shaytan was speechless, gawking at the sky, unable to believe what was happening. That was my split second to try to move back before he registered my presence again. I was the closest he could take his wrath out on.

"You," he said, his sword arm trembling from the rage as he looked down at me. "You did this. You... You ruined everything!"

I held my breath for a moment, quickly and quietly assessing my physical state. My chest wound was closing up, but I only had seconds to get away from Shaytan. That had just become an impossible mission, since his red eyes were fixed on me once again.

My sword was within my reach, inches away from my fingers.

"I told you we'd do it," I muttered. "Not my fault you didn't believe me."

"You think your people will take me down?" Shaytan replied, raising his voice. He was having trouble controlling his breath. His fury was going to be the end of him—and I was hoping that would come sooner, rather than later. "I'm undefeated! I am the champion of Neraka! The undisputed king!" he roared.

"Then why do you reek of fear now?" I asked, spotting Ramin on the roof of the Palisade.

There was something different about that bird. As it ruffled its feathers, sparks flew from every plume. It was weird, but it filled me with energy—like the kind I needed to move. I realized then that it wasn't the Hermessi giving me anything. It was me, channeling the ounce of life force I had left inside me to make the final push.

Shaytan sneered and narrowed his eyes at me.

"It's time for you to die, you filthy little—"

I cut him off. "It's time for you to experience defeat!"

He snarled and raised his sword over his head again, ready to bring it down and kill me.

"Harper, no!" Hansa screamed.

I heard the others gasping and struggling to get back on their feet. They were desperate to stop Shaytan. All I could focus on was the daemon king, blocking everything else out until the flutter of wings made my heart skip a beat.

My hand found my sword. His blade came down. I was ready to block it, hoping I had enough strength to stop it from slicing me open.

The Ekar bird shot through my field of vision. It burst into horrendous flames as it hit Shaytan right in the head. The daemon king was caught by surprise, grunting as he moved back, trying to fight off the Hermessi. I was stunned, watching as the fire spread quickly and ate his whole body up.

"I'm not done here! No! I'm not done!" he cried out, his arms flailing as he fought against the flames to no avail.

I managed to get up and grabbed my sword. He dropped his with a painful clang.

It was as if I were watching a tragedy unfold in slow motion, only there was barely a sliver of sadness left for me to feel toward Shaytan's demise. I didn't like taking a life, no matter whose it was. But, still, I knew I had to, and boy, did he deserve it!

I was amazed by Shaytan's ability to resist the flames. He muttered a variety of protection spells, hundreds of tattoos lighting up beneath the blaze. Too little, too late, as the fire kept eating away at him.

His eyes glowed red through the flames. He roared and came at me with his bare claws.

I broke into a cold sweat and swung my sword out. I cut his forearm first.

He growled and tried to attack me again, while I kept my distance from the fire that had engulfed him.

"I'm not done here!" he cried out.

"Denial isn't the mark of a leader," I muttered, then retaliated with multiple sword hits.

I managed to cut through his chest several times. He howled from the pain, but still, he didn't stop. This was his Hail Mary attack. It was no longer either my death or his. We both had to go, in his twisted mind.

"I will not be defeated!" he screamed, the fire burning through his flesh.

The smell became unbearable. I had to end this.

"You don't get it, do you?" I replied, then raised my sword, the tip pointed at him. "You were defeated the moment you ate the first soul."

I didn't give him a chance to respond. I wasn't even sure he could. It was a miracle he was still standing, at this point.

I dashed forward and jumped. I drove my sword through Shaytan's neck as I tackled him.

We both fell. I landed on top of him, refusing to let go of my sword.

"Harper!" Fiona screamed. "Harper, get out of there!"

The flames were licking at me. But they didn't burn. It was a strange sensation.

Beneath me, Shaytan was unrecognizable. His beard and hair had been destroyed by the flames. His skin was gone. The flesh and bones beneath were blistering as the Hermessi kept burning him from head to toe. And yet, all I felt was warmth.

I looked down at myself and exhaled. Ramin was keeping me safe.

My blade had gone straight through Shaytan's throat.

He stared at me, choking and gurgling, finally giving in to it all.

I watched the life dim in his red eyes, before the flames consumed them and turned them into goo.

"Harper!" Hansa cried out. "Harper, get away from there!"

"It's okay," I replied, unable to take my eyes off Shaytan. "It doesn't burn."

I was straddling the mountain of flesh that was—or, until a second ago, had been—Shaytan. The daemon king was dead. I'd killed him. I'd kept my word.

Heat filled my body. I needed the warmth.

My whole being hurt, but I pushed myself back up and stepped away from Shaytan's burning carcass. It was over.

I watched him for a while.

One deep breath. Another deep breath. By the third, I started tearing up, as I looked to my left and saw Caspian on the ground, burned to a crisp. But his eyes were wide open and fixed on me. He blinked once, as if telling me yes.

Fiona and Zane were better, and so were Avril and Scarlett. Hansa and Jax. Patrik and Ryker. Caia. Rayna and Idris... Wyrran... Peyton... There were Adlets and rebel Imen and Maras standing up again, unable to take their eyes off Shaytan. Those whose emotions I could see spoke for all of us—hope and relief surged through them. Joy and determination.

I rushed to Caspian's side and dropped to my knees, leaving the daemon king's corpse behind me. Hansa, Jax, Caia, and Rayna were the first to reach us. Caspian couldn't move. He was in a lot of pain. I could feel it all, clutching my heart and squeezing so tightly it made me sob.

"You'll be okay," I whispered in his ear, then bit into my wrist and gently pushed the open wound against his crusty lips. "Drink, Caspian."

Hansa and Jax stared at me, wide-eyed, as they took out all their healing potion satchels and started applying the paste to Caspian's body. Rayna moved next to me and cut her own wrist, motioning for me to take mine away.

"Harper, you're weak," she murmured. "Let me do this."

I nodded slowly and gave her some room, watching all my friends gather around us. Whoever had blood to give, they offered it—a collective Pyrope of sorts. The others brought out more healing paste from their satchels and spread them over Caspian's legs, while Hansa and Jax handled his torso and head.

Caspian didn't take his eyes off me. There was pride surging through his very soul as we looked at each other. I gave him a weak and hopeful smile.

"You'll look like crap for a little while, but you'll live," I said.

Fiona left Zane's side and rushed to hug me. She held me tight, sobbing, and, for the first time since we'd started this mission, I relaxed into her arms and cried as well. Zane got up, though he was still a little wobbly, and stared at his father's corpse for a while.

He sighed, then looked at me and bowed curtly. "Thank you, Harper. You did something I couldn't."

"I wouldn't have done it without..." My voice trailed off as I looked at Shaytan. The flames had died out, but there was no sign of the Ekar. The Hermessi I'd known as Ramin was gone. Everything he'd told me was true. I felt it—I believed it—deep in my heart. The elemental spirits were very much alive. Ancient powers that had been forgotten. "The Hermessi," I murmured.

"The Hermessi?" Zane replied, frowning and genuinely confused. "Those are legends. Wait... I saw the bird turn into flames. Was... Was that a—"

"Hermessi, yes," I said, nodding. "They're real, Zane. And one of them helped me. Otherwise I'd be dead right now."

I lowered my head. Fiona dropped a kiss on my temple, holding me tight.

"Babe, the daemon king was a monster. Not one of us alone could have defeated him," she said softly. "It's a miracle you held your own against him for so long. If you're doubting yourself as a fighter, please stop. You're the strongest warrior I know."

"You did incredibly well, Harper," Hansa added, offering me a warm smile as she continued to spread the healing paste over Caspian's severe burns. "We're alive because of you and your determination."

Tears rolled down my cheeks again. We'd been through so much to get here. "You were all amazing. Each and every one of you," I replied. "We're in this together," I added, listening to the war continuing on the lower levels. "We still have some fighting ahead of us."

They all nodded.

"The shield is down, but it will take a little time for our people to come through," Jax said. "We need to hold the daemons at bay and get the innocents and wounded to safety."

"Okay, let me—" I said, trying to stand up, but fell backward. My knees were too weak. "Dammit." I cursed under my breath.

"Sweetie, you've done enough for today," Fiona replied as she helped me up into a sitting position. "We need to get you, Caspian, and everyone else who can't fight up onto the seventh level. Hundurr is there, keeping an eye on Rowan and Farrah. The rest of us should go down to the lower levels and assist our allies."

"I agree," Jax muttered. "We've got it from here, Cucumber."

I looked up at him, overwhelmed by a sense of gratitude and hope. The worst part was over. Without their leaders, both the Maras and the daemons were going to fail. Their time had run out, and our people were coming. It was only a matter of time at this point.

Shaytan still had plenty of sons leading his armies, but, without a king, they were going to struggle. The last thing a warrior nation needed during a battle was a power struggle. The daemons were greedy and impulsive. They were bound to be at each other's throats for the crown.

The Maras, on the other hand, were already at a massive disadvantage, since we'd taken down their Lords. They had nothing left to fight us with.

I gazed at the sky, hoping to catch a glimpse of a ball of light carrying our people.

Fiona was right. I'd done my part.

My soul had been partially consumed by Shaytan. The thought pained me, but I held on to the hope that there could be a way to fix this. Lumi was more powerful and more capable than the stories about swamp witches had mentioned. She had enough knowledge and resources to undo most of the damage that the daemons and the Maras had caused to Neraka.

Maybe she could fix me, too.

29

DEREK

Hours had passed since we'd had to settle on one of Neraka's moons, unable to get through whatever shield surrounded the planet. Most of us were pacing around the main chamber of the capsule, while Viola feverishly flipped through her swamp witch magic notes, looking for a way in.

My nerves were stretched and close to snapping. I occasionally glanced out through the main glass pane that gave us a full view of... well, nothing. We couldn't see Neraka, anyway.

"There must be some way for us to get through that damn thing," Jovi muttered, scowling at the view.

"Our magic doesn't work against it," Corrine replied, massaging the back of her neck in order to relieve some of the tension that had gathered since we'd landed.

"Well, at least we didn't blow up when we first made contact with the shield," Draven said, as Serena leaned against him. They'd kept to their seats, for the most part, leaving the rest of us to claim the walking space for our nervous pacing.

I had to give the kids credit. In some ways, they seemed more restrained than us. Maybe it had something to do with their experiences on Calliope. After all, the Daughters had shielded Eritopia in a similar fashion for hundreds of years. Draven, Serena, Jovi, Vita, Bijarki, Phoenix, Viola, and the others had been on the other side of the problem.

At least, in this case, our memories were intact. We had not forgotten about our children. It was hard to look for a bright side at this point, but I had to, for everyone's sake. Personally, I was beginning to grow tired of these challenges and mishaps. This was supposed to be a routine recon mission on Neraka. We were now actively trying to rescue our people, after having been duped for days by impostors through Telluris.

"This has to be the work of Exiled Maras," one of Jax's wards said, staring at the tattoos on his bare arms. "I can feel Jax, you know. The closer we are to him, the more attuned we are to him, as his wards."

The others in his group nodded. "They're definitely down there," a second ward said.

"That's a good thing, right?" Serena asked, then gave Tejus and Hazel a concerned look. Her parents were obviously distraught and worried sick over Harper. They'd been through this kind of scare before. This time, however, it was worse for them, because they were aware of it all.

The first ward sighed. "Yes. It means he's alive. We'd feel something if he died, too. So, there's that."

"How many days has it been? Four?" Heath asked, his brow furrowed.

Draven nodded. "Approximately, yes," he replied, then looked at the first ward. "I think we should keep some reserve in pointing out potential culprits, for the time being. They reached out to us for help, after all. Maybe whoever is doing all this is also responsible for all the abductions they've been dealing with."

"But this is definitely swamp witch magic," Phoenix chimed in. "And Rewa clearly said they rescued a Druid delegation with a swamp witch on board. She also said she waved them goodbye, but the delegation never made it back to Neraka. This could all be some kind of ploy."

"But for what purpose?" I asked, shaking my head slowly. "I've been going over everything, repeatedly, and I cannot, for the life of me, find motive."

The first ward scoffed, bitterly amused. "The Exiled Maras were terrible creatures. I wouldn't be surprised if they continued to promote the toxic culture that got them thrown off the planet in the first place. Some of us never learn, to be honest."

"But why would they reach out to us, then?" Sofia replied. She made a very good point.

The ward's shoulders dropped, and he rolled his eyes. "I don't know."

I turned to face the Daughters, who kept to themselves in a corner of the main chamber. They'd taken off their golden masks, and they were quietly looking at each other. They were flawless and beautiful, and brimming with supernatural powers.

"Do you think you could try something on that shield?" I asked them. "Anything?"

Safira was the first to stand, exhaling. "We can try. But, like I've said, we are not as strong out here as we are back in Eritopia. Our solar system gives us the energy we need to do what we do."

"It's worth a shot, instead of not doing anything," Viola muttered, exchanging irritated glances with her sisters.

Draven got up, his expression suddenly illuminated. "I could try something," he muttered. "And the Daughters could give me the energy I'd need for this. It's serious dark magic. I've never done it before, because it would drain the life out of hundreds of creatures in order to work. But if I get my energy from the Daughters, instead, I could pull it off."

"What are you thinking of doing?" I asked.

"There's an attack spell," Draven explained. "It's a pure energy pulse. That's why it needs so much of it. It can generate enough power to shatter almost anything. I don't know if it's ever been tried against a shield of this magnitude," he added, pointing at the invisible planet, "but it's definitely worth a shot."

I nodded, willing to try anything. Our people were down there, and we had no idea what state they were in. The longer we took to get to them, the more they could be at risk... or worse.

"Okay. Let's try it. What do you need from us?" I replied.

Draven shrugged. "Nothing. I just need you all to move back and clear this area for the Daughters and me," he said, pointing at the front area of the chamber.

Corrine, Ibrahim, Serena, Viola, Phoenix, Shayla, and Arwen moved back with the rest of us, while the Daughters came forward, joining Draven in front of the arched windshield. They gathered behind him in a semicircle as he drew a flurry of Druid symbols in chalk on the metallic floor.

Serena stilled, gazing out the windshield. "Draven, stop. Stop," she muttered.

I followed her gaze and found myself holding my breath. Gasps erupted from our group, as we all stared at the seemingly empty space between two planets, where Neraka was supposed to be. The shield started to burn off the invisible globe, its shrinking edges glowing gold until it all went away.

Holding my breath, I watched Neraka as it revealed itself to us in all its splendor—its blue oceans and vast continents, the wisps of white clouds gathering on the side of sunset... Finally, we could see our destination.

"Good grief, it's beautiful," I heard myself whisper.

"Corrine, can you have a look through your telescope?" Viola interjected, then opened her backpack. "I'll get the travel spell ready."

Phoenix grabbed two glass helmets from a side compartment and gave one to her. "Here, babe," he said. "I'll come with you outside, so we can speed this along."

Corrine nodded, then angled the hybrid telescope toward the

now-visible Neraka. She pointed at the glass helmets. "Put the small metal collars on first, then the helmets," she said. "It's the only way you'll lock the ambient oxygen in."

Both Viola and Phoenix nodded, and they geared up and headed toward the exit hatch. Corrine had designed an exit chamber for situations like this, making it safe for us to get out and explore a planet without an atmosphere or with toxic air—without compromising the capsule itself.

My heart skipped a beat, watching Viola and Phoenix as they stepped into the exit chamber. The glass door slid closed and sealed them off, then decompressed the exit chamber and opened the main hatch leading out to the moon's surface. They both bounced out, unbound by gravity, and vanished to the right as they proceeded to draw the swamp witches' interplanetary travel spell on the ground.

I then shifted my focus to Corrine, who was busy looking for signs of life through the telescope. I instantly noticed her concerned frown.

"What is it?" I asked.

She looked at me, then let out a long and heavy sigh. "Well, our team is having a little bit of trouble."

"Define trouble." Hazel shot to her feet, concern etched into her beautiful features.

"War. Mostly. I mean, there's some weird stuff going on down there as we speak, but, from the looks of it, all our GASP team is still alive," she replied.

I rushed over and looked through the telescope myself. The hybrid telescope offered a highly detailed view of Neraka's surface.

"War?" Hazel gasped. "We need to get ready," she added, then looked at Tejus, who gave her a reassuring nod.

"We're almost there," he said, his voice low and calm. "The dragons we've brought are more than capable of ending whatever is going on down there in a matter of minutes."

"Damn straight," Heath replied, his tone clipped as he gripped the edges of his seat. If he squeezed any harder, the entire thing was going to come off with a snap.

I took my time to analyze the area that Corrine had pointed at through her telescope. It was a large mountain surrounded by a curtain of gorges. Its eastern side faced the ocean. That was Azure Heights, just like Rewa had described it when we'd first met her.

My stomach churned at the sight of an army laying siege against the city. I couldn't see what sort of creatures they were, exactly, but I could tell that Blaze didn't like them. He was in full dragon form and was delivering a veritable firestorm against their ranks. They'd come with large war machinery—catapults and ballistae—but Blaze seemed to do a pretty good job of avoiding them.

The city of Azure Heights cascaded across seven levels, massive terraces carved into the southern mountainside. I could see the buildings and narrow streets, many of them on fire and riddled with a variety of strange creatures, especially on the ground floor.

"Corrine, is there any chance we could see closer?" I asked.

She fumbled with the lens controls next to my visor. In an instant, I had an even better view, and it instantly filled my entire body with burning tension.

"There's definitely a siege going on there," I said. "I'm seeing some of our own and the locals. There's an army of massive warriors with... horns, attacking the city. I see Blaze at the bottom, burning them in troves, but he's not enough. Most of our team are moving down from the top to the base, to join the fight. They're not going to last for much longer. There are thousands of these horned creatures, and—" I froze, watching Jax and Hansa leading the charge against a crowd of Exiled Maras on the third level. "You were right."

A couple of moments passed as I kept watching.

I took a deep breath as soon as I heard the outside hatch open. Viola and Phoenix were back.

"The Exiled Maras definitely have something to do with this," I said, looking at the wards. "You were right."

"Dammit," Jovi muttered. "I was hoping they'd learned something from this whole exile thing."

"Everybody gear up and get ready to fight," I said, raising my voice. "We're going in hot. Telluris is probably working again, now that the shield is down, but with the fighting is going on down there, I would hate for us to distract our team with it."

Heath nodded, then motioned for his dragons to line up by the door, just as the cabin regained the interior pressure levels, its door sliding open to let Viola and Phoenix back in.

"Come on, guys," Heath said. "We'll be the first line of attack. My boy needs us."

The wards shot to their feet and assumed the second line in front of the main exit, their weapons ready. The rest of our crew gathered behind them, checking their swords and combat gear.

Viola took the central position in what was basically the middle of the swamp witch pentagram she'd drawn outside, then began chanting the incantation for the interplanetary travel spell. She brought one of Rewa's red beads to her lips, closing her eyes.

We all backed away, while Corrine and Ibrahim resumed their positions by the control board.

"We'll need the Daughters to stand by and help steer this thing down there," I said, as the capsule began to whine and creek. "We can't land on the mountain at this point. We have to land in the field and attack the army from behind."

The Daughters nodded, then moved to stand closer to Viola.

Once her incantation was complete, a great ball of light swallowed the capsule and temporarily blinded us all. I closed my eyes, wrapping an arm around Sofia's shoulders and holding her close to me.

The capsule trembled as it lifted off the powdery ground.

We all wobbled when it took off and shot toward Neraka.

"This is it," I murmured against Sofia's temple. "We're getting our people back."

I braced myself for what came next. There were creatures out there, thousands of them, looking to hurt our family, our friends, and our allies. Under no circumstances could we let that happen.

Heath gave me a sideways glance and a brief nod. I could see the fire in his sky-blue eyes.

Like all of us, he was determined to lay waste to the enemy, and obliterate anyone who threatened the lives of those we loved and held dear.

30

VESTA

It drove me crazy to sit in a tree and watch thousands of daemons attacking the city.

Laughlan's blue lens worked to help us see, better though, and in great detail.

Dhaxanian frost did a good job of crippling their offense, but there were too many of those horned bastards and not enough of our own. However, I could breathe a little easier, as we'd all watched the shield go down.

The sky didn't look any different. With the cloaking shield gone, it still carried its afternoon hues of pink and orange. Black smoke billowed from different levels of the mountain. Had it not been for the sounds of swords clashing, screams of agony, and Blaze's bloodcurdling roars, this would've been a beautiful and tranquil afternoon.

"I know you're anxious," Laughlan said quietly.

I looked to my right and found him watching me intently from another branch. I replied with a shrug.

"Aren't you?" I asked.

"Of course," he replied. "But the shield is down. Which means that, any minute now, their people will be coming down from the sky."

"I know." I sighed, then let out a frustrated groan. "But we don't know what's going on in the city now. I don't have Harper's True Sight. I can't see who's still standing, or whether the daemon king is still alive. We don't know anything!"

"I can see Hansa and Jax from here," Rush murmured, taking his hood off and squinting toward the mountain through the blue lens. "And Fiona, Caia, Avril, Scarlett, and Patrik. They're down on the third level now, headed for the fight. They left a trail of headless Maras behind them."

"Hah!" I chuckled, my heart swelling with pride. "Knew they were hardcore," I added, then frowned. "What about Harper?"

"She's on the seventh level with... I think Caspian," Amina chimed in, looking through the lens as Rush held it up for her. "He's pretty banged up, and... Oh, no." She instantly teared up.

"What?" I croaked, mentally preparing myself for bad news. It was bound to come. We were at war, after all. "Amina, what is it?"

"It's Colton," she breathed, her lower lip trembling. "He... He didn't make it. Neither did Arrah." She shook her head slowly, then wiped the tears streaming down her cheeks. "It's best if we don't think about the casualties for now. Let's get this over with first."

Amina was the first to get down from our safe tree spot, followed by Rush.

I watched them both as they headed out into the field. The sun was setting beyond the gorges to the west. My heart was aching at the thought of Arrah and Colton gone. Arrah, especially, had suffered enough already. She deserved better.

"What are you doing?" I asked, swallowing back my own tears.

"We should move out into the open," Amina said. "The sun is going down. Once the others come from the moon, we need to be able to spot them."

"She's right," Laughlan said, then jumped off his branch and landed in the tall grass. I joined him, and we walked over to Rush and Amina.

A spine-tingling groan erupted from the mountain base. The daemons had set the catapults off, hurling large stones at the third and fourth levels of the mountain. A variety of Druid spells prevented most of the projectiles from hitting the people and some of the buildings. The shimmering sheets of gold and blue pushed the stones away—they crashed into the second and first levels, flattening entire neighborhoods in the process.

My breath hitched, and I wondered if anyone was anywhere near the impact areas when the stones came down. I had no choice but to hope that they weren't. There was enough anguish and anxiety building up inside me, and, like Laughlan had said, I needed my wits about me.

"At least Arrah's brother is still alive," I murmured, following Rush, Amina, and Laughlan deeper into the field. Amina gave me a sad look. "She fought hard to get him out of there and to keep him safe. So, there's that."

"Arrah died a hero," Laughlan replied. "So did Colton and anyone else we've lost today. We knew this would happen, from the moment we agreed to help the GASP crew. But they did it. They brought the shield down."

I stilled, staring up at the sky. My heart jumped into my throat.

"Whoa," I croaked, my jaw dropping. A bright light twinkled between two strips of white clouds. "I think they're here."

I pointed at the light, which grew bigger with every second that passed.

Laughlan produced a handful of rough gemstones from his pockets, which he tossed around us in the grass, in a wide circle. He then joined me in the middle, motioning for Amina and Rush to move back. Rush frowned, then shook his head.

"No, you Druids need energy for your dark magic," he said. "Take some from us, if you need to. Don't push us back."

"I'm not pushing you back," Laughlan replied dryly. "The spell won't work with you in it. Oh, and thanks for offering your energy. I was going to help myself, anyway."

Amina chuckled, then crossed her arms. "Not a fan of consent, are you?"

"Sorry," Laughlan replied with a half-smile and a shrug. "I forget I have to say these things out loud. I've been locked in that damn meranium box for so long, my social skills are comatose."

He then muttered a spell under his breath. He clapped his hands once between each sentence of the incantation. With each clap, a gemstone lit up in the grass. When the last one ignited, bright white light swallowed us as the beacon shot through the sky.

Rush and Amina glowed as Laughlan's Druid spell drew some energy from them.

The beacon was about fifteen feet thick. It could probably be seen from outer space.

Laughlan took my hand and whispered another spell. All of a sudden, I could see him again, despite the blinding light.

"I need you to focus now," he said. "This beacon doesn't just draw the interplanetary spell close; it also amplifies your elemental abilities and my magic. We've only got a minute before Rush and Amina are drained and we miss our window of opportunity."

I nodded and focused my senses on the winds rising around us.

Humming, I put my arms out, then aimed them both at the interplanetary spell hurling toward the surface. It was round, and it glowed white. I summoned the winds, using an internal voice to ask for their help.

Come on... You've done it before, you can do it again. Help me.

It didn't always work, but when it did, I could even hear the winds whispering as they did my bidding. With Neha's stories about the Hermessi now in the back of my head, I was beginning to wonder whether there was any truth to them.

Please, winds. Help me.

They did. They howled and swished around us, then expanded into powerful gusts that knocked both Amina and Rush down before they headed toward the light orb.

I wiggled my fingers in an attempt to finetune the winds' direction. Each current felt like an extension of my own body, perfectly attuned to my needs and my intentions. They worked seamlessly, albeit a tad roughly for my taste.

They knocked into the light orb, stopping its trajectory in midair. They swirled around it, then bumped into it and pushed it toward us.

"It's coming!" I shouted. "It's coming! I'm doing it!"

I laughed. I'd never accomplished such a feat before, not at that large a scale, anyway.

I could feel the energy flowing through me, as if every particle in my body was a part of the wind—weightless and timeless. It was strange, but I couldn't get enough of it. It filled my heart with unprecedented joy, making my pulse race and my lips stretch into a grin.

"This feels... different," I added, moving my hands and coaxing the large light orb closer.

Laughlan watched me with renewed interest. The shadow of a smile flickered across his face.

"I'm not surprised," he said. "You're a fae."

"No, this is different," I replied. "It's... much more powerful. It's as if I'm connected to everything. I'm having a hard time explaining this, but I can almost hear the wind whispering actual words in my ears."

He frowned slightly. "Do you know what they're saying?"

I shook my head. "Not really. I don't recognize the language. But I've got a good feeling. It's positive, I think."

Laughlan scoffed lightly. "I'm starting to think that those

Hermessi stories are real. Maybe the elements *are* helping you. I mean, it would make sense, if you think about it. Neraka is a powerful world all by itself. The strength of its waves. The resilience of its stone. The power of its winds. The devastation of its fires. It's all there."

I thought about it for a while as I kept my gaze focused on the approaching light orb. I found myself nodding slowly. Laughlan gave me a soft nudge, then put his arms out.

"Legends aside now, are you ready?" he asked. "Here comes the hardest part."

"What's that?" I replied, slightly confused.

"Steering and landing."

My eyes grew wide, watching the interplanetary spell sphere get bigger. It was less than a mile away, and it was coming at us extremely fast. Whether it was my wind power or its own design, the light orb was going to smash into us if we didn't help it slow down and land.

My heart skipped a beat.

"You've got this, and I'm here," Laughlan added, as if sensing my frayed nerves.

I took a deep breath and focused on the orb.

We were so close to ending this war, once and for all.

31

DEREK

Once we breached Neraka's atmosphere, the interplanetary spell stabilized itself.

We shot through the sky at an incredible speed, and yet we were so far from the surface it seemed as though we weren't even moving.

A beacon of light shot out of the field between Azure Heights and the gorges. It was thick and bright, and my instinct told me to follow it. I looked at Viola.

"Can we land there?" I asked.

Sofia gently squeezed my arm. "Are you sure it's a good idea? What if it's a trap?"

"I doubt it's a trap," Corrine interjected. "Someone took the shield down so we could come in. There's a war going on at the base of the mountain, but there's a beacon out in the field. I'm inclined to think they're with us and they're trying to signal us away from the mountain."

She looked through her telescope, then frowned slightly.

"Who do you see?" I asked.

"Four people. Two of them Maras, a Druid, and... a fae, I think," Corrine replied.

I looked at Viola again. She nodded once. "I can head toward it, yes," she said, then gave her sisters a sideways glance. They all huddled together, humming as they lit up in a bright shade of hot pink. Viola put her arms out, muttering a spell as she helped guide the orb toward the beacon.

"Everybody, hold on!" Safira said, closing her eyes. "I can feel something coming."

My heart skipped a beat. "What do you mean?"

"I'm not sure I can explain it," she replied. "But as Daughters of a galaxy ourselves, we feel the planet's energy. And right now, it's aimed at us. It's as if Neraka knows we're coming and it's reacting."

"Is that good?" I asked.

Safira shrugged. "I have no idea, but—"

Something hit our capsule hard. It knocked me down. I caught Sofia and held her close as I fell backward, cushioning her landing. I heard the others grunt. Corrine and Ibrahim held on to the control board. Only the Daughters stayed upright, all of them glowing pink and shutting their eyes as they focused on steering the orb.

I looked around, then at Sofia. "Are you okay?"

She nodded. "Mm-hm. But what was that?"

"Wind," Corrine answered. "Extremely powerful wind. I think Safira may be on to something here," she added, looking at the multiple glimmering lights on her control screen.

"What do you mean? What's happening?" I asked, suddenly overcome with concern. There were many of us on board. At this altitude, an impact could do a lot of harm to half of our group. Our chances of survival were even slimmer if our travel spell exploded. Until our feet reached the ground, I had no choice but to stay on edge.

Safira groaned, then chuckled softly, her eyes still shut. "It's the wind. It's rough, but it's actually helping us. It's steering us toward the beacon."

"Wait," Corrine murmured, looking through her telescope again. "The fae... The fae and the Druid. I'll bet they have something to do with this."

I looked out through the windshield, then got back up and took a seat, with Sofia next to me.

"Maybe we should buckle up," I said.

"No need," Corrine replied, shaking her head. She gave me a brief look over her shoulder and smiled. "We're steady now."

"We're too fast, though," Ibrahim interjected, looking at the controls before him. One of the screens blared red. "Pink ladies, can you help us slow down?"

Viola chuckled softly, then continued with her incantation.

"We're working together here," Corrine replied. "We're slowing down, and, judging by the wind direction, the fae is doing something on her side to help us, too. It's pushing back against the capsule now."

I took several deep breaths, holding Sofia's hand. I felt the capsule tremble, hurling toward the surface of Neraka.

"Everybody, hold on!" Corrine said. "We're landing."

The impact wasn't as bad as I'd thought it would be. The dragons and the wards lost their footing as soon as we hit the ground. They fell and toppled one another like bowling pins, grunting and cursing as they struggled to get back up and retain a sliver of dignity.

I stifled a chuckle, as did Jovi and the others. Heath gave me a joking death stare, prompting me to offer him a smirk in return.

"You all right there, Heath?" I asked dryly.

He scoffed, then got back up and stretched his arms out.

The capsule settled on the ground, just feet away from the beacon.

We all got out through the main hatch. Two at a time. Sofia and I rushed around to the front, where the beacon died out. In its place, four creatures awaited, as described by Corrine. A Mara couple, a Druid, and a young fae.

They all stared at us with wide eyes, measuring each of our crew members from head to toe.

Corrine and Ibrahim joined our side, while the others gathered around the gemstone circle left in the tall grass. The air was clean and fresh—though I could smell the burning wood and flesh from the city. It made my spine tingle, and not in a good way. It was the smell of death.

"I guess a thank you is in order?" I asked, looking at the four strangers.

They all bowed before us. The Druid then stepped forward.

"I didn't think we'd see Eritopians again," he said, and offered his hand. I shook it firmly. "I'm Laughlan," he added, then pointed at the fae and the Mara couple. "These are Vesta, Rush, and Amina. We're part of the Druid delegation that crash-landed on Neraka a long time ago."

"Oh, wow," Draven exclaimed, coming around to get a better look at them. "You're... You were with the swamp witch, right?"

Laughlan nodded.

"What's going on back there?" I asked. "Where are our people? How are you still here? What happened?"

Laughlan, Vesta, Rush, and Amina looked at each other, bitterly amused.

"There's a war going on back there, but before you go in, there are a few things you need to know," Laughlan replied.

We all huddled closer and listened as Laughlan and his group brought us up to speed on what had been going on in this world for the past eight or ten millennia. My stomach dropped as I heard about the Exiled Maras' inability to turn their lives around and their horrible treatment of the Imen, along with other endemic species.

We learned about the daemons and their addiction to eating souls. That alone required a lot more clarification, but, given the war transpiring less than a mile away from our location, we had to make do with what the Druid could tell us.

We found out about Lumi and how she'd been abducted by the Exiled Maras, then tortured and shared with the daemons for her spells. Ten minutes later, we had a much better picture of what had been going on here. And it made my blood run infinitely colder. On top of that, there were a lot of gaps that needed filling, and details that didn't fit the overall picture.

Sofia was the first to spot the most important anomaly. "Hold on," she said, shaking her head. "You said our people have been here for weeks. How is that possible? They left Neraka four days ago."

Laughlan stilled, his eyes widening as he realized something. "It wasn't just a cloaking shield, then," he muttered. "It was a—"

"You've got to be friggin' kidding me!" Jovi snapped, suddenly exasperated. "It was a time lapse!"

"No," Phoenix gasped. "Like in Eritopia?"

"Kind of? I guess?" Jovi replied, shrugging. "It's only been days, though, not years. Plus, it's reversed. Last time, we were the ones slowing down, while The Shade was going twenty years faster. Dammit, we really need to scrap this type of spell out of any recorded document. People can't just screw with time like this again!"

Laughlan watched the exchange, somewhat confused.

"We've been through something similar before, where the flow of time is concerned," I said, trying to speed things along.

"So, you're saying the Exiled Maras and the daemons have been working together for thousands of years, bleeding Imen dry, wiping out the other species, and consuming actual souls?" Tejus asked, taking a step forward.

"Pretty much," Vesta replied. "They've been keeping the surviving delegation members prisoner. They've been draining this world dry."

"And the reason they reached out to us was so they could

capture some of our people and force them into breeding camps?" Tejus muttered, his hands balled into fists. I could see rage swelling his veins already.

"Yes. Which explains why they shifted time within the cloaking spell," Laughlan said. "They needed more time to figure out the best way to capture your people. They'd been putting on an elaborate play and looking for the right angle to attack. You see, they didn't know you had dragons. That threw them for a loop, and they had to improvise. It didn't work out too well for them because your kids are sharp."

Heath chuckled, crossing his arms. He could see his son spitting fire over the daemon hordes at the base of the mountain. We could all hear them screaming.

"That's my boy," he muttered.

"Anyway, long story short, your people found us and freed us. They found out what the daemons and Maras were doing. We teamed up, we found allies in the Manticores, the Adlets, and the Dhaxanians still living in remote parts of the continent, and, well, here we are," Laughlan explained. "We weren't looking to start a war, but Shaytan, the daemon king, decided to rescind his alliance with the Maras and fight us all. Hence this," he added, pointing over his shoulder at the mountain.

"We sabotaged several daemon locations until we found out where they were keeping the swamp witch, Lumi," Vesta added. "We knew that our only chance to put an end to this was to have her bring the shield down so we could reach out to you."

I nodded slowly, taking it all in.

"Okay then, ready to go?" I asked our crew.

Vesta came closer. "Hold on!" she said. "There's a problem. You can't just unleash your dragons on the city. We have allies up there. Hundreds of innocent Imen who are still alive and scattered throughout the levels. They can't get off the mountain with all those daemons working their way up."

"She's right," Corrine said. "We can't kill them all in one strike."

"What do you suggest, then?" I asked.

Corrine exhaled, then motioned for Ibrahim, Arwen, Shayla, and the Daughters to come closer. "I've got an idea for how we can evacuate all the innocents and allies safely," she replied. "I'll work out a quick plan with our resident warlock, witches, and Daughters. We'll be ready to go in five minutes. We'll deploy first."

"Once you get everybody out, we'll unleash the dragons," I said, then glanced at Jax's wards and the rest of our crew.

"The rest of us can stay on the outskirts, around the mountain base," Field suggested, motioning at the allied troops that we'd brought with us. They all wanted to be a part of it. Lucas and Marion, Pippa and Jeramiah, Hazel and Tejus, Grace and Lawrence, Anjani and Jovi, Dmitri and the Hawk brothers... They were all here, along with our additional succubi, incubi, and fae fighters, our werewolves and Druids.

"Sofia and I will stay back here with the parents," I replied.

"What? No, I'm going to—" Lucas tried to say, but I cut him off.

"Don't be ridiculous. We've got fire and ice dragons. It's more than enough," I said. "Besides, our kids need us here. Once Corrine and her group get them out, they'll need some familiar faces."

Corrine came back from her brief powwow with Ibrahim, the witches, and the Daughters.

"We're ready," she said. "We're going in now. Once we get everybody out, we'll give your dragons a signal."

"Once the innocents are out, you're free to level the whole damn mountain, if you want," Vesta replied, crossing her arms as she looked at the city.

A bright red light shone above it. Smoke billowed out of most buildings. Bodies were scattered all over. The streets and stone steps were covered in blood. There was nothing but pain and despair oozing out of Azure Heights. There was a terrible story in that place—a story I knew we'd hear in full as soon as we brought this fight to an end.

"It's time for the grownups to get involved, then," Tejus said, scowling at the mountain.

Laughlan chuckled, prompting all of us to stare at him. "Don't worry. Your kids have already done most of the hard work. I think you people are, at best, the cleanup crew."

I couldn't help but laugh, resting a hand on Tejus's shoulder.

"Why am I not surprised?" I asked rhetorically.

"Because our team is fierce, and they've been trained well?" Tejus replied.

Sofia smiled. "Good. I didn't expect anything less from our Nerakian team."

Laughlan had a point, though. Our team lacked the numbers they needed to take on an army of daemons and hostile Maras. And yet, they'd managed to free the swamp witch. They'd brought the shield down, and they'd made it possible for us to come in and provide assistance. They'd definitely done most of the hard work.

"Should I reach out to them via Telluris?" Draven asked. "It probably works now."

"I would advise against it," I replied. "They could be fighting as we speak. We cannot distract them in any way."

Draven nodded slowly. We all made room for Corrine, Shayla, Arwen, Ibrahim, and the Daughters to gather in the middle. Corrine had brought with her a bag filled with tiny gemstones. She emptied it into multiple satchels, which she handed over to the others in her first intervention line.

She then turned around to face us and smiled.

"Okay. We're off now. See you old farts in a bit!" She giggled, then vanished into thin air.

One by one, Ibrahim, Arwen, Shayla, Viola, and the Daughters disappeared. They teleported onto the mountain to begin the evacuation procedure. I wasn't exactly sure what it entailed, but I had all the faith in her and the others. I'd been fortunate enough to cross paths with some of the most incredible creatures across multiple worlds.

I had a feeling that, despite its turmoil, the Nerakians held the same extraordinary potential.

We all watched the mountain, waiting for Corrine and her crew to do their thing. The daemons were ruthless, but those on our GASP team were admirable adversaries, to say the least. I was stuck in limbo, somewhere between concern and pride. I wasn't going to breathe easily until they were all out of harm's way, but, at the same time, I knew they were going to come back to us.

Because they were blood of our blood.

They were fighters.

32

HANSA

There was a sense of urgency burning through me as we fought our way down to the third level. Looking farther down, I saw the thick frost walls that the Dhaxanians had put up, blocking access into the city from the first level. They'd isolated several daemon squadrons from the rest of the army, and, with the help of Manticores, Adlets, and rebel Imen and Maras, they'd managed to kill most of them off.

It didn't help that there were still Maras loyal to the Lords down here, but my crew and I had cut off plenty of their heads along the way. I estimated at least a hundred, maybe a hundred and fifty Exiled Maras left in the city. The streets and market squares were littered with bodies, blood glazing the cobblestone and smoke coming out of partially torn-down buildings.

The daemons were launching rounds of stones and flaming projectiles into the city and past the Dhaxanian frost, in a bid to destroy Azure Heights's structures. It was the daemons' way of telling us that we couldn't hide behind the ice forever.

The daemon army roared at the bottom, hitting their meranium shields with their swords. Blaze flew over them and delivered fiery jets at them, while the daemons scrambled to move their ballistae and get him with the massive steel arrows. Unfortunately for them, the dragon had learned valuable lessons back at Ragnar Peak. However, one dragon wasn't enough to destroy thousands of daemons at once. It was only a matter of time before somebody shot him down.

Things were eerily quiet on the second level. The front part of the neighborhood had Manticores, Adlets, and Dhaxanians lined up and aiming their crossbows at the frost walls below. The infirmary was partially demolished, with clouds of dust billowing out. Our crew spread out, picking up bows and quivers and crossbows from the fallen rebels. The Imen were putting up a good fight, but they'd also registered the largest number of casualties. It broke my heart to watch them point their arrows at the frost walls, while doing their best not to look back and get glimpses of their fallen comrades.

"What's happening here?" I asked one of the Dhaxanians.

He pointed at the frost walls. "Those won't hold for much longer," he said. "We're not giving up on this level yet. We're looking to bottleneck the daemons once they break through the frost, before we retreat up to the third level."

I nodded firmly, then pointed at Scarlett, Patrik, and the others. "You've got us here, too. Whatever you need, you tell us."

"We could use a couple more of those dragons," the young Dhaxanian replied with a smirk.

"They're on their way," I said. "The shield is down. It's a matter of minutes now. But, until then, we need to hold out here."

"What happened to the infirmary?" Jax asked, frowning as he stared at the ravaged structure.

"Catapults," the Dhaxanian replied. "I just hope your people got out of there first. We can't spare anyone to look for survivors now. We've lost dozens of our own and—dammit, it's coming down!" he shouted, readying his bow.

I followed his gaze and froze. A large crack stretched from the top to the bottom of the ice wall, just where it encompassed the main road into the city.

Jax motioned for Patrik to keep the crew in their positions. "Get ready, Druid! Cover the allies! Hansa and I will check the infirmary!"

Patrik replied with a nod, then moved toward the main road, joined by Scarlett, Fiona, Caia, Rayna and Idris, Ryker, Wyrran, Peyton, and their rebels, as well as the Adlets. The daemons were smashing swords and axes against the frost wall. Soon enough, they were going to breach it.

"Oh, no. Heron!" Avril screamed.

She darted from my side and headed for the infirmary, where chunks of stone started to move. Jax and I followed. My heart jumped into my throat as fear clutched me. Harper had told us about the switch, which meant that if Heron was there, so was the swamp witch.

"How do you know he's there?" I asked Avril.

She jumped over a pile of rubble and feverishly started digging through the ruins. "I caught his scent!" she replied, her voice trembling. "Heron! Heron, can you hear me? I'm coming!"

Jax and I joined in and started pulling the rubble back, looking for Heron and the witch. To my surprise, we found Velnias first. He was unconscious and severely wounded, but still breathing. It took both Jax and me to pull the big guy out.

We found the floor beneath the debris. It was covered in daemon bodies and coagulated blood, dirt, and dust. I caught a glimpse of a hand, its fingers long and its skin pale. I prayed to the Daughters that it was one of ours and that its owner was still alive.

Avril kept digging through the rubble, tossing large stones aside like they were made out of paper. The adrenaline was coursing through us all as we kept clearing the front room of the infirmary. I got the second guy out. It was Nevis, and he was severely wounded as well. Next to him was a burly, dead daemon. Jax turned the horned head around for me to see.

"That's a high-level warrior," I breathed.

"Look at this," Jax muttered, picking up a piece of a broken sword. There were swamp witch symbols engraved into the blade, much like the ones we'd seen on Shaytan's sword. "Soul-eater."

I gasped, then checked Nevis from head to toe. "Oh, dear," I murmured, discovering a nasty wound in Nevis's shoulder. The broken tip of the daemon warrior's soul-eating blade was lodged in there, the symbols still glowing yellow. I pulled it out and tossed it to the side, then put pressure on his wound. "I'm out of healing paste!"

Jax fumbled through his pockets and found another satchel. He brought it over, giving Nevis a concerned frown. "How is he?"

"Unconscious and with his soul probably in tatters, but alive," I muttered, spreading the healing paste over his shoulder wound. His armor had partially come off, the white silk blouse beneath covered in blood.

Nevis stirred and groaned. His eyes peeled open. Jax bit into his wrist, drawing blood. He pushed it against Nevis's lips. "Drink, friend. You'll be okay," he said.

The Dhaxanian prince looked at us both, then nodded and drank some of Jax's blood.

Avril yelped. She'd found Heron. Jax left me with Nevis and rushed across the piles of rubble to help her. Nevis and I watched as they pulled Heron out, then Lumi. Avril took care of Heron, while Jax helped Lumi back to consciousness. They were both okay, just dazed and severely cut up. Nothing that couldn't be healed with some vampire or Mara blood.

Relief washed over me, and I shifted my focus back to Nevis.

"What happened?" I asked him.

He grunted from the pain and forced himself into a sitting position.

"They were holed up in the infirmary," he replied, slowly

looking around. "Daemons started coming in. Lumi's protections weren't permanent, and she needed to finish her incantation to take down the shield. Velnias, Heron, and I fought the daemons. Sienna and Tobiah, and Dion and Alles, plus a few others, had taken positions outside."

"Those daemons were from Shaytan's private guard," I said.

"Well, they got more backup quickly after that." Nevis scoffed. "Lumi took the shield down. I moved to freeze everything but got attacked by a considerably large daemon. The bastard had come from the first level. He'd broken through our frost with his stolen swamp witch magic. What's worse, he had a nasty blade. Whenever it cut me, it drained my energy. It got to the point where I couldn't make any ice, at all. I was reduced to fighting him physically. Then there was the blast. I'm guessing catapult?"

I nodded. "Yes. As for the fiend, he's dead. And his sword was a soul-eater. I've only seen this on Shaytan's blade earlier," I replied. "It drains your soul whenever it hits your sword. It's a lot worse if it cuts through you."

Nevis's eyes grew wide with outrage. "Are you telling me that horned bastard ate my soul?"

"Some of it, yes. I'm so sorry."

"They're okay!" Jax confirmed, prompting me to look at them. I smiled at the sight of Heron, Velnias, and Lumi fully conscious.

"Hold on!" Nevis barked, visibly infuriated. "He ate my damn soul! My frost! I can't..." He shook his head slowly, raising his hand and staring at it. "I can't make any ice. I'm... I'm powerless."

"Come on, let's get you up and worry about your frost later," I said, then put his arm over my shoulders and pulled him up. "We need to get you all out of here and onto a higher level."

I heard Avril gasp. "Oh, no..."

Both Nevis and I followed her gaze. She cleared more rubble from the southeastern corner of the infirmary, revealing Dion and Alles. They were both dead. They'd been crushed by the broken walls. I instantly teared up.

"What about Tobiah and Sienna?" Heron asked, looking around.

He stilled, spotting something under a large chunk of stone. He rushed over and pulled it back. Jax quickly came to assist him. They cleared the spot, then got Tobiah and Sienna out—the daemon had shielded the young Mara with his body. They were both severely wounded, but they would eventually heal.

"We need to get them all out of here," I said.

We could all hear the daemons roaring. They were seconds away from breaking through the ice wall. Nevis cursed under his breath. Velnias managed to stand.

"They're coming through," he muttered, frowning at the cracked frost.

"Well, I certainly can't help at this point, since a daemon chomped on my damn soul!" Nevis snapped.

"Hey! Calm down! We'll figure something out," I shot back firmly. "Before anything else, we need to get you all back up there. Especially you, Nevis. You're injured and weak."

"Both of which haven't occurred to me since I was a little boy," Nevis muttered. "The perks of being friends with you people, I suppose."

Heron chuckled. "Well, he's still snappy, so that means he'll be just fine."

Nevis gave him a deadly stare. Heron was unimpressed. He picked up Sienna, while Velnias took Tobiah. Avril took care of Lumi, and Jax came back to Nevis and me. We got away from the infirmary and were headed back up the road leading to the third level, when the allies' shouts stopped us in our tracks.

"Get ready!" one of the Dhaxanians said.

I glanced over my shoulder and groaned. "Ugh, they're about to break through."

"We need to move—" Jax didn't get to finish his statement, as Corrine appeared out of nowhere, right in front of us.

I gasped. "What in the ever-living—" I started, but she cut me off.

"I cannot tell you how glad I am to see you all here," Corrine said, beaming with joy.

"Good grief, you're real," I breathed.

"Corrine! You're really here!" Avril exclaimed.

"There's no time now," she replied. "Take these. One for each."

She handed us a handful of gemstones. We each took one, as instructed. I put one in Nevis's hand, while Jax and Heron did the same with Tobiah and Sienna.

"What are these?" I asked, frowning at the small crystal in my palm.

"Your way out," Corrine replied. "Ibrahim, Shayla, Arwen, and the Daughters are here, too, doing the same with all the survivors and innocents. It's about to go down here, but we need you out first."

"Wait, what?" Avril blurted out, somewhat confused.

Corrine smiled. "Sweetie, it's time to go. Your parents and friends are waiting out there in the field. We need to get everyone out because there are dragons coming."

"Oh. Dragons. Plural..." Velnias murmured, his eyes nearly popping out of their orbits.

"Wow, you're a big guy," Corrine exclaimed, looking him from head to toe with an appreciative smirk. Velnias couldn't help but grin, all of a sudden flattered.

"I don't look my age, I know," he replied.

"And you're not an enemy, either," Corrine concluded. "I see lots of your people trying to kill mine down there."

"Not something I want to see happen again, rest assured," Velnias said.

Corrine clapped her hands once. "Okay now! Everybody out, while I get the others!"

"Out where?" I asked, but quickly got my answer when she snapped her fingers.

One by one, my crew disappeared. Poof. Like clouds blown away by a sudden gust of wind. I lost all sense of time and space. For a split second, everything went dark.

I'd been decomposed into the tiniest of particles, soon to be reassembled elsewhere.

I was out of Azure Heights. Away from the war.

33

HARPER

I stayed by Caspian's side after we were helped up to the seventh level. Hundurr circled around Colton's lifeless body, occasionally growling at Rowan and Farrah. Patrik had put them both inside a Druid mandala-type of chalk drawing, a spell designed to keep them from running off.

Zane was right next to us. His breathing was even, and he was slowly recovering, drifting in and out of consciousness just to check on the two Mara Ladies. A part of him refused to let himself rest. There was so much death and devastation around us that tears kept streaming down my cheeks—my heart burned for every life we'd lost along the way.

Arrah's body had been laid next to the other Imen. The ones we'd managed to rescue had huddled inside Emilian's mansion. Despite the ravaged front wall, it still provided them with cover. I heard them gasp whenever an explosion tore through the lower levels. The daemons' catapults weren't able to hit the sixth and seventh levels. Not yet, anyway. I had a feeling that they would, provided they were angled properly.

Caspian sighed, most of his body still covered in horrific burns. But he was calm, and he was healing. In a day or two, he'd be as good as new. I dropped a kiss on his tender forehead. He groaned softly.

It killed me to see him like this. Most importantly, the damage that Shaytan had done to my soul hurt even more. I had to do something to make that pain go away, or at least simmer down. I instinctively pulled my combat suit zipper down, revealing the medallion that Serena had given me before I left Calliope.

I spent a minute staring at it. I pressed my lips against it and closed my eyes.

The world around me seemed to vanish. Matter warped into a different setting. I wasn't on Neraka anymore. I was back home in The Shade, with Mom, Dad, Serena, and Phoenix, during our first family dinner after we got both of my siblings back from Luceria. We laughed. We were happy. We talked about building a GASP base on Mount Zur. I begged Dad to let me get on the Calliope detail. I wanted to be close to Serena.

That was my fondest memory. Dinner with a complete family. We were all at peace, smiling at one another and looking forward to the future.

I shuddered, opening my eyes and realizing I was still on Neraka. There were still daemons below, laying siege upon the city. My lips were soft and warm against the cool medallion that Serena... I started sobbing like a little girl. I missed them. I needed to see them again. But, deep down, I did feel a little better. I had something to look forward to.

Any minute now.

"There is some water in the kitchen," a young Iman girl said.

I looked at her as she stood in the broken doorway of Emilian's mansion. She was shaking like a leaf, her aura beaming in red and yellow—a mixture of pain, grief, and fear. Despite what she was feeling, however, she sounded calm and reserved. She held it all inside, most likely so as not to startle or worry the others.

I gave her a weak smile. "I'm okay, thank you. But I think our pit wolf here would appreciate some," I said, nodding at Hundurr.

The pit wolf stilled and stared at the Iman girl for a minute. She was fearful of him, but still, she nodded, went back inside, and then came back with a large pan filled with water. She placed it at the bottom of the porch stairs, then stepped back, watching Hundurr as he trotted over and started lapping away at the water.

She smiled. "He's so... different."

"That's because he's an Adlet," I replied. "Pit wolves are not inherently evil or savage. They're merely the result of the corrupted swamp witch magic that they were subjected to. Once you take off the charmed collars that the daemons made them wear... Well, you can see for yourself."

"Is it over?" she asked, giving me a hopeful glance.

I shrugged. "I don't know. I don't think so."

I looked around. Ramin was definitely gone. Whether I'd dreamed it all or he was actually real was something I would dig into later. For now, I focused on keeping the survivors in one place and, hopefully, seeing my family and friends again soon. I'd seen the light cut through the sky.

They were down there, somewhere.

"Harper," Zane muttered, blinking several times as he came to again. "Where's Fiona?"

"She's down on the second level with Hansa and the others," I replied. "Are you okay?"

"I feel like I've been hit by a mountain. Other than that, I'm great. You?"

I let out a long, tortured sigh. My lungs were weak. My heart wasn't pumping as fast as it should. My body temperature was even lower than usual. I was weak and cold, holding my knees up to my chest. My wounds had closed, but something was missing.

"Tired," I replied. "I now know what it's like to have your soul eaten. I wouldn't wish it upon anyone."

Farrah scoffed. Rowan was still unconscious, but Farrah had

her eyes wide open. With one arm left and a shoulder wound that would take a long time to heal, she was also extremely bitter and mean.

"You should try eating one," she said. "Once you're on the other end, trust me, it's an incredible feeling. The power surge... It's like being constantly weightless and—"

"How about you shut the hell up and focus on what your life will be like inside a cage, with only one arm and a string of failures and murders tied around your neck, instead?" I shot back, my tone clipped. "No one's interested in hearing how 'cool' your addiction is. You've done enough harm as it is."

"I only speak the truth," Farrah retorted. "Just because you refuse to see it—"

She yelped and went quiet all of a sudden. In a split second, Hundurr had gone back to her, towering over her with his fangs out, eager to tear her to shreds.

"I suggest you keep your mouth shut, unless you want the pit wolf to rid you of the other arm, too, and make you even," Zane replied, chuckling. He then looked at Caspian. "How is he?"

"I think he'll be okay," I said. "Provided the daemon army doesn't make it up to this level. In which case, we'll be a little screwed."

Viola appeared out of nowhere, right in front of me. I gasped. My heart nearly stormed out of my chest. She smiled.

"Hi, Harper," she murmured. "Sorry I'm late."

"Whoa," Zane breathed, looking up at her in awe. His jaw was close to hitting the ground.

"Viola... How... When... You made it!" I croaked, then jumped to my feet and instantly lost my footing. I was still so weak.

Viola giggled and caught me in her arms, breaking my fall. I hugged her tight, thankful to hear her, to see her, to feel her in my arms. Her presence here meant that it was all over, and I could truly breathe again, for the first time since I'd left Calliope.

"You're not well, are you?" she asked, helping me stand on my own as she measured me from head to toe.

I shook my head slowly, then pointed at Caspian and Zane. "None of us are," I replied. "But hey, we've made it this far." I chuckled.

"No, I mean, there's a part of you that's missing," she said, as if she could see right into my crippled soul. There was no way for me to describe the emptiness I was feeling. On one hand, I was thrilled—or should've been thrilled—to see her... and yet, I felt desolate. Nothing felt right.

"The daemon king ate chunks of my soul, if that makes sense," I muttered.

She caressed my cheek and gave me a soft smile. "It will be okay. We'll figure something out."

"What are you doing up here? Where are the others?" I asked, looking around and hoping to see my parents and the rest of our family.

"They're waiting for you. I'm here to get you and everyone else out," Viola replied, carefully checking out our surroundings.

Zane managed to get up, then offered her a curt bow. His reverence made me smile. I had a feeling he'd realized just how powerful Viola could be as a Daughter of Eritopia.

"This is Zane," I said. "He's our friend and ally. This is Caspian," I added. "Also our friend and ally."

"He's more than that, isn't he?" Viola asked, wearing a half smile.

I nodded. "Good grief, your intuition scares me sometimes," I murmured.

She took a deep breath, then exhaled. "Okay. We need to go. The dragons are coming."

"Yes!" I squealed, momentarily energized. "Wait, how do we... Never mind, you literally popped out of nowhere. I'm guessing we're all getting out the same way."

"Indeed." She chuckled softly, then handed me one of the

pouches she carried on her dress belt. It was filled with tiny gemstones that glimmered in a variety of colors. I looked at her with my eyebrows raised, waiting for an explanation. "Hand one to everyone you need to get out of here safely. Once you're done, I'll get us out. It's a little trick that Corrine employed for mass evacuations."

"Okay. Okay, got it," I replied, then started distributing the gems around the seventh level, while Viola waited patiently.

I handed one to Zane, then slipped one into Caspian's hand. I put one in Rowan's dress pocket, then gave another to Farrah, who scowled at me. I responded with a low growl.

"You're going to pay for all your crimes, Farrah," I said. "I'm going to make sure of it."

She tossed the gemstone away. "Go to hell. I'm staying here."

I scoffed, then grabbed her by the back of the head and shoved another gemstone down her throat—in a most literal sense. She coughed and gagged, but she ended up swallowing it. She cursed under her breath and bared her fangs at me. I chuckled.

"You still don't get it, do you?" I replied, then got back up. "You lost. We won. Now, take it like a big girl."

I walked over to Hundurr and offered him a gemstone.

He looked at it, then at me with big, curious red eyes.

"I think you need to swallow it, buddy. You're coming with us," I told him. Hundurr groaned, then briefly glanced back at Arrah and Colton, before looking at me again. "We'll take them with us, too. They deserve a proper burial."

He nodded, then licked the gemstone out of my palm and swallowed it. I put one in Colton's mouth and another inside Arrah's short tweed jacket. I ran my fingers over the bloodstains, then brushed a few loose strands from her face.

I couldn't help but burst into tears again. "I'll find your brother, I promise. You fought well, Arrah. Hopefully, there's something better waiting for you on the other side."

Five minutes later, I'd shared my gemstones with all the

surviving Imen hidden inside Emilian's mansion. I made sure to mark all our fallen allies as well. They all deserved a ceremony. They were all heroes.

"What now?" I asked Viola, while the Imen gradually came out of the mansion.

She smiled. "Now, we go," she replied, then snapped her fingers.

One by one, all the Imen and our fallen allies vanished like wisps of smoke in the evening breeze. Hundurr was next. Then Rowan and Farrah. Zane gasped before he disappeared. Caspian followed.

Next thing I knew, I was weightless.

I, too, was gone.

34

HARPER

I t felt like only the blink of an eye.

I found myself transported to the field, about a mile away from the mountain.

"Harper!" My mother's voice cut through my consciousness. "My baby!"

Before I could register what was going on, I was wrapped in my mother's and my father's arms. I burst into tears as soon as I saw their faces. They, too, were crying—mostly with relief and the joy of having me close again.

"Sis!" Serena yelped and joined in the group hug.

I laughed. From the bottom of my heart, I laughed. Phoenix's long arms seemed to bring us all even closer, tighter than ever. Despite the hole in my soul, I was happy. I was free. I was with my family again.

We stayed like that for a while, while more of us appeared out of nowhere—both from our team and from our allies' ranks. Corrine, Ibrahim, Shayla, Arwen, and the Daughters did a stellar job of rescuing everyone we needed from Azure Heights. Adlets and Manticores, Dhaxanians, Imen townspeople and rebels, surviving Exiled Maras, and Peyton's fighters, too.

All of a sudden, we'd all been transferred off the mountain and into the field, while the daemon army continued to push through the city.

"You're okay! Thank the stars that you're okay," Mom breathed, covering my face with feverish, loving kisses.

"You know me, Mom. I'm not easy to kill." I chuckled, resting my head on my father's shoulder. I then gave Serena and Phoenix a warm smile. "Now I know how you two felt when we found you in Luceria."

"Best feeling in the world, isn't it?" Serena asked, grinning like the Cheshire cat. She came in closer, holding me tight.

"Thank you for this," I murmured, holding up the medallion for her to see. "It definitely helped. Nothing like the vivid memory of your loved ones to keep you going."

"You're okay. It's going to be okay," Serena replied.

I nodded slowly, then glanced around once more. We'd all made it back.

Fiona was sandwiched between Yelena and Benedict, as expected. Lucas and Marion held Avril in their arms, while Pippa and Jeramiah showered Scarlett with loving words and kisses. Vita, Bijarki, Grace, and Lawrence had Caia, and Jax, Hansa, and Patrik were all surrounded by their people.

Blaze had flown away from the war zone and had just landed in the field, just twenty feet away from Heath and the other drag-ons. They all rushed to greet him. Heath was beside himself, as expected. My heart swelled to three times its original size once the last batch of Dhaxanians was brought back from the mountain.

Nevis, Tobiah, and Sienna were severely injured. Neha and Pheng-Pheng were okay. Peyton and Wyrran, too. We'd lost plenty of people out there, but we were now surrounded by some of the most powerful supernaturals to come out of The Shade, and Eritopia, as well.

Derek and Sofia were with us, too, going around from one group to another, to hug us and to express how grateful they were that we were still alive. Rowan and Farrah were restrained, as were the other Exiled Maras we'd captured from different levels. There was an overall feeling of weight still pressing down on our shoulders, though.

"We didn't know," Derek said as soon as he reached our side. "We had no idea this was going on."

"You couldn't have," I said. "I know, don't worry about it," I added, then nodded at the mountain. "What about them? It won't be long before they figure out we're all gone."

Derek glanced over his shoulder, then gave me a confident smile. "Don't worry, sweetheart. We brought dragons." He winked and shouted at Heath. "Come on, you grumpy old lizard! Get out there and show these daemons who they're dealing with!"

Heath scoffed, the shadow of a smile fluttering across his face. "You don't have to tell me twice," he said, then looked at Blaze, who'd already been given an extra pair of pants. "You ready to let loose, Son?"

Blaze smiled. "Thought you'd never ask," he replied, then gave Caia a brief wink.

The dragons lined up on the edge of our group, slipping out of their clothes and stretching their arms, as if getting ready to run a triathlon. My cheeks caught fire at the sight of so many naked butts, but I couldn't look away, as the ice dragons were the first to shift and fly out.

"What are they doing, Grandpa Derek?" I asked, watching the majestic creatures cut through the early evening sky.

"Well, first we need to isolate the daemons and stop them from getting off that mountain," Derek replied.

We all gathered behind him, as if we were about to watch one hell of a show. Knowing the dragons' flamboyant theatrics in battle already, I knew we were in for a treat. Caspian stayed back, still unconscious and in the care of Corinne, who'd already started applying some of her proprietary healing potions to speed up his recovery.

"You know we're going to have to talk about him at some point," Mom said gently. She, too, was watching Caspian while Corrine administered some of the good stuff in her healing arsenal. Mom could read me like an open book, anyway. It didn't come as a surprise that she'd already figured it out.

I rested my head on her shoulder, then sighed. "Soon, Mom. Soon."

"I know, baby," she replied and dropped another kiss on the top of my head.

We were all still on edge, somehow. It was as if none of us could rest and relax until the mountain was purged of daemons. There were still thousands of them, now roaming freely through the city's levels. I used my True Sight to follow some of them around. They were looking for us, for the Exiled Maras and the allies. Their red eyes glimmered with the hunger for violence. They wanted us all dead, after all. They'd been indoctrinated to the point of no return.

"Rush, Amina, Laughlan, and Vesta have brought us up to speed," Derek said, keeping his gaze fixed on the ice dragons as they approached the mountain. "They told us everything, from the beginning of the daemon and Exiled Mara alliance to the present day. Based on their accounts, we've concluded that the only way for us to push the daemons into submission and force them to agree to a peace treaty is to beat the fear of GASP into them."

"Therefore, we need to set an example," Field added, standing next to him and Sofia. "The remaining daemon cities will now see who they've messed with."

Zane chuckled softly, lying on his side in the tall grass. "They've been asking for it for millennia. It's about time someone put us back in our place."

He briefly exchanged glances with Fiona, who was just ten feet away with her parents, before they both resumed watching what was about to unfold.

"First, we need ice," Derek muttered.

The ice dragons flew around the mountain base and riddled it with billions of ice shards. They raised a thick and extremely tall wall around Azure Heights and extended a mile-and-a-half stretch around the base, as well. It sealed the daemon army in.

I could see the confused and fearful looks on the daemons' faces as they realized what was happening. Some of them rushed toward the base and tried to get off the mountain but couldn't. The ice was thick and sturdy enough that not even their catapults could break it. They did try, though.

And they failed miserably. Soon enough, panic struck them.

Blaze, Heath, and the other fire dragons flew out next, while the ice dragons returned to our side. Thousands of daemon soldiers were stuck in Azure Heights. They could see the fire dragons coming their way. Blaze had obliterated the Death Claws in the early stages of the siege. Their ballistae were partially disabled. There were too many fire-breathers this time.

I could see the daemons' expressions change as they understood what was going to happen next. They were pale and wide-eyed. Some tried to hide. Others hit the ice wall with their hatchets and swords even harder. But nothing would stop the ensuing inferno.

The fire dragons converged on the mountain and released thick showers of flames. Fire engulfed the mountain from top to bottom. Nothing and no one was spared. Within seconds, the whole of Azure Heights was burning. Orange flames licked at the evening sky. The mountain had turned into an enormous torch.

The daemons screamed as they were burned alive. The pit wolves we hadn't managed to rescue from their ranks were lost, too. The bodies we hadn't been able to recover were suddenly given a funeral of sorts.

Zane stood up, watching the mountain as it burned. He walked forward and stopped in front of us, facing the inferno. He sighed, then put his arms out.

"Forgive them. They knew that what they were doing was wrong, but they've paid the price now," he muttered. I wasn't sure who he was praying to, in particular, but someone did need to say a few words, anyway. I felt sorry for the daemons, despite everything they'd put us through. They'd been so brainwashed and taught to hurt and feed on the innocent, that there wasn't much of a way back out of the darkness for them. "Welcome them," Zane added. "For they were innocent and did not deserve to die like this. Spare us. We've tried to restore the balance. Guide their souls into yourselves, Hermessi. Welcome them into your arms. Tomorrow, they will flow with the rivers, they will grow with the trees, they will fly with the winds, and they will grow with the flowers."

Only when he mentioned the Hermessi did I realize that Zane had started to believe in them for the first time since he'd heard the legends. He'd seen what had happened to Shaytan. He'd heard me talk about Ramin. He'd understood that the elements were real and indeed powerful on Neraka.

Maybe that was a good place to start Neraka's healing, in a way —with the forgotten forces that still animated it, that gave life but also took it away.

We all stood there, quietly, as the dragons torched the entire damn mountain, from top to bottom, until not a single scream could be heard. All the daemons were dead. Everything was gradually turning to ashes as black smoke billowed and stretched above it.

"And that's the end of Azure Heights," I whispered.

"The end of a pretty-looking hell," Fiona added.

Part of me couldn't believe it.

After everything we'd been through, it was finally over. We'd experienced a lengthy and intense nightmare over the past couple of weeks—which, by the way, felt more like years. In the end, it had brought us closer together. It had put us through incredible trials and tribulations. We'd walked out of it all still breathing, albeit a little roughed up.

There was a hole in my soul.

But hope was blossoming in my heart again.

35

SCARLETT

It took a while for all of us to get together and just... talk.

Azure Heights burned in the background, while we set up camp by one of the rivers flowing through the field. The witches cast a protective spell around us, making sure that no other daemon would be reckless enough to disturb us. We'd been through enough already.

The body count was exceptionally high, but the worst part was over. There was a new world order coming to Neraka, and it started with Zane nominating Velnias as his right hand. He tasked him with reaching out to the daemon cities and conveying Zane's message: either they all got on board and backed away from hurting the Imen and other Nerakians, or they died.

To make sure that his point got across, Velnias enlisted the assistance of several fire and ice dragons to join him, along with the fighters that Derek had brought over from Calliope.

Once we were made aware of the time discrepancy that Lumi's protective shield had caused on Neraka, we became even more aware of the damage that could be done if the wrong people got their hands on swamp witch magic.

We brought our parents and families up to speed with every detail of our mission, from the moment we'd set foot on Neraka until the moment they came to fetch us with their little gemstones. It took us several hours to cover every essential topic, to explain what had driven the daemons and the Exiled Maras to band together, and what they'd gotten wrong when they reached out to us for "help".

"So, in the end, it all came down to the dragon," Derek concluded, after he'd listened carefully to all our accounts. "They didn't know we had dragons."

"Basically, yes," Harper replied with a nod. She sat by Caspian's side. He'd been enveloped in a glowing blue spell designed by Corrine to speed up his healing process. "They would've handled us swiftly, otherwise. I've seen what tricks they employed and the lengths that they were willing to go to in order to get what they wanted. But when they saw Blaze, their whole plan was turned upside down, and they had to improvise while they got to know him better. Unfortunately for them, they could never catch him alone."

"And the longer they spent trying to fool us, the more cracks appeared in their story," Fiona added, sitting next to Zane and her parents. They'd already made the introductions, and, based on Yelena and Benedict's expressions, they were still adjusting.

Corrine took a seat in the tall grass next to Lumi and the Daughters, offering Lumi a bowl of water with a mixture of herbs inside. "Drink this, little witch," Corrine said, smiling. "It will give you some strength."

"Thank you," Lumi murmured. She took long sips from the herbal water, watching us all with curiosity.

"What about the souls?" Tejus asked, giving Harper a brief, worried glance. "Can they be healed?"

Lumi nodded slowly. "I need to fix myself, first. It will take a few days, but I can help with that. Soul-eating itself was discovered by accident, but it has roots in swamp witch magic. We don't know who came up with it first among the daemons, and therefore we can't investigate its origins as a ritual. But I've seen it done before in other worlds throughout my travels. A consumed soul can be fully healed, provided it wasn't consumed in its entirety. If there's even a wisp left, I can fix it with my magic."

"Just like with Neraka, I suppose," I muttered. "It will take some time, but it will recover, eventually."

Neha smiled. "We wouldn't be here if it weren't for you," she said, then looked at our parents and elders. "You are all lucky to have brought such noble creatures to life. Cherish them."

"We most certainly will," Derek replied. "This was supposed to be a simple recon mission, and yet they managed to overthrow an entire kingdom. There isn't a day that goes by that I'm not in awe of what our people can do."

"You were all unbelievable," Sofia added. "You've managed to pull through some truly extraordinary circumstances. Your critical thinking and fast reflexes have put you ahead in the game. It didn't matter how well armed or magically equipped the enemy was. Their numbers didn't matter, either. You analyzed the situation and went straight for the right scenario. We are proud of you all."

I couldn't help but blush.

We went on talking for a while, and Derek and Sofia got better acquainted with Neha and Nevis. Lumi had already been brought up to speed with what had been happening in Eritopia. She'd been under such duress that she hadn't even had the time to grieve her sisters' deaths properly. I could see the sadness in her white eyes, though. It was going to make its way to the surface, soon.

Fortunately for her, she had the Daughters and our Shadian witches with her. Lumi, the last of her kind, wasn't truly that alone. Especially since all it took was one swamp witch to create another.

"You said swamp witches are made, not born," Corrine said, watching her intently. "How does that work?"

Lumi sighed, staring at the campfire just fifty feet away. "A swamp witch picks an apprentice," she explained briefly. "First, there's a trial of trust. The swamp witch must be able to trust the apprentice with all the knowledge, including the thousands of words we didn't record in that triple-tome. Then comes the theory part. That's just a lot of reading, really. Then comes the practice. The beauty of the power of the Word is that, as long as the pronunciation is flawless, a spell will be cast. With experience comes the witch's ability to write the spells from memory. Once the teacher decides it's time, the apprentice will be subjected to one final test, before she's given her markings," she added, pointing at her tattoos.

"What's the test about?" Viola asked.

"It's different from one apprentice to another. But they all involve pain, misery, grief, and sacrifice. The apprentice must be tested. Her resolve must be flawless. Her dignity unbreakable. Her loyalty eternal," Lumi said.

"I'm still amazed at how you managed to survive for so long," I replied, shaking my head slowly. "How did you keep your sanity throughout the years?"

Lumi smirked. "Who said I'm sane?" she shot back, chuckling. She then exhaled, resuming her serious face. "I tried to kill myself many times," she added, her voice low. "Whenever they took the gag off, it was the first thing I attempted. After a while, though, understanding that the daemons and the Maras weren't going to let me die so easily, I started bracing for the future. I lived for the day that I would be free again, so I could watch the city burn."

She pointed over her shoulder at Azure Heights, which was still blazing behind her.

"Achievement unlocked, then." I scoffed. "It's why you were really selective about the spells you gave them, right?"

Lumi nodded. "Absolutely. My luck was that they weren't aware of how much a swamp witch really knows. We keep our secrets well-hidden. Even the Maras couldn't tell if I was holding out on them or not. They had no choice but to take what I gave them."

I shifted my focus to Patrik, who was sitting by the fire with Draven, Laughlan, Ryker, and the other Druids who had come on the rescue mission. We exchanged glances and smiles, and Mom nudged my shoulder with hers.

"Are we going to talk about that yet?" she asked, raising an eyebrow.

My face caught fire. "About what?"

"Are you serious?" She chuckled softly, while my dad watched our exchange with childlike confusion.

"What are you two talking about?" he asked.

Mom gave him the "are you blind?" look, then grinned. "You of all people should be able to tell when a guy is completely and utterly in love with a girl," she said.

That just confused my dad even more. I sighed in response.

"Well, it's only been days for you guys, but for us it was weeks," I replied. "To be honest, I've had a bit of a crush on him since before we got here, but—"

"He was grieving, wasn't he?" Dad asked. "The Lamia. What was her name?"

"Kyana," I muttered. "Yeah. He's still grieving, I guess. But we just got closer, and... Well, you know."

"Know what?" Dad replied, now feigning confusion.

I couldn't help but roll my eyes, while Mom groaned. "Oh, come on, Jeramiah. It's obvious our little girl can't share the details of her relationship with a Druid we barely know anything about!" she said, and I did not miss the double-edged blade there. My mom had a way of using sarcasm to her advantage.

I laughed. "Mom, I promise, I will dish as soon as we decompress properly," I said. "And, Dad, try not to intimidate him or anything. After what he's been through, believe me when I say you won't scare him."

"That's a shame," Dad replied, grinning. "I had this whole hazing ritual planned out. Sort of a 'welcome to the Novak family' ceremony."

My stomach churned. "Ugh, please don't. Not that you'll scare him off, Dad, don't get me wrong. It'll just be... lame."

We all laughed this time. I'd missed this. The little stings we delivered. Our inside jokes. The feeling of calm and hope that my mom and dad constantly inspired me with. They were truly irreplaceable. I would've been miserable without them in the long run.

Good thing that shield came down.

I wanted to say something, but my attention was captured by a spine-tingling roar. I jumped to my feet, instantly recognizing it. Hundurr was still by Colton's body, refusing to leave his side. Jovi and Dmitri were trying to coax him into doing just that, so they could prepare Colton for the funeral ceremony in the morning.

"Whoa there, boy," Jovi muttered, putting his hands out in a defensive gesture. "Nobody wants to piss you off, now."

I rushed to their side and reached out to Hundurr. Both Jovi and Dmitri were stunned by the sudden change in his behavior, as he stilled and lowered his head, allowing me to touch him.

"Cuz, I didn't peg you for a pit wolf charmer." Dmitri chuckled.

"Well, I didn't either, but we seem to get along," I replied, then focused on Hundurr. "It's okay. We need to prepare Colton for his funeral, Hundurr. I know. I know you're grieving. I know it hurts. We have to bury a lot of friends in the morning, but... we have to. You know that."

He whimpered softly, then settled on the ground, next to Colton.

Tears streamed down my cheeks as I got closer to him. It hurt me deeply to see him like this, but I had to break him out of his state. It was time for the real Hundurr to come back out.

"The pack leader is dead, Hundurr," I said, keeping my voice low. "He took your place, you know. Your pack needs a new alpha now. What are you going to do?"

Hundurr looked up at me, his red eyes sparkling with an emotion I'd yet to understand.

"Will you wallow here in misery, or will you snap out of it and assume control of your people once more? They need someone to lead them, Hundurr. You've been on the other side; you know what to do. You know what works, what doesn't... Come on," I added.

He exhaled, then put his head down, breathing heavily.

I watched him for a minute, then moved back and turned to face Jovi and Dmitri. "I think you guys should give him another hour or two," I murmured. "He's obviously in a foul mood. I mean, understandably so. He just needs some time."

Jovi and Dmitri's expressions froze when they looked behind me. Their eyes nearly popped out. Their jaws dropped. I glanced over my shoulder and lost my breath, too.

Hundurr was lying on his side, heaving and whimpering. His bones started to crack. His skin began to ripple. His muscles twitched, and he howled from the pain. We all stood back as we watched him transform.

Patrik rushed to my side, watching the entire extraordinary scene unfold before our very eyes. Hundurr was turning! His reddish mane emerged from the top of his head as he regained his humanoid figure.

One head, two legs, and two arms. A broad chest. Strong back with ropes of muscle.

His skin turned white. His hair grew long, wavy, and orange-red.

He grunted and groaned as he rolled over in the grass. For the first time, he'd managed to return to his Adlet form, after two years trapped inside the body of a pit wolf.

I gasped when Hundurr raised his head and looked at me. The only aspect of him that I still recognized were his big, beautiful red eyes. Those stayed the same—perhaps like a scar of his pit wolf existence.

"Hundurr?" I murmured, staring at him.

He looked down at himself, panting, then stood up in all his naked glory. Jovi, Dmitri, and Patrik were the first to grumble and turn around. Hundurr was a gorgeous creature. His frame was imposing, his limbs long and muscular. His abs were perfectly sculpted, and the human expression on his face could make any girl simply swoon.

Had I not been in love with Patrik already, I would've definitely fallen for Hundurr because... *Good grief, he's superb.*

"Can someone get this guy some clothes before Scarlett passes out?!" Jovi cried out, prompting Dmitri and even Patrik to burst into laughter.

Blaze showed up with a pair of pants, which he handed over to Hundurr, who stared at them as if he didn't know what purpose they served.

"It's okay, just put them on," Blaze said. "I'm guessing it'll take a while before more of your fur comes back, and we're all squeamish about naked dudes here, for some reason."

"Yeah, *you'd* know!" Jovi shot back.

Hundurr nodded slowly, then put the pants on and looked around, still speechless and in shock.

"You did it!" I said, moving toward him.

He nodded again. I ran toward him quickly, then jumped and hugged him, in his humanoid form, for the first time. He stilled. Then I felt his arms wrap around my waist as he reacted and hugged me back. Half a minute later, he breathed deeply, then stepped back and gave me a soft smile.

"I did it. Thanks to you," he said, his voice low and raspy.

Patrik joined us and rested a hand on Hundurr's shoulder.

"Good to see you made it out in the end," Patrik said.

"You and Scarlett helped me. I... Sorry," Hundurr replied, shaking his head and frowning. "I'm still trying to adjust."

"Take your time," Patrik said. "It takes a while. It's okay."

It was okay. It really was.

This was beginning to look more and more like a good conclusion to our Nerakian adventure. If anyone deserved a damn good happy ending, it was Hundurr. He'd been through hell and back. And now, he had his body back.

36

HARPER

None of us could take our eyes off Hundurr, especially those of us who had had the good fortune of fighting with him. He was tall and handsome, with a feral beauty that was otherwise difficult to reproduce. He was a little dazed and was still adjusting to his body, but the smile on his face said everything.

The Adlets who had helped us back in Azure Heights all jumped to their feet and gathered around him, lavishing him with praise and tight hugs. I had a feeling his kids would be over the moon the next time they saw him.

I then looked at Caspian, pleased to see over forty percent of his body already healing. The glowing membrane that Corrine had put around him was certainly working. Soon enough, he'd open his eyes and meet my family.

"You really love him, don't you?" Mom asked, then dropped another kiss on my forehead.

I gave her a weak smile and a nod. "I mean, it's obvious, isn't it?"

"You're beaming like the morning sun," Serena replied, grinning with delight. "Honestly, I didn't think it would happen this soon."

"Me neither," I said, then chuckled softly.

"Well, I was hit over the head with a boulder when I met your mother," Dad replied. "Figuratively speaking. You never know when or how it happens. But, when it does, you just have to ride it out. Chances are it will last a lifetime."

"You'll like him, I'm sure of it," I murmured. "He nearly got himself killed for me."

"Frankly, I'm liking all of your new friends," Dad said, nodding at our allies.

What wasn't there to like, anyway? Neha and Pheng-Pheng were unbelievably fierce. The Adlets were loyal and brave. The Imen were extraordinarily resilient, with a rich cultural heritage—they knew how to make the most of their short lifespans. They pursued art, beauty, and education. They made the world a better place. The Dhaxanians were cold and distant, but they could be extraordinary allies and were true to their word, despite their unconventional techniques. They'd understood that with great power came some responsibility.

The Maras... Most of them had been horrendous, but that was simply because of the toxic culture that their forefathers had perpetuated from the moment they'd come to Neraka. They didn't know any better. They didn't want to stray from the herd—those who did were quickly ostracized and punished, or, in Caspian and Sienna's case, for example, forced into a blood oath. There was good among them. We'd saved those who had turned against their people and had understood that killing innocent creatures for pleasure or to chase a temporary high was wrong.

And even the daemons were subject to massive changes. Unlike the Maras, however, they required a firm and brutal hand to put them back in their place. They didn't respond to other kinds of reinforcement, unfortunately. But it was all for the greater good. Whether they liked it or not, they were going to change their ways.

They were going to stop hunting Imen. They were going to wean themselves off the souls. That was just so wrong and unnatural, so cruel and vicious. There was no room in this world or any other for such behavior.

Peyton and Wyrran brought Farrah and Rowan closer to the fire, and we all gathered around them. Rowan had come to and was clearly unhappy with where she was. Farrah was quiet and gloomy, most likely getting used to the idea that judgment and punishment were coming. Sienna was fighting back tears as she leaned against Tobiah and stared at her mother. Rowan sneered at her.

"You're a traitor to your people," Rowan said. "I'm ashamed to call you my daughter."

"Tough luck, Mom. I'm the only one you've got," Sienna shot back.

Derek and Sofia came closer, accompanied by Jax and Hansa. Peyton and Wyrran took a few steps back, while Nevis and Neha watched from the edge of the circle we'd formed around them.

"We didn't get all the Exiled Maras, did we?" Derek asked.

Jax shook his head. "No. Some definitely escaped before the mountain base was sealed off. There were plenty of tunnels they could've reopened to get out of the city."

"That's fine," Nevis replied. "They will all be captured, eventually. They will pay for their crimes."

"We'll take these hostiles back to Calliope for judgment, though," Derek said.

Rubia, one of the Daughters, scoffed. "We won't be as forgiving as the last time, rest assured."

"I would like to kindly request that we form a tribunal and judge each of the Exiled Maras individually," Jax interjected, his brow furrowed. "Some are guiltier than others. We'll need to ascertain who was deliberately working with the Lords to perpetuate these horrors, and who was simply afraid or under an oath."

"Do you not agree that they deserve punishment?" Safira asked.

"I most certainly do," Jax replied. "I just think the penalty must also fit the crime. They will all pay, of course. But I trust we are able to quantify the damage they've done and to punish them accordingly. I will make sure to set a noteworthy example."

"Oh, please!" Rowan groaned, rolling her eyes. "Just because we found a way to elevate our existence doesn't mean we're guilty of anything. It was always about the survival of the fittest. It's not our fault we're designed to lead!"

"That's a load of crap," Jax hissed. "You had a chance to do something better with yourselves, without destroying the lives of thousands of Imen. You squandered the opportunities you were given, and you *chose* to torture and kill. At least the daemons ate souls to prolong their lives. Not saying they had a better reason, but you were in it for the temporary high, and nothing else. That is insanely superficial, and it's what led to your downfall."

"Well, that and their greed," I muttered from the side. "They nearly wiped out the Iman population and decided to bring in some Eritopians to replenish their soul food source."

"Yeah, you picked the wrong supernaturals to mess with this time," Derek replied, raising an eyebrow. "A new age is dawning. We embrace diversity and peace. Your 'survival of the fittest' is just a shtick, a pathetic excuse to justify your cruelty and evil ways. We all see right through it. Which is why you're now here, in such a pathetic state."

"Time's up," Hansa added with a cold smirk.

A groan next to me made my heart skip a beat. I looked down to my left and saw Caspian open his eyes and blink several times. The glow dimmed down but stayed present, as the spell continued to work on him. His eyes found mine, and he exhaled sharply.

"You're okay," he murmured.

I leaned forward and kissed him softly. His lips and most of his face had healed. His jade eyes glimmered with relief and hope as he looked me over from head to toe, then smiled.

"Of course," I replied. "In part, thanks to you."

"You drew Shaytan away before he could finish me off."

I nodded. "Well, what kind of world was I fighting for, if it didn't have you in it, huh?" I said, smiling.

Mom, Dad, and Serena came closer, giving him warm smiles. I couldn't help but chuckle at the confused look on his face.

"Caspian of House Kifo, this is my family," I added. "Hazel, my mom. Tejus, my dad. And Serena, my awesome sister."

"Aww." Serena giggled. "I think we're both competing for that title," she said, then shifted her focus back to Caspian. "It's an honor to meet you, Caspian. And don't worry, we'll totally drill you with lots of uncomfortable questions once you're back on your feet. No one gets away from the Hellswans' fiancé probe."

Mom dropped to her knees and placed her palm on Caspian's chest. "I know you're connected to Harper now. And I know you're becoming one of us, in a way. Like Serena said, we'll definitely get to talk later, but, for the time being, thank you."

Caspian blinked several times. "What are you thanking me for?"

"For saving our daughter's life, more than once," Dad replied firmly. "We know everything you've done for her and for GASP. The Hellswans are forever in your debt."

Caspian nodded slowly, his aura blooming into a bright gold hue. I could feel him again—his love for me, his hope returning, his awkwardness in front of my parents... his relief. He could breathe again, much like the rest of us.

After Rowan and Farrah were put away inside a charmed circle in the capsule, the rest of us caught up with our friends and family. We introduced our beaus and better halves to everyone. Caia and Blaze, however, kept quiet for a little while longer—though everyone could see right through them. Heath, in particular, was struggling not to chuckle whenever the dragon and the fae exchanged longing glances before focusing on the group conversation again.

About an hour later, we all had a pretty good idea of what we needed to do next, at least where Neraka was concerned. Caspian was up in a sitting position, his breathing even and his vision cleared. Nevis's wounds had closed, too, but, just like Lumi and me, pieces of his soul were missing. It was impossible to describe how that felt, but the looks we exchanged spoke volumes instead.

"I think it's best if all the Exiled Maras are repatriated to Calliope," Derek suggested, looking at Draven and the Daughters for their approval. They all nodded in return.

"The guilty will stand a fair trial," Draven replied. "The rebels who worked with GASP to overthrow the Lords of Azure Heights will be allowed to return to White City."

"You're all welcome," Jax interjected, looking at Caspian, Sienna, Peyton, Aymon, and all the other rebel Maras who had survived. "White City will be your home, and you will live among Maras who respect all living creatures and give grace for every drop of blood they get to drink."

His wards stood behind him, carefully analyzing each of the rebel Maras and Imen. One of them placed a hand on Jax's shoulder. "Milord, what about the Imen? They've been repeatedly mindbent. Their memories and wills require a cleanse."

Jax nodded. "Yes. First thing in the morning, we'll summon all the Imen to this camp. We'll override their mind-bending en masse, now that I have you, my faithful wards, back in the fold."

"Wait, en masse?" Wyrran asked, frowning slightly.

"It needs to be done. We have to make sure that the Exiled Maras no longer have any control over you or your people. We've seen it with Alles and Dion, may their souls rest in peace," Jax replied. "Neither of them was aware that Alles had been mind-

bent as a sleeper agent. There are many of them in similar condi-
tions across Neraka. It's better to just wipe the slate clean."

"You'll wipe our memories?" Wyrran muttered.

Jax shook his head. "No. I can only do this with my wards'
assistance. Consider it a cleanup operation. I'll simply remove all
the Exiled Mara corruptions. Your memories and your wills will be
all yours—even what was repressed."

Neha then stepped forward, smiling at us.

"I believe it's time we discuss our roles, as separate species,
going forward," she said. "I will continue to lead the Manticores.
Our culture remains, and our people will thrive. However, I think
it's time we all sit down and discuss a peace treaty among
ourselves—the Manticores, the Dhaxanians, the Adlets, and the
Imen. Our alliance should be strong and tight before we engage in
any kind of peace talks with the daemons."

"I agree," Nevis said. "The Imen were left on their own when
the daemons and the Maras banded together. We allowed them to
divide us further, and we wound up isolated, stuck in desert gorges
and patches of woods and two measly mountains. This time, we all
need to stand together. The daemons must understand that if they
mess with one of us, they mess with all of us."

We all nodded in agreement. Scarlett smiled, then looked at
Hundurr.

"What do you think, pack leader?" she asked him.

Hundurr's red eyes lit up as he smiled. "I haven't heard that in a
while," he replied. "But yes, I agree. The Adlets are on board."

Behind him, the Adlets growled their approval. The Imen, on
the other hand, seemed a little lost, looking at each other and
shrugging. Wyrran noticed their expressions and came forward,
wearing a strained smile.

"You know, the Imen have been through a lot," he said. "Right
now, we don't really have a leader, someone to speak on our behalf.
But, if all the Imen present agree, I'd like to put myself forward as a

representative, at least until we come together, resettle, and hold an election."

The other Imen hummed and nodded. Once Wyrran was pleased with their reaction, he turned to face Neha, Nevis, and Hundurr, and bowed reverently.

"Then, on behalf of the Imen, it would be an honor to join this alliance. You are right. We are all stronger together. I think this alliance should extend, as well—not just to defense against the daemons, but also across economic and social aspects of our life on Neraka. We will have to agree on territories to occupy, and that should also include shared regions, where everyone is welcome. I know the Dhaxanians and the Manticores, in particular, like to keep to themselves. But we, as Imen, are very inclusive and welcoming. We will gladly offer our cities for open markets and neutral territories."

"The only way for Neraka to not repeat its past mistakes is for us to move forward," Zane interjected, then stood up. He looked around and smiled at each of us, his gaze temporarily softening on Fiona. "I will assume the daemon throne. Velnias and GASP's troops are already out there, conveying my message to my people. And I agree. You all need to band together. Once your alliance is set in stone, I will gladly sit down and negotiate a peace treaty. I'll make sure to rein the daemons in, from now on. Technically speaking, I should tell you not to worry, that everything will be okay, now that I'm in charge. But we all know that that isn't always going to be the case. Something might happen. I could very well die at some point. And my successor might not be as tolerant as me. So, yes. Be good friends and stand up tall. Don't let us think you'll allow us to walk all over you, ever again."

Nevis smirked. "Spoken like a true king."

"Hear, hear!" Neha exclaimed, then clapped her hands.

Soon enough, the thousand-strong crowd erupted in cheers and applause. Our celebration echoed across the field and trickled into the gorges. I glanced over my shoulder and spotted the mass of red eyes watching us from the pitch blackness of the Valley of Screams.

"Daemon hunters are out," I muttered.

"Good," Zane replied. "If they're smart, they'll be here by morning, pledging their allegiance to me. Oh! And before I forget, though I shouldn't, because it's a critical issue and part of why we were in this mess in the first place... There will be no more soul-eating. It will be made illegal and will be punishable by death. It's the only way that it'll get the daemons to stop."

Once more, we cheered and applauded. I caught a glimpse of Fiona—she encouraged Zane with her bright eyes and smile, but, whenever he looked away, I saw the faint sadness pulling her shoulders down. I had a feeling she was concerned about the status of their relationship. My guess was that she was still wondering whether she should stay here or not. Zane had just made it clear that he wasn't going anywhere.

"You know, we've done this with Eritopia already, and it's proven to be extremely successful," Derek then said. "What do you, leaders of the Nerakian people, think of GASP opening a base here? We would bring our agents to train and introduce your fighters to our methods and policies. We would help you police your criminals and maintain peace. Most importantly, should talks of war ever emerge, GASP will help mediate and protect the Nerakian people, no matter what. That includes protection from outside forces."

"The In-Between is still a vast unknown to us," Sofia added. "We've barely identified and recorded a few galaxies. There is much of it that we've yet to understand. Should there be an external threat against Neraka, GASP will come to your aid. Always."

"Well, my daemons do need fear struck into them," Zane replied with a shrug. "Provided you bring some dragons into the mix, I'll be more than happy to support your proposal," he added, grinning.

Nevis, Neha, and Hundurr nodded.

"Sounds reasonable," Neha said. "I'm profoundly impressed by GASP agents already, and so is my Pheng-Pheng." She chuckled softly, nodding at her daughter, who, in return, gave her a grin, then winked at me. "I would love nothing more than to see what your expertise can do here, on Neraka, on a large scale."

Caspian slowly leaned against me, so he could whisper in my ear.

"You do realize I'm not going to White City unless you come with me, right?" he asked.

For a split second, I was thrilled to lose myself in his dark jade eyes again. "I'm with GASP. I live in The Shade. I mean, I'll be moving around a lot, anyway, with whatever missions I get."

"Then I will go with you, wherever GASP takes us," he said, then frowned. "Provided they accept my application."

Dad chuckled. "Don't worry about that, Lord Kifo. You're already in. Harper tells me your combat skills are impressive. You'd be a valuable asset to GASP."

"There you go," I said to Caspian, giving him my warmest smile. "It's settled."

Caspian smiled. It had been a while since I'd seen him so full of life and brimming with energy. I was pale by comparison but being connected to him as a sentry seemed to make it all better—if only for a while.

The worst part was over now. We had a great future ahead of us already.

37

FIONA

Corrine set up a temporary hospital and treatment area along with our camp, by the river. With Ibrahim, Arwen, and Shayla's help, she also added lodging and basic amenities to our temporary settlement. We knew it would be a while before we'd leave—not because we couldn't, but because we all had unfinished business here. It was all about Neraka. Its people deserved a clean, fresh start, and we'd promised we'd help.

Our parents and friends stayed with us, too, as well as Derek and Sofia. Aida had a good hold on Calliope for the time being, and Ben and Rose were more than capable of managing The Shade in Derek and Sofia's absence, even with the island extension works still in progress.

We gave ourselves some time to get our affairs in order, to bury our dead, and to assist Neha, Nevis, Hundurr, and Zane in establishing peace terms and alliances. As expected, the daemons didn't immediately jump on board. Velnias, the pacifists, our dragons, and GASP troops had to put their feet over the fire, almost literally, to get the entire kingdom to understand and accept that change was coming.

It was going to take a while, but it was worth it. With Shaytan dead and the Council virtually obliterated, Zane had little trouble gaining control over the daemon kingdom. About five days after we destroyed Azure Heights, all the daemon cities had conceded and accepted Zane's rule, albeit begrudgingly.

Zane established his leadership and enlisted the pacifists on his Council, with Velnias as his right hand. Mose and his brother both had survived and had also made it into the daemon government system in high positions. Firm elders were needed to guide the daemons, particularly the younglings. All the Iman, Manticore, Adlet, and Dhaxanian prisoners were released and returned to their people. The pit wolves were freed and reunited with the Adlets—Hundurr made sure to help them all regain their natural forms.

The daemons were put on a "detox" program. Some didn't fare very well and required imprisonment. Those who flat-out rejected Zane and tried to organize a rebellion were promptly arrested. Those most culpable in their support of Shaytan and his murderous policies were not given a second chance—they were deeply and irreparably addicted to souls. There was no way out for them.

Some of Zane's brothers repented and bowed before him. Shaytan's harem was disbanded; all his wives were given their own homes wherever they wanted. Some moved to other cities altogether. The only one who stayed in the palace was his mother. She'd earned her seat next to her son's throne, after all.

I didn't go with Zane. We didn't even get to talk about our relationship, and for good reason. Fixing his kingdom was a matter of the utmost urgency, and I had a ton of GASP issues to deal with by the river, including a solid debriefing and assisting the locals and our witches in rebuilding Azure Heights. My strength helped speed certain things up.

The mountain was cleansed by the dragon fires. We repopulated its flora and fauna, then proceeded to rebuild each level of the city. Azure Heights was designated as the new capital of the Iman state. The allies engaged in lengthy talks over territory distribution and the sharing of certain resources. Trade routes were established, and there was a consensus for a comprehensive Nerakian legislation to which all species would adhere—this had to do with the basics, like murder, theft, corruption, and so on.

As expected, the territory splits were pretty straightforward. The Dhaxanians stuck to the northern parts of the continent, where the temperatures were below zero. The Manticores preferred the hot and dry areas, as well as the marshes. The Adlets stuck to the hills and densely forested areas, while the Imen were perfectly happy with plains and southern mountain chains, as well as shoreline territories.

The daemons kept to the underground cities, with hunting areas carefully outlined in specific locations, including the Valley of Screams. No one was allowed to hunt or feed off the Imen. That was punishable by death, with no exception. It worked as a deterrent.

Jax and his wards gathered all the Imen and performed the mass cleansing he'd talked about. They were all cleared of previous mind-bending, their memories fully restored. Demios was brought back from the ocean-shore village where Arrah had kept him safe. Once he remembered everything that had happened, he knew what he had to do—he applied to become a part of the newly formed Iman government and put forward his candidacy for mayor of Azure Heights. He was going to compete against Wyrran, but they were both willing to support one another, no matter who won. Demios didn't have too much time to suffer over Arrah's death. The Imen kept him constantly busy, helping him get involved in crucial legislative and territorial conversations.

Most of the Exiled Maras who had fled were eventually captured. The rebels were kept separate, while Caspian, Sienna,

Peyton, and Cadmus helped identify those who could be repatriated to White City. The others faced prison for a minimum of five
hundred years for what they had done.

Caspian was going to be with Harper, and we all welcomed
him as a part of GASP. Tobiah insisted he go with Sienna—they
would've been allowed to stay on Neraka, given his daemon
heritage, but he wanted a fresh start. White City sounded like a
good place to do just that, as long as Sienna was with him. Their
bond was strong, and I couldn't help but admire their dedication
to making that relationship work.

I knew I needed to talk to Zane about us, but I didn't even
know how to bring it up. It took hours to travel from Neraka to
Calliope, and the Daughters didn't have the juice to create portals
here like they'd done between Calliope and The Shade. The
distance wasn't an issue, per se. But Zane and I were barely getting
to know each other. Yes, we were deeply in love, but we both
needed to commit and talk about how we would make this work.

As I stood in the special guests' area at his coronation ceremony, just outside the royal palace in Infernis, I knew it was only a
matter of time before we sat down and discussed things. It was just
hard to find the right moment.

It was eerie to be back in Infernis, surrounded by thousands of
daemons, along with our friends and allies. Nobody wanted to eat
our souls or kill us this time. The palace itself had been restored to
its former glory, with gold leaf and precious gemstones encrusted
in intricate details across the walls. Fires burned in massive, cere-
monial pits. Flower garlands dressed the front columns from top
to bottom.

"It's obnoxiously hot down here," Derek grumbled, loosening
his shirt collar.

None of our Shadians or Eritopians seemed comfortable,
except for those of us who had spent days down here already. I
actually enjoyed the heat. My vampire nature kept me cold, but all
the lava lakes bubbling nearby did a good job of making me feel a

bit more human. It was the one thing I'd missed since I'd been turned, along with the inability to stuff my face with a decent burger without retching. I couldn't fix the latter, but Infernis was definitely helping with the former.

"It's actually grown on me," I replied with a giggle.

"It makes sense. You've only been a vampire for what, twenty years?" Derek asked, and I nodded. "You're still in touch with your human side. I've long since gotten accustomed to my cold nature. I doubt I would ever readjust to these temperatures comfortably."

"Oh, shush." Sofia chuckled. "I'm willing to bet we'll all miss this once we go back to The Shade. This place feels like a spa, complete with a lava sauna!"

"Mm-hm, does wonders for my complexion," Hazel chimed in, making us giggle.

I stayed with my crew throughout the ceremony. Velnias and the pacifists organized the entire thing. The majority of the attendees were pleased to see Zane ascend to the throne. Some were quite miserable, judging by the sour looks on their faces, but they had no choice. Change was coming, and they couldn't stop it.

Zane's mother, Derya, stood by his side, clad in a gold dress. Her long hair was braided with a million tiny diamonds, and her red eyes twinkled with pride as she watched her son bow before Velnias, so the former High Warden could put the crown on his head.

The crowd erupted in cheers as Zane straightened his back and took center stage, looking at his people. His gaze traveled across the square, finding me among my family members and friends. He gave me a brief, soft smile, then took a deep breath and spoke up, his firm voice thundering across the square.

"I solemnly swear to uphold our new constitution, to pursue peace and righteousness, to protect my people, and to help my kingdom thrive. We are all equals here, and we abide by the rules. We've given in to our weaknesses for far too long, brothers and sisters. It's time for a change, because our nation needs saving," he said. "Our kingdom needs to grow and step away from the vileness. We are not superior. We are no better than the blades of grass above the ground. No better than the rivers flowing through the Valley of Screams. We live, we die, we breathe, and we dream, just like our brothers among the Imen, the Dhaxanians, the Adlets, and the Manticores. We will not thrive until we learn to respect and cherish life. All life!"

The crowd murmured. A round of applause rumbled through the square.

Not everyone was on board. Not fully. Zane smiled. I could tell from the look on his face that he was well aware of that. But they all just needed time and a firm hand. He had both, plus a brilliant mind.

"We will see better days, soon enough," he added. "We do not need to crush those we could instead help thrive along with us. Neraka is our home. The Imen, the Adlets, the Dhaxanians, and the Manticores... They are our people, too. There's a whole universe out there, waiting for us to discover it. The time of petty feuds and frivolous deeds is over. The era of progress and greatness is upon us. I will show you a better way. And I am honored to call you my people. I am proud to represent you and to lead you into the next stage of our existence. I am humbled to wear this crown and establish peace throughout the kingdom. The future is ours, brothers and sisters. Let's make something of it."

The crowd reacted differently this time—better, in fact. Applause thundered in copious rounds. Cheers whistled across the square. Arms were raised, and words of encouragement made it to his ears. Zane couldn't help but smile as he bowed gently before his people.

Shaytan's sons were now free to live as they wished, and so were their mothers. That alone had been incentive enough for them to stand by Zane. The pacifists had done a good job of swaying the public opinion in his favor. The dragons had been equally persuasive with those who weren't willing to cooperate. In the end, most of them did. Most of them accepted their new king.

I knew, deep in my heart, that I loved him now more than ever. However, I didn't know if he still wanted me in his life. Or if this would work. I should've gone up to him that day, but I lacked the courage. I watched him go inside the palace with his new Council, his mother, and his extended family, as his subjects continued to cheer him on.

Maybe a good night's sleep would help me see things more clearly in the morning. Whatever happened next, I knew I had to mean it, to truly want it. And it had to be mutual. In a way, the ball was now in Zane's court. He had the kingdom and the throne. All he had to do was ask me. I probably would've said yes.

38

HARPER

A week had passed since we'd brought Neraka's ordeal to an end. It seemed like yesterday, though. Azure Heights had been rebuilt—this time it was even more beautiful and was filled with open-air public spaces. There was no social segregation of any kind, either. This was a city of Imen that welcomed everyone, from all walks of life.

The Valley of Screams was reassigned to the Imen. Only ten gorges were given to the daemons for hunting. Lumi made sure to set up alarm spells to notify the Imen if anyone broke the territorial rules. After she healed herself and replenished her soul through a comprehensive ritual, she gifted the Imen with swamp witch charms to use in the future—to improve their crops, to preserve their food supplies, to grow their trees, to heal their wounds, and to protect them from any kind of attack. It was her gift to them, the little she could do after thousands of years spent in utter misery.

Caspian made a full recovery. We spent a lot of time together—in one of the bedrooms in the newly rebuilt Palisade, which was now a luxury hotel, or with the others, helping the Imen open new stores and businesses on different city levels.

We spent our evenings walking the streets and talking about what had been, and about what would come to pass. Lumi had given us both something extraordinary. First, she'd removed Caspian's blood oath. He could speak freely again, and he had so many stories to tell.

Second, she subjected me to a ritual to replenish my soul. I felt whole again. I could smile again. I could breathe and relish every second, once more. *The difference that a complete soul makes.*

Of course, she did the same with all the Imen and everyone else who had had their souls nibbled on by the Exiled Maras and the daemons. Nevis was all proud and smirking again, thrilled to have regained his full powers. The Dhaxanian prince's unbreakable frost had returned, and the first thing he did with it was, of course, troll the hell out of Heron. It took Avril a while to explain to both Lucas and Marion that this was just the usual mischief between the Mara and the Dhaxanian.

"I will return to White City and bow before Jax," Caspian muttered as we settled on the edge of an artesian fountain on the fifth level, overlooking the fields, our camp, and the Valley of Screams. Even the air felt different. Better. "He's the Lord of Maras on Calliope, after all. It will be an honor to serve him," he added.

"And you'll be a part of GASP, too," I replied, smiling.

He nodded slowly. "For a minute there, I felt a little lost. Lacking direction. I wanted to thank you and your parents for backing me up on this whole GASP thing. I wasn't sure you'd feel the same way a few days later. You know how emotions can get the better of us, sometimes."

"Don't be silly," I said, watching his hand cover mine on the fountain's edge. "Honestly, I will live anywhere, as long as you're with me. Whether it's The Shade, or Calliope, or, hell, even Neraka. Or any other place. It doesn't matter to me, as long as we're together. We're bound, Caspian, in ways that no one can ever understand—except other sentries, of course."

"I like feeling you this way," he breathed, unable to take his eyes off me. "I don't think I'd ever be able to go back to my life, the way I was before I met you. You're an indelible part of me, now."

"And you're a part of me," I replied. "Therefore, don't ever think my feelings will change. Not even in a thousand years. Maybe it works differently with Maras, but sentries are different. Once our souls are bound, that's it. Game over. I am yours and you are mine for life."

He exhaled sharply, then looked out into the distance and smiled. "I think my parents would've loved you."

"My parents already love you." I giggled. "When Serena and Phoenix decided to stay on Calliope, it shocked Mom and Dad. It took them a while to adjust, even though they fully supported them. Plus there's the portal between Calliope and The Shade. This time, it's a little different. Maybe because they've already had two kids leave to be with their soulmates. It didn't hit them so hard this time around."

I fumbled through my shirt pocket and took out the pendant that Serena had given me. This charmed little trinket had made my misery feel less rancid in the minutes after I'd defeated Shaytan. It had brought back one of my most beautiful memories, in full and vivid color. It had felt as though I'd been right there, with my entire family, around the dinner table.

I wanted Caspian to experience the same—to lovingly remember those he'd loved and lost. So I put the medallion in the palm of his hand and smiled.

"I want you to have this," I said, my voice trembling.

He looked at it for a while, unsure of what it was or what it did. "Thank you," he murmured, then gave me a curious look. "There's a story behind this, huh?"

I chuckled softly and closed his fist around the medallion. "I want you to close your eyes and think about your family. Deep in your mind, hidden beneath years of abuse and suffering, are moments that made you smile... that made you happy. Think of those."

He did as I asked, closing his eyes. He sucked in a breath, his lips stretching into a smile.

"This... This is incredible," he said.

"What do you see?" I asked, my heart swelling at the sight of him looking so happy.

Tears started streaming down his cheeks. "My mom and dad. I'm so tiny. I'm looking up at them. We're on the rooftop, looking at the stars. My dad's telling me about the moons and the legends behind them."

He gasped, then took a deep breath and opened his eyes. The love surging through me like liquid sunshine was all him. He wrapped his arms around me and pulled me close, his mouth crashing into mine as he kissed me with everything he had.

I was overwhelmed. I teared up as well, relishing the taste of him, his emotions burning through me and bringing me even closer to him.

"There isn't much I can do to match this extraordinary gift you've just given me," Caspian said, pulling himself back. He fumbled through his jacket pockets, frowning slightly. He was looking for something. "All I can give you, over and over, is my heart. And... well, this."

He held up a diamond ring, exquisitely crafted in silver. It was beautiful, yet simple.

My heart stopped. I held my breath. My brain just stopped functioning, as I tried to figure out what was going on. Caspian was giving me a ring...

He slipped it on my finger without taking his eyes off me.

"Don't think of it as a proposal," he said. "I know we're still at the beginning of this journey, and I wouldn't want to pressure you in any way. I'm not a stickler for traditions, anyway, and, frankly, after my last experience with an oath," he added, chuckling, "I'm not too nuts about making another one any time soon. But I want you to accept this as a token of how I feel about you."

"Caspian, I..." I croaked, unable to formulate a coherent thought.

"It's the only thing I've got left from my parents," he muttered. "It was my mother's. And I want you to wear it. Whenever you look at it, I want you to remember how much I love you. I'm alive today because of you, Harper. Not just because of what you did with Shaytan, but because of how you pulled me out of my personal darkness and set my soul on fire. I love you."

I broke down, sobbing like a little girl. "I... I love you, too," I managed.

He chuckled. "Then why are you crying?"

"Because I love you, and there are so many feelings bursting through me right now, yours and mine. I'm a little overwhelmed," I replied between hiccups.

Caspian laughed wholeheartedly, then took me in his arms and covered my face in hot, sweet kisses. I welcomed his embrace, hiding my face in that warm space between his head and shoulder, taking deep breaths and savoring his natural, musky scent.

"We're bound, Harper," he whispered. "We're looking at an eternity together. Wherever we choose to spend it, we'll be together."

"Forever," I breathed.

"Mm-hm."

I liked that. I liked that a lot. With my soul complete and my heart filled with undying love, the prospect of being with Caspian for the rest of my life was something that fueled me, much like three suns fueled the entire galaxy and gave life to Neraka.

An eternity together... Yup. Sounds good.

39

FIONA

Two weeks had passed since Zane's coronation. Neraka had made incredible progress since, with substantial help from our witches and the Daughters. Safira and her sisters said that assisting the Nerakians in rebuilding their world was the least they could do, given that they'd been the ones who had allowed the Exiled Maras to get another chance. They were wise and mature enough to take some of the blame, though they couldn't possibly have known what the Maras would do with that opportunity, anyway.

We'd set up a consistent travel schedule with Eritopia, using the interplanetary spell. Most of the GASP troops that had come to Neraka were now solely focused on finalizing the peace treaties and supporting the Imen where appropriate.

New cities were coming up. Trade routes and laws were being established. And Azure Heights was the gem of the entire region, once more. Its white marble buildings and golden towers glistened from afar, overlooking the fields and the Valley of Screams.

Derek was already in talks with Nevis, Neha, Hundurr, Zane,

and Wyrran to set up a GASP base on Neraka. They were looking at potential locations, and Ragnar Peak was brought up. The mountain was down, but the location was still highly advantageous and was at the intersection of multiple roads. It was perfect for what they needed.

The area around the base of Azure Heights had just become home to a very special monument—a stunning work of art created by Corrine and Ibrahim, with plenty of help from our crew and allies. A white marble statue had been erected for every fallen Iman, Mara, daemon pacifist, Manticore, Dhaxanian, and Adlet who had fought against the daemon-Exiled Mara coalition. There were hundreds of them, each made in the appearance of the creature it was commemorating. Lumi had helped with a few spells, digging through thousands of memories to accurately reproduce these marble portraits.

Lumi had added her extra touch to each of them, too. The statues were imbued with protective charms and alarms, designed to keep the city safe, going forward. From afar, it looked as though the mountain was guarded by hundreds of beautiful statues. From up close, the Guardians of Neraka, as they'd been dubbed, stood tall and proud—timeless in their heroism. I walked among them for a while, recognizing Arrah, next to Dion and Alles. Colton was right behind them.

I cried, unable to stop my tears from rolling down my cheeks. At first, I'd thought it was because of the monument, but, after some reflection, I had to admit that I was crying because of Zane.

He hadn't spoken to me since before his coronation. Not a single word.

I knew he'd been insanely busy with his kingdom. The daemons required his undivided attention; otherwise, he risked a rebellion. The purpose of these new alliances had been to restore the peace and balance, and to prevent further bloodshed, after all.

But it still hurt, because I needed some pointers from him on where our relationship was going. I'd talked about this with Mom and Dad already. I'd put forward the idea of staying here, but I'd yet to exclude the possibility of leaving. I was horribly confused, and my parents had tried their best to listen to me and advise me as selflessly as possible. Of course, they didn't like the idea of me living so far away from them, but, at the same time, they respected my freedom and said they would adjust to whatever decision I made.

What decision am I making, though?

After a long walk, I went back to the newly rebuilt Palisade, where I'd been given a gorgeous suite. I noticed the daemon guards standing outside the building. I was still getting accustomed to the notion that they were all peaceful now. They all bowed politely as I passed by.

I made it upstairs, then opened the door to my room—and froze. My heart skipped a beat.

Zane was standing in the middle, tall and gorgeous as ever. He'd opted for a black leather tunic with gold thread embellishments and gemstone buttons, simple but classy, hugging his muscles and adding some gravitas to his already-imposing figure.

His horns were fully covered in gold, and he'd settled for a smaller, simpler gold crown to casually wear while out in public. His red eyes found mine, and my heart stopped beating altogether. All of a sudden, I was conflicted. *Should I be happy to see him? Or should I be angry that I'm only seeing him now?*

"Hi," he said, his voice low and raspy and already doing all kinds of things to my senses. I replied with a brief nod. "Can we talk?"

A part of me had slapped the panic button already. All systems were full steam ahead, preparing for the worst-case scenario I'd been imagining, where Zane would tell me that we were better off going our separate ways, that the urgency of our situation with Shaytan had brought us too close, too fast... and so on. My soul was already aching as I got ready to put on a straight face and keep it cool.

"Yeah, sure," I mumbled.

He hadn't even touched or kissed me. He wasn't even smiling.

Ironically, he'd been the one coming after me during our dark adventure. He'd kidnapped me, he'd saved me, he'd let me go, and then he'd saved me again—over and over, in fact. And, as soon as everything had fallen into place, he'd gone silent. It hurt me, because I'd fallen for him. I'd fallen so deeply that I wasn't at all sure I'd be able to take a breakup well.

Seconds went by. He seemed to be looking for the right words. I waited patiently. What was an extra minute in these circumstances, anyway?

But my pulse raced, and I caved in.

"Look, I can leave, and we can just pretend—" I started, but we spoke at the same time.

"Marry me," he said.

I blanked out, completely.

"Wait, what?" I croaked.

"I mean... Hold on, you want to leave?" he replied, frowning.

We both looked at each other, equally confused. I blinked several times, then shook my head. Honesty was the best way forward.

"You want me to stay?" I breathed.

He shrugged. "Of course," he said. "I mean, I stand by my question. You can say yes, or you can say no. Or not yet. Or... I don't know. Whatever you want, I'm fine with it. Whatever your decision, that is. I just want you to know that I will be extremely miserable if you leave."

I was out of words. I couldn't believe it. He'd baffled me with such precision that I had a hard time getting my brain to function. Zane didn't seem comfortable with my silence, so he kept on rambling.

"The Daughters don't have enough power out here to set up a portal, but an interplanetary travel spell takes only hours," he said. "If you choose to stay here, you could do that to see your parents and friends whenever you want. Plus, we'll have GASP here, so they can always come visit, too. I've been thinking about this for a while. I'm sorry I didn't come see you sooner, but I completely underestimated the complexity of my role. And I didn't even know what to ask you, or how to ask you to stay. I... I'm babbling."

"You are," I murmured, then took a deep breath.

Everything sort of came into focus then. I loved him. That was the only undeniable fact that I could cling to, no matter what. And Zane had just asked me to marry him.

Holy smoke.

"It's okay if you don't want to marry me—" He tried to continue, but I quickly shut him up, as I rushed across the room, jumped on him, and wrapped my arms around his neck. He caught me, holding me close. I kissed him—hungrily, feverishly, desperately. I'd missed him so much.

"I love you," I whispered against his lips.

"I love you, Fiona," he replied softly, his red eyes drilling into my soul.

I teared up, then chuckled to stop myself from crying like a little girl. "I'm not accepting your proposal. Yet," I said. He stared at me, unsure of how to respond. "First of all, you need to propose properly. Dinner, music, ring, the works. Don't make it sound like a royal command," I added, then mimicked him, lowering my tone. "'Marry me.'"

He scoffed, slightly amused, as he analyzed every feature of my face, further making my heart soar and struggle against my ribcage.

"So, what? It's a no?" he asked.

"No. It's not a yes, either. It's a half yes," I replied, smiling. "I'll stay. Shall we start with that, then work our way forward? I mean, what if you end up hating me in a year or ten?"

He laughed, then kissed me. This time, he was sweet and gentle. It felt so profound that tears rolled down my cheeks. I was beside myself. Weeks of uncertainty had just flown out the window.

"How could I possibly hate you, Fiona? You're a part of the reason I'm still here, looking forward to every moment I've got in this world," he said, then settled me back on my feet and ran his fingers through my hair. "I'm having serious trouble imagining life without you in it."

Several moments passed as we lovingly gazed at each other.

"I will make you pay for these weeks," I muttered. "You know that, right?"

He nodded, then put on a playful smirk. "I know. I've been a bad daemon."

I giggled, then gasped. "Oh, dear. We need to tell my parents."

"Think they'll be okay with this?" he asked.

My father's voice cut through the room and made us both freeze. "Well, we're not jumping for joy, that's for sure."

We both stepped away from each other, and I turned to face my parents. Mom was tearing up already, and Dad wore an indelible frown on his face. They definitely didn't look happy, but I was going to hold them to their previous statements nonetheless.

"Mom, Dad... How much did you hear?" I managed, my voice higher than usual.

"We've heard enough," Dad replied, then exhaled sharply.

Zane was motionless, as if he'd just stepped on a mine and the slightest movement would blow him to bits.

"Mom, I—" I tried to speak, but she cut me off.

"Sweetie, I... Your dad and I stand by what we said earlier," she replied, wiping her tears. "We'll adjust to this. Your happiness is all that matters to us."

"Sure, we're selfish and want you with us," Dad added, "but, let's be realistic. We can't have everything we want. Zane has a kingdom to rule, and he loves you. You obviously love him, so... there's not much we can say here, at this point. Whatever you two do, make sure you're happy."

Mom sniffed, then put on a serious face, pointing a finger at Zane. "And if you hurt my daughter in any way, I will rip your throat out."

"Honey, that's *my* line," Dad muttered.

"Well, then, I beat you to it," Mom replied.

We all burst into laughter, as Mom and Dad came into the room to hug and congratulate us both. I teared up again, thankful to have been raised by such amazing creatures.

"You are always welcome on Neraka," Zane said to my parents. "Anytime."

"You bet your ass," Dad shot back, smirking. He then shifted his focus to me. "So! That makes you what, now? Queen of daemons, if you accept his proposal?"

"Holy crap," I gasped. "Yup. That's right. Queen of..." I murmured, then looked at Zane. "Daemons."

Zane's expression said everything. There was love and excitement glimmering in his eyes. This was a whole new era we were entering together. The daemon kingdom had never had a queen before, just the king's concubines. Then again, the daemon kingdom had never had Zane as its ruler. That, alone, was a critical upgrade.

Whatever came next, I was ready to tackle it, especially since I had Zane by my side.

40

BLAZE

I'd been putting off talking to my father about the celibacy oath.

With everything now calm and running smoothly, Caia and I were getting closer than ever. There was no way that we'd be able to keep ourselves away from one another. She burned so hot in my presence, and I was head over heels with her.

While I understood the value of a celibacy oath, I didn't feel like it would do much to influence my success as a dragon anymore. I'd slayed many daemons and I'd helped save thousands of innocent lives. I'd done my best to keep my people safe, too. It just didn't make sense to me, when all I wanted was to be with Caia and experience the world together.

"Are you sure you want to do this?" Caia asked me as we stopped outside the former Palisade, overlooking the now-peaceful fields and gorges.

I nodded slowly. "Absolutely," I said, then gently brushed my knuckles against her cheek, feeling my heart go on a crazy race whenever she smiled at me. "I don't want us to stay apart and suffer because of an old tradition."

She chuckled. "I thought you were all *for* traditions."

"Yeah, but then I kissed you, and it pretty much flew out the window," I replied with a shrug.

"There you are!" My father's voice made me jump.

I quickly turned around to face him and smile. My palms were already clammy, and my throat was slowly but surely closing up. He was in a good mood, from what I could tell. That was a good sign for me to get right to it.

"Dad, thanks for coming," I said. "I know you've been busy with the daemon rebels here..."

"That's fine," he replied. "They never last against fire anyway," he added, then smiled at Caia and me. "What did you want to talk about?"

I looked at Caia, then exhaled and shifted my focus back on him.

"Look, Dad," I said, my voice already shaky. "There's no other way to say this but... Caia and I, we're in love."

Dad frowned slightly, but there was a flicker of amusement in his blue eyes that confused me a little. He crossed his arms as he kept his gaze fixed on me.

"Way to state the obvious, son," he replied dryly. "I noticed that the first time I saw you two together."

I paused, suddenly blank. Caia and I had been careful around him, mainly because I'd yet to find the courage to tell him that I wanted out of the celibacy oath, and because Caia, ever the sweet and supporting fae that she was, didn't want him asking questions that I wasn't ready to answer.

I blinked several times, trying to find my words.

"You know..." I managed.

"Of course," he shot back, genuinely amused. "I wasn't born yesterday. I know love when I see it. I would never be upset with you about it—" He added, then raised both his eyebrows. "Is that why you two have been sneaking around like thieves in the night?"

My cheeks flared. I gave Caia a quick glance and noticed her flushed face and wide eyes. "Oh, so your father knows..." she murmured.

My dad laughed wholeheartedly. "Darling, I know everything my son does and wants, even when he doesn't," he replied. "Just like I know he's about to ask me to release him from his celibacy oath, but he's not yet sure how to do it without making me angry."

I froze.

But then Dad gave me a warm and understanding smile, causing a wave of sheer relief to wash over me.

"Son, times have changed," he said. "Our dragon traditions won't all survive in the future. We used to take celibacy oaths for reasons that were always deeply personal to us, but that doesn't have to apply to all dragons."

"Dad, I just... I don't want you to be disappointed in me—"

"That's ridiculous!" He cut me off. "Why would I be anything but proud of you, after what you've accomplished here? Blaze, you're more of a dragon than I ever was at your age. You don't need the celibacy oath to validate you. I would've appreciated you seeing it through, since you went ahead and took it, but... honestly? It's not a big deal."

It took me a few seconds to properly digest what he'd just said. My heart swelled with gratitude and love for him—he had a way of confusing me sometimes, but that was just a part of who he was.

"So... You're okay with me not fulfilling the oath," I said, trying to get him to say it again, just so I'd make sure I was in the clear.

"Son, you can do whatever you want," he replied, grinning. "You proved your worth long before you even set foot on Neraka. If being with Caia makes you happy, I'm fully behind you on this."

In a split-second, I'd already wrapped my arms around him, pulling him into a tight hug. He was still bigger than me, but even he couldn't resist his son's embrace. He hugged me back, chuckling softly. As soon as I stepped back, I nodded.

"Thanks, Dad," I muttered.

"Nothing to thank me for, son. Traditions can be overrated, if you ask me," he replied. "We could start some new ones instead."

I laughed lightly, then took Caia's hand in mine. She was once again relaxed and smiling, as if the weight of the whole world had just been taken off her shoulders. Dad gave her a brief, albeit not-that-serious scowl.

"You'd better not break his heart, little fae," he said firmly. "My fire is stronger than yours."

It was Caia's turn to blink several times, unsure of how to respond to what had sounded like quite the threat. Knowing Dad, however, I chuckled, helping her loosen up a little. I swallowed my humor when he then glowered at me—he wasn't joking this time. I could feel my spine tingling.

"And you. If you make this girl cry anything other than tears of joy, I will beat you into a pulp and then some, you hear me?" he muttered.

I nodded vehemently. "Yes, sir!"

He then smiled and took both Caia and me in his arms, keeping us close. We laughed, as he refused to let us go. Caia giggled, looking up at him.

"Thank you, sir," she said softly. "I do love your son, you know..."

"I know you do. And call me Heath. Only he gets to call me 'sir'," he replied, nodding at me.

It felt good to have that celibacy oath off my plate. I'd come to Neraka thinking I'd be okay with it. But the closer I'd gotten to Caia, the more difficult it had become for me to envision myself making it to twenty-three without being able to make love to her.

Eloping to New Zealand suddenly became the next thing on my to-do list.

Just me, Caia, and the colorful volcanic lakes of Rotorua... I was going to spend the rest of my life loving her and making her happy. And she looked more than ready to do the same.

41

AVRIL

For the first time since we'd brought the Neraka madness to an end, Heron and I actually got to go on a first, proper date, prior to going back to Calliope. We'd held off on leaving Neraka sooner, so we could help the locals get all their ducks in a row. It was worth it, too. We were leaving a better world behind.

The new Palisade had a gorgeous restaurant on the ground floor, complete with an open-air terrace. At night, it was simply stunning, surrounded by flowers and flickering oil lamps. Heron and I sipped on our spiced blood flutes, thrilled to have this moment all to ourselves, after everything we'd been through.

Every moment I spent with him simply reinforced the fact that we were meant to be together. We couldn't get enough of each other.

"No sign of Ramin, huh?" Heron asked, his hand covering mine on the table.

The white linen tablecloth felt soft and smooth against my fingertips. Heron's skin came on top like silk. Each of these little details made life an absolute pleasure—and Heron was at the very center of it all.

I shook my head. "Nope. Harper hasn't seen him since Shaytan kicked the bucket," I replied. "But still, it's good to know he exists. That the Hermessi exist."

"Yeah, Neraka does need some supernatural oversight, in a way," he muttered. "If anything ever goes wrong again, the Hermessi may be able to intervene."

"Do you think they'd be responsive, though?"

He shrugged. "I don't know. They haven't manifested since Shaytan died. They could be like the Daughters used to be in Eritopia. Distant but ever-present. What matters is that the people believe in them. As long as they believe, the Hermessi will gain enough power to manifest. Neraka's special because it's got powerful Hermessi to begin with."

I nodded slowly. "I wonder if we would ever be able to reach out to the Hermessi on Calliope. Or Earth. Or anywhere else, for that matter."

"Well, according to what Ramin said to Harper, they exist everywhere. They're universal entities, and they fuel the fae. I'm inclined to believe that fae planets definitely have stronger Hermessi," Heron mused, then smiled. "It would be pretty cool to try to reach out to them, now that we know they exist."

"You heard Harper. If you believe in them, chances are they'll manifest," I said. "We should totally try this when we go back to Calliope. You never know, right?"

He sighed, gazing at me as if I were the single most precious thing in his life. He'd already made that clear, verbally, but it was nice to see it written all over his face, too.

"Stay with me," he croaked, his voice trembling. "In White City."

I blinked several times, surprised by the sudden turn in our conversation.

"Wait... What?" I managed. "You want me to move in with you, in White City?"

Be still, my beating heart.

He nodded. "Yes. I love you, Avril. I want to be with you. That counts for something, right?"

"Of course." I chuckled, suddenly loving him even more.

"I mean, even Blaze had enough balls to tell his dad that he's with Caia, celibacy oath be damned. Scarlett's parents are adjusting to the idea of Patrik. Yelena is still sobbing about Fiona staying here, but... Anyway, point is, I'd like to make this official. With your parents."

"Oh, wow," I murmured, my eyes widening. "I am genuinely impressed. You know my dad's a serious badass and will tear you to shreds if you screw this up, right?"

Heron's lips stretched into a grin. "I'm aware, yes. I'd be the lowest of life forms if I hurt you, anyway. I'd definitely have it coming if it came to pass," he replied. "Avril, I... I love you. I do. I'm a reckless, foot-in-mouth pretty-boy with a penchant for disasters, and there's a lot I should probably fix about myself. But you, you're the only thing I got right. And... I want to be with you. Always."

Tears stung my eyes as I pressed my lips together, then exhaled sharply.

"I love you, too, Heron," I breathed. "You stomped your way into my life and then refused to get out, and now... Well, now I'm hopelessly head over heels with a reckless, foot-in-mouth pretty-boy with a penchant for disasters."

He chuckled softly, then leaned in to kiss me. Our lips met and, as always, so did our souls.

"Although, I disagree with you having a lot to fix about yourself," I said, smiling. "You could improve the timing for some of your jokes, maybe, but I hardly think it's a requirement. You're you, and that's what I love about you, anyway."

Heron moved to kiss me again, then stilled, his lips inches from mine. He groaned, then rolled his eyes. It suddenly got unseasonably chilly.

"Son of a—" Heron muttered, looking down.

I followed his gaze and burst into laughter. Dhaxanian frost had covered him, all the way up to his waist.

"My apologies," Nevis said from the other side of the terrace. "There's only so much sweetness I can put up with before I start gagging. And the food here is phenomenal; I would hate to regurgitate it."

"Dude, seriously," Heron grumbled, leaning back in his chair. "Cut it out."

"I figured it was the best way to help you... cool off," Nevis replied with a shrug, then waved the Dhaxanian frost away. It disintegrated into a thousand snowflakes, each sparkling and unique.

I gave Nevis a half smile. "I see you're doing better."

"Absolutely. It's amazing what having a complete soul can do for a Dhaxanian." He sighed. "Not that I'm apologizing for interrupting your dinner, but I wanted to talk to you before I head back to Athelathan tomorrow."

I motioned for him to take a seat at our table. He gave Heron a brief nod, then joined us.

"What's up?" I asked, holding Heron's hand under the table. We had trouble staying away from each other, in general. Even the slightest touch was enough to keep us grounded when we were together.

"I've already expressed interest in joining the Nerakian GASP branch," Nevis replied. "But I would like you to put a request in for me when you get a chance. I think it will carry more weight if it comes from you."

I frowned slightly, somewhat confused. "I can try."

"Well, it's simple. I'm open to taking foreign missions," he said.

That came as a surprise for both Heron and me. Nevis wasn't the type to even leave the Athelathan Mountains—it had been a miracle to have him assist us against Shaytan and the Mara Lords in the first place. The guy was a hermit to the core.

"You. You want to get off the planet," Heron replied dryly.

"Yes. I may not look like it, but I *am* a curious and independent soul," Nevis said. "I didn't get out much over the past ten thousand years because I had a mountain to protect from daemons. The circumstances have changed now. The In-Between is vast and full of mysteries. I mean, what's the point of living for as long as I will, if I don't get out and see the world?"

I smiled. "That makes sense," I replied. "I'll talk to Derek, I promise."

"Thank you," Nevis said. "I appreciate it."

"You'll owe me a favor, though," I shot back.

Nevis's forehead smoothed. "What do you want?"

I shrugged. "I don't know yet. I'll figure something out," I said, offering my hand, to shake on it.

He thought about it for a minute, then nodded and squeezed my hand in his.

"I'm curious, though," I added. "Why come to me with this? Why not go directly to Derek? He would have no problem with your request whatsoever."

Nevis exhaled sharply, then tucked a lock of his long white hair behind his ear.

"It's common courtesy, I think. I don't know Derek as well as I know you," he replied. "Besides, you're the best person I could think of for a reference."

"Aww." I giggled. "Well, count on me, Nevis. I'll put in a good word for you. I'd love to see you more often after we go back to Calliope. You're cool."

Nevis smirked. He gave Heron a brief glance, then looked at me again. "You know, there are a couple of beautiful places to consider for your honeymoon here, on Neraka. There's a beach down south I'm sure you will—"

"Wait, what honeymoon?" I cut him off, chuckling. "Heron just asked me to move in with him. We haven't discussed marriage yet. I mean, I appreciate the suggestions either way. We could both use a vacation after all this."

Nevis froze, then frowned at Heron. I followed his gaze and noticed the look on Heron's face. He was paler than usual, his eyes wide and glassy, as if he was stuck in a slasher movie and he was next in line to get slaughtered.

"You asked her to *move in* with you?" Nevis muttered.

When Heron didn't answer, I felt the need to intervene.

"Heron, what's wrong?"

"He's been rehearsing a proposal for days now," Nevis retorted, somewhat irritated. "Building up the courage to ask you to marry him. He even got a ring and—"

"Whoa!" I gasped. "How did *you* know?" I asked, then looked at Heron. "Is he telling the truth?"

Nevis scoffed. "I don't lie," he shot back. "I found him talking to himself the other night, in front of a mirror."

"And you promised you'd keep your trap shut!" Heron hissed, now blushing like a peony.

I was stunned. My face caught fire. My pulse went on the rush of the century, making me a little lightheaded.

"Heron..." I murmured, struggling to formulate a full sentence, a response of any kind.

"I thought you'd proposed already!" Nevis replied, raising his hands in a defensive gesture. "I figured that's why you were both smooching and tearing up."

"Which makes your interruption even worse," Heron retorted. "Imagine I'd proposed, only to have you troll me with your frost!"

"Guys!" I raised my voice. "Shut up!"

I took several deep breaths, staring at them both.

Heron opened his mouth to say something, but I shushed him.

"Let me see the ring," I said.

Heron blinked several times, then produced a small velvet box. Inside was a gorgeous meranium band, encrusted with diamonds and red garnet flakes. It was beautiful, and it made my heart swell. I could hardly breathe.

"I mean... Will you?" Heron mumbled, giving me a worried look.

"Will I what?" I managed.

"Oh, for the love of—" Nevis blurted, then stopped himself halfway through and exhaled sharply.

"See? You ruined it!" Heron reprimanded him.

"Fine, I'll fix it," Nevis replied, and gave me a stern look. "Avril, if you don't accept his marriage proposal, then you are not as smart as I thought. I would be thoroughly disappointed if you were unable to see what an extraordinary creature he is. After all, you rejected my affections in favor of this guy. At least commit. What's the worst that could happen?"

Heron sighed. "Divorce."

"Shush!" I snapped, then put my hand forward, no longer able to control myself. My heart was galloping at full speed, filled with the kind of love I knew I wouldn't find anywhere else in this universe. "Yes. Okay? Yes, Heron."

"Yes what?" he murmured, as if lost in space. I scowled at him for a second, enough to make him understand that this was real, that it was happening. "You will?"

I nodded. "I'll marry you. And don't even think of divorce. If you screw this up, you won't live to see a divorce," I replied.

Heron was beside himself. I could almost see the concerns wafting away like a dark cloud blown off by the evening breeze. He lit up like a Christmas tree as he slipped the ring on my finger with a trembling hand, then jumped to his feet and took me in his arms.

We both heard Nevis groan with feigned disgust, but we didn't care. We kissed, deeply, as we looked past our differences and embraced the future together. We'd been through quite a challenge already. We'd both nearly died and lost one another. We'd experienced joy, fear, and anger. We'd fought by each other's side and—good grief, we made one hell of a team.

We didn't have to tie the knot anytime soon. I knew that. Heron would never pressure me. Clearly, he'd asked me to move in with him first because he didn't want to rush me. But we had an eternity ahead, anyway. And we were bound, body and soul. I was thrilled by the prospect of a lifetime with Heron.

Let's hope Dad takes it just as well.

42

SOFIA

Our family was once again reunited. Our new friends were safe. Neraka was now seeing better days, defined by peace and progress. There were deep wounds that needed time to heal, of course, but the Nerakians were ready to move forward. The Imen, in particular, were willing to forgive.

Three of the fire dragons and the auxiliary troops we brought from Calliope were temporarily assigned to Neraka, along with Arwen and Shayla. The witches took it upon themselves to build the new GASP base where Ragnar Peak had once stood, while the fighters were there to ensure that all peace treaties were followed to the letter. Even Zane was aware that some of his daemons may be tempted to stray off the path, and he'd actually insisted that there be dragons present.

Fiona was going to stay with him, as well. Benedict and Yelena were quite sad about it, but, at the same time, they were proud and thrilled to see their daughter happy and in love. She'd decided to support Zane. Soon enough, she was going to marry the daemon king and become queen herself. I welcomed the idea—after all, other than Tejus, we didn't have any other royalty in our family tree!

We gathered on the main terrace of the city's seventh level, ready to bid our new allies goodbye, and to go back to Calliope and The Shade. Derek was going to nominate a senior GASP agent to take over the Nerakian branch within the next couple of weeks. In the meantime, we could all get back to business.

Neha and Pheng-Pheng, Hundurr, Nevis, and Wyrran came to say goodbye, along with Zane and Fiona. Chances were that Wyrran was going to be the next leader of the Imen—preliminary polls spoke in his favor. He'd already agreed with Demios that they would support each other, no matter what the election results would be.

The Daughters stood on the edge, while Viola prepared the interplanetary spell. We'd left the capsule in the field for the locals to use in case of emergency. Our way back was straightforward and no longer required the vessel, anyway.

Harper and Caspian, Heron and Avril, Caia and Blaze, Jax and Hansa, and Patrik and Scarlett took turns hugging everyone they were going to leave behind. They promised they would visit as often as they could. Nevis was due for a chat with Derek, anyway, sometime in the next few months, to discuss his involvement in Eritopian and other In-Between missions.

Lumi said goodbye to the Nerakians as well, leaving another armful of spell scrolls with Wyrran.

"These are for you," she said. "Just some fertility and protection spells. I think you'll find them useful."

"Thank you," Wyrran replied, smiling. "You've already done so much."

"It's the least I can do for all the spells I was forced to surrender to Shaytan and the Mara Lords. They all hurt you. It's just my way of making some amends," she said.

"What will you do next, Lumi?" Derek asked, standing by my side.

Lumi shrugged. "I'm the last of my kind, for the time being," she answered. "First thing I'm going to do is find a cozy spot to live on Calliope, followed by a long, hot bath. After that, I'll take on new disciples and rebuild the swamp witches' coven. We're still needed."

"I agree," Corrine replied. "Your magic is truly exceptional; it would be a shame for it to go away. In all fairness, that triple-tome is great, but you've clearly been holding out on all the good stuff."

Lumi chuckled softly. "That's true. Well, let's hope I find some good disciples to work with. They're not easy to come by these days. The power of the Word must continue to transcend, and I will do everything that I can to make sure of that."

"Okay, everybody ready?" Viola joined us.

The interplanetary spell was ready. We all huddled in the middle of the massive pentagram—our children and their parents, our friends and new couples, including Tobiah and Sienna.

"We'll prepare the prisoner and Mara refugee transports for tomorrow," Wyrran said. "Rowan, Farrah, and all the other fiends will get to you first. The Maras for White City will follow."

"Thank you, Wyrran," Derek replied. "I shall see you again soon enough!"

We'd already established a Telluris link between the Nerakian leaders, Draven, and Field, as part of a constant connection to Eritopia. If anything happened, if anything came up, GASP was ready to come to their aid, one way or another.

With an ever-growing network of friends, partners, and long-term allies across the In-Between, I looked forward to the future. As we all came together while Viola muttered the travel spell incantation, I felt Derek's hand gently brushing against mine. I looked at him and found myself in awe of what we'd accomplished —not just ourselves, but our offspring, as well. We'd come a long way from those first dark and cold days in The Shade.

"I'm proud of you, darling," I whispered in his ear.

He smiled, then dropped a kiss on my temple.

"I'd be nothing without you, Sofia," he said.

We looked at our Nerakian allies one more time, waving them goodbye, as the bright spell light swallowed us. The giant orb lifted us off the ground, humming softly.

"I can't wait to get home," Caia said. "Don't get me wrong, Neraka's cool and all, but dammit, I miss my Shade."

"Here, here, Cuz!" Dmitri chuckled.

"You're all aware we're having a massive dinner tonight, right?" Serena asked. "Aida will kill us if we don't attend. She's been preparing it for a week. And given her, um, condition, I don't think it would be wise to poke the... wolf."

Jovi burst into laughter. "I absolutely agree. I mean, cravings are one thing, but having her set up a dinner for nothing? Nah, that would be suicide."

"I don't know why you're laughing, though. I'm the one who looks after her cravings, anyway," Field muttered behind him.

We all chuckled, relieved to be united again.

The light orb shot through the sky and pierced Neraka's atmosphere.

Within seconds, we were all at the heart of a shooting star, traveling through the vast vacuum of the In-Between, fluttering past thousands of other galaxies and wandering asteroids. There was life out there.

There were more species thriving in this universe. Creatures I looked forward to discovering. We'd definitely come a long way, from expanding our Shade to restoring peace across the In-Between. And there was still room for much more.

43

HARPER

There months.

Time did fly after we went back to Calliope.

Heron and Avril moved in together. They had their own place in White City. Caspian and I had our little penthouse there, too, on one of the higher levels. But we spent our time equally between Calliope and The Shade, where I'd been given my own treehouse.

Patrik and Scarlett settled on Calliope, as well. Serena insisted that they take one of the private suites in Luceria, complete with all the amenities. Jax and Hansa were also together—she was the first succubus to settle in White City. It took the other Maras some time to adjust, but they all came to adore her spunk and straight-forward nature. Soon enough, they all agreed that the Lord of Maras had certainly found his match.

Fiona and Zane came to visit us on Calliope once every couple of weeks. Caia and Blaze were dating—though I had to admit, there was a lot of fire between those two! Quite literally! They were deeply in love with each other, and it showed. I was relieved to hear that Heath was cool with their relationship, too, and that he didn't care about the celibacy oath as much as we'd thought. Time had a way of changing views, I guessed...

Vesta and her parents were brought back, along with Ryker, Laughlan, Rush, and Amina. They were all resettled in new homes. The Mara couple stayed in White City, while the others accepted Draven's invitation to live in Luceria. That castle was huge, and there were still plenty of unoccupied rooms. Vesta was adjusting to her new life, though she went back to Neraka once in a while to check on her Imen village. In a way, she had two homes.

Caspian started training with Jax's wards as part of his GASP induction. On top of that, his sentry abilities were truly coming out —his ability to mind-bend other Maras would come in handy. It scared some of them, but, at the end of the day, Jax was pleased to know it was possible. He was even considering wards for Caspian. Lumi had already indicated that she would mark some for him, if they agreed on it. Wards would allow Caspian to perform mass mind-bending on Maras, too. If ever they needed to regain control of a large group, Caspian's ward-amplified sentry skill would sure come in handy.

Mom and Dad got their own suite in Luceria in the end. With all three of their kids living here, we'd figured it was only a matter of time before they joined us. The Shade was just one portal away.

Good news was coming out of Neraka, too. The Imen were on their way to repopulating the planet. The peace treaties worked smoothly. And Zane and Fiona ruled over the daemon kingdom with firm hands—the daemons had come to both fear and respect our petite vampire, whose strength had put many of their Legions to shame.

The Exiled Mara rebels were successfully resettled, too. In fact, they were welcomed with arms wide open. Sienna and Tobiah were well-adjusted and thriving, and they'd also joined GASP.

Farrah and Rowan had been sentenced to life in prison. That was an eternity behind bars. Farrah had tried to persuade the judges and jury that she was willing to mend her ways, but it didn't do her any good. Rowan stood her ground until the gavel came down. Upon hearing the sentence, she broke down in tears. I didn't feel sorry for either of them. The other Exiled Maras were also subjected to their individual trials. Sienna, Tobiah, Cadmus, Peyton, and Caspian had done a marvelous job of gathering evidence against those who had aided the Lords in their genocide.

In the end, fifty life sentences were handed out. The rest each got between one hundred and five thousand years. In some cases, the judge was lenient and sentenced a handful of younger Maras to hard labor and service to Luceria, as servants.

Vita was pregnant, though it was Bijarki who was positively glowing—literally, his silvery skin shimmered all the time. His emotional state was far too powerful to contain. We'd organized a double baby shower, for both Vita and Aida, whose baby bump was starting to show. Corrine kept a watchful eye on both of them, given that their babies were going to be hybrids.

We were all dying to see what they would turn out like. Would Aida and Field's kid grow wings or turn werewolf? Would Vita and Bijarki's little one take on his father's silvery blood and complexion, or become full fae? There were lots of unknowns in our cross-couplings, but they all filled us with hope and wonder.

As I looked back on my Nerakian stint, I found myself fully energized and eager to tackle the future. There were some important celebrations and anniversaries coming our way over the next few months, so I figured I'd do my part and get something organized. I wanted to make sure that Derek, Sofia, Lucas, Marion, Xavier, Vivienne, and all the "old guys and gals' club" knew how much we loved and admired them.

So, one late night, I left Caspian to discuss the possibility of wards with Lumi, while I snuck into our base on Mount Zur and called a secret meeting for all the Shadian kids. Serena had been kind enough to drag Phoenix out of bed and bring him over, too. We'd agreed to leave our better halves behind. Not that they weren't family, but we were trying to keep a low profile and organize a surprise for the elders. It would've been suspicious if all of us were missing at the same time, over the next six months or so.

Serena, Phoenix, and I sat in the grand meeting room on Mount Zur, next to one of the fire training halls. We stared at the touchscreen that had been incorporated into the long table surface, with a satellite connection and some magic amplifiers mounted underneath to increase its reach. It gave us the ability to connect to Corrine's wicked telescope and get real-time glimpses into neighboring galaxies.

"I can't believe we've already got satellites in Calliope's orbit," Phoenix muttered, swiping across a galaxy and randomly zooming in and out on different planets.

"You can thank Viola for that," Serena replied. "She loves our tech."

"Okay, so..." I said, checking the meeting list I'd hastily put together. "The others should be here soon."

"Who did we bring into this, again? Did we tell Rose and Ben?" Serena asked.

I nodded. "Yeah, but they said we should go ahead and plan whatever. They'll do their part when the time comes. They trust us to pick the right place."

"Oh, that's wonderful," Serena replied, beaming with excitement.

"Do you think they'll agree, though?" Phoenix sighed, his brow slightly furrowed. "Derek's a workaholic. What are the odds he'll say yes?"

"Well, that's where River and Ben come in," I said, grinning like a devious little devil.

The double doors opened wide, prompting the three of us to stand and welcome the rest of our organizing crew—Caia, Vita, Fiona, Avril, Field, Scarlett, Dmitri, Jovi and Aida; Elonora, Ruby and Ash's daughter; Kailani, Arwen and Brock's daughter; and Blaze.

"How did you all get here at the same time?" I asked, surprised to see everyone at once.

Elonora, one of the few vampire sentries in The Shade and one of my closest friends, pointed at Caia. "Little Miss Fiery Fae here made sure we all met outside first," she said, giving Caia a brief smirk. "Her organizational skills will serve her well in the future."

"Wait, are you being sarcastic?" Caia replied, somewhat confused.

The thing with Elonora was that sometimes it was difficult to tell whether she was joking, or she was serious. In hindsight, I might've rubbed off on her a little.

"No, I'm giving you a compliment," Elonora said. "I *wish* I had my crap together as well as you do. Honestly."

"Yeah, but then again, you're a freaking monster under pressure," Kailani interjected, chuckling softly. The young witch had recently been approved into GASP's Eritopian base, and she'd been getting along surprisingly well with Lumi. I hadn't said it out loud yet, but I was willing to bet that Lumi would offer her a disciple role. After all, Kailani already had the magic gift. Amplifying it with swamp witch magic would be the icing on the cake.

"She meant that in a good way," Vita said to Elonora.

"Let's get down to business," Field said. "Our future mommies need their beauty sleep."

Aida shot him a cold glance, raising an eyebrow. "What's that supposed to mean?"

"Uh-oh." Jovi chuckled. Aida playfully smacked him over the back of his head. "Ouch!"

"Wait till Anjani gets pregnant," Aida replied, grinning.

"I will feed her well, I promise!" Jovi shot back.

We all laughed, as Vita took a deep breath. She wasn't showing yet, but she was definitely dealing with pregnancy symptoms already. Spiced rosewater helped her and Aida a lot, as it soothed their bouts of morning sickness. Their cravings were hilarious, though—mainly because we got to watch both Field and Bijarki scramble to get their soulmates everything they needed, even if it meant going across the entire continent in a heartbeat for a sweet fruit.

"Well, thank you all for coming," I said, starting the meeting. "As we all know, we've got some important milestones coming up! We've just completed the new extension to The Shade; we've got peace missions fully accomplished in Eritopia and on Neraka, with new GASP bases on both... and, most importantly, The Shade itself is entering its six hundredth year of existence!"

They all cheered and clapped, while I pulled up a satellite image of a foreign galaxy. It was a beautiful sight to behold—an ample spiral in glowing shades of blue, white, and pink, riddled with millions of stars and mysterious planets.

"This, in my humble opinion, calls for a serious celebration," I added, "which is why you're all here tonight. Now, I'm not able to get this done all by myself, obviously, and frankly, I think we all have a part to play in this, because it's about rewarding our parents, our grandparents, and our wonderful founding great-grandparents for everything they've achieved so far."

"So, Harper and I have been thinking," Serena chimed in, pointing at the colorful galaxy. "Our elders deserve a big, beautiful, and relaxing vacation somewhere to celebrate all this. Somewhere new and amazing, somewhere they've never been before. We need to wow them."

"We found this place, with Jovi's help," I said, then zoomed deeper into the galaxy. I pulled up a solar system. "It's in the Meahiri galaxy. It's a remote solar system with a single massive star, called Aylara. Mind you, this is what we've managed to confirm with Draven from his Druid astrology archives."

Jovi smirked. "Glad to hear we're doing Strava, then!" he quipped, then touched the table surface and zoomed in on the planet in question. It was a blue gem, the perfect paradise with turquoise waters, white sand-beds, and clusters of small islands and archipelagos. "It's a tropical haven," he added. "There are only two seasons, one hot and dry, the other warm and wet. In about six months, it'll be perfect for this vacation thing."

"We've been monitoring the planet," I said, pulling up some geographical and astronomical details on the table screen for everyone to see. "We'll need to scope it out first, but it looks uninhabited. There's an atoll I think will be the perfect place for us to set up a temporary vacation resort. I'm talking the full-service works. The beach is perfect, the flora is lush and abundant, and from what I can tell, there are plenty of wild animals to hunt."

"Ben and Rose have agreed to take over The Shade for a month," Serena continued. "Otherwise, it would be impossible for us to get Derek to stay away from work for more than a week. I mean, sure, he was on Neraka for what, three? Four weeks?"

I nodded. "Yeah, but it was still work-related, and he had both Ben and Rose on Telluris speed-dial at all times," I replied. "We need to get them to fully disconnect and just... relax. Enjoy themselves. Be together, and all that good stuff!"

Everyone was immediately on board.

"Grandpa and Grandma will definitely welcome the idea," Dmitri said.

"Yeah, Vivienne and Xavier haven't been on a long vacation for... wow, for centuries. Good grief!" Serena exclaimed.

"Okay! Yup! We're in!" Elonora replied. "What do you need from us?"

Phoenix cleared his throat. "I'm going to have a talk with Viola, Lumi, and Arwen, so we can organize a brief expedition to Strava. We'll need to check the place out, particularly that atoll, and make sure it's safe and habitable. The last thing we want is to get our grandparents stranded in the middle of nowhere, somewhere in a galaxy far away," he said, chuckling.

I couldn't help but burst into laughter, doubling over. "We have a terrible track record as a family in foreign places, huh?"

"Hey, we'll do our homework this time!" Jovi shot back. "Whatever you need, we're here. We'll give Derek, Sofia, and our grand-parents the vacation they deserve."

"Oh, we most certainly will," Aida replied, her lips stretching into a grin.

I nodded slowly, looking across the table. I loved that image of all of us together, gathered around the live snapshot of a distant galaxy—all of us ready to go farther into space, ready to explore and discover new incredible places.

For a second, I wondered if Strava's Hermessi would be as powerful as Neraka's. I would love to meet more of them, as I was still reeling from my experience with Ramin, the fire spirit of Neraka.

Either way, Jovi was right. Derek, Sofia, and the other founders of The Shade deserved a break. After everything they'd been through, and after everything they'd accomplished, the least we could do was give them the perfect month in a heavenly corner of the In-Between.

They'd come a long way.

They'd earned it.

IT'S THE END OF A SEASON,

BUT IS IT THE END OF THE SHADE?

Dear Shaddict,

Thank you for reading the final book of Season 7, *A Battle of Souls*.

I'm excited to announce that the Shade series will continue for another season!

Book 1 of Season 8 is called **ASOV 60: A Voyage of Founders**, and with The Shade's sixth hundredth anniversary approaching, there will be an extra special return of your favorite original characters—along with the younger Shadian generations and some unexpected new faces... :)

A Voyage of Founders releases <u>May 31st, 2018</u>.

Order your copy now: www.bellaforrest.net

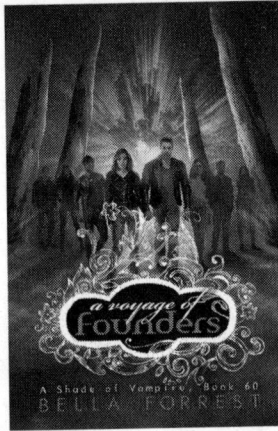

See you soon!

Love,

Bella x

P.S. Join my VIP email list and I'll send you a reminder as soon as I have a new book out. Visit here to sign up: **www.forrestbooks.com**

(Your email will be kept 100% private and you can unsubscribe at any time.)

P.P.S. Follow The Shade on Instagram and check out some of the beautiful graphics: @ashadeofvampire

You can also come say hi on Facebook: www.facebook.com/AShadeOfVampire

And Twitter: @ashadeofvampire

READ MORE BY BELLA FORREST

HOTBLOODS

(New supernatural romance series!)

Hotbloods (Book 1)

Coldbloods (Book 2)

Renegades (Book 3)

Venturers (Book 4)

Traitors (Book 5)

Allies (Book 6)

THE GIRL WHO DARED TO THINK

The Girl Who Dared to Think (Book 1)

The Girl Who Dared to Stand (Book 2)

The Girl Who Dared to Descend (Book 3)

The Girl Who Dared to Rise (Book 4)

The Girl Who Dared to Lead (Book 5)

The Girl Who Dared to Endure (Book 6)

The Girl Who Dared to Fight (Book 7)

THE GENDER GAME

(Completed series)

The Gender Game (Book 1)

The Gender Secret (Book 2)

The Gender Lie (Book 3)

The Gender War (Book 4)

The Gender Fall (Book 5)

The Gender Plan (Book 6)

The Gender End (Book 7)

A SHADE OF VAMPIRE SERIES

Season 1: Derek & Sofia's story

A Shade of Vampire (Book 1)

A Shade of Blood (Book 2)

A Castle of Sand (Book 3)

A Shadow of Light (Book 4)

A Blaze of Sun (Book 5)

A Gate of Night (Book 6)

A Break of Day (Book 7)

Season 2: Rose & Caleb's story

A Shade of Novak (Book 8)

A Bond of Blood (Book 9)

A Spell of Time (Book 10)

A Chase of Prey (Book 11)

A Shade of Doubt (Book 12)

A Turn of Tides (Book 13)

A Dawn of Strength (Book 14)

A Fall of Secrets (Book 15)

An End of Night (Book 16)

Season 3: The Shade continues with a new hero...

A Wind of Change (Book 17)

A Trail of Echoes (Book 18)

A Soldier of Shadows (Book 19)

A Hero of Realms (Book 20)

A Vial of Life (Book 21)

The Secret of Spellshadow Manor (Book 1)

The Breaker (Book 2)

The Chain (Book 3)

The Keep (Book 4)

The Test (Book 5)

The Spell (Book 6)

BEAUTIFUL MONSTER DUOLOGY

Beautiful Monster 1

Beautiful Monster 2

DETECTIVE ERIN BOND (Adult thriller/mystery)

Lights, Camera, GONE

Write, Edit, KILL

For an updated list of Bella's books, please visit her website:
www.bellaforrest.net

Join Bella's VIP email list and she'll send you an email reminder as soon
as her next book is out: www.forrestbooks.com